Spawned Secrets

Jay Verney

ZEN KETTLE BOOKS | BRISBANE, QLD

Zen Kettle Books

Email: steaming@zenkettle.com
www.zenkettle.com

Publisher's Note: This is a work of fiction. Names, characters, places, and incidents are products of the author's imagination. Locales and public names are sometimes used for atmospheric purposes. Any resemblance to actual people, living or dead, or to businesses, companies, events, institutions, or locales is completely coincidental.

Book Cover Design: © Zen Kettle Design at zenkettle.com

ISBN: 0987377914
ISBN-13: 978-0987377913

Dedication

To all those who suffered during and after the Global Financial Crisis, this book is for you. I hope you'll enjoy this small offering of fictional catharsis.

OTHER BOOKS BY JAY VERNEY

FICTION

A Mortality Tale
Percussion
Summon Up The Blood

POETRY

The Mindful Art of Verandaku: Micro Poems in a Macro World – Volume 1
The Mindful Art of Verandaku: Micro Poems in a Macro World – Volume 2
Zenku 365

MEMOIR

The Women Come & Go and The Women Came & Went: A Memoir & An Essay

NON-FICTION

Creating A Custom Fit In An Off-The-Rack Genre World: The Proximal Investigator, The Corpse of Convenience, and Their Family of Circumstance in Crime Fiction

Acknowledgements

To Lorrie Lawler, thanks for all the fish, not to mention many other delightful sources of inspiration, and scones.

No writer worth her salt (not to mention cinnamon sugar on breakfast bananas and rice cakes) is complete without her demanding moggies. To Dotty and Mottle (ectoplasmic, but always in our hearts, sweet Mot), thank you little furbies. As Leonardo Da Vinci so accurately said: *The smallest feline is a masterpiece.*

The rainforest has always spawned secrets.

Janette Turner Hospital

CHAPTER 1

OPERATION BLUEWATER POLARIS #001

It was Dave Brubeck. Listen to the tempo, Dave on piano, the maestro leading them out, turning back, in and around, sliding between bass and drums And the sax, by turns liquid and jaunty, joyful, feisty, the coolest of the cool. 'Take Five,' blasting from somewhere behind him in the darkness. One of his favourites.

He wasn't sure which bed he'd stumbled into tonight, but it didn't matter; his daughter, Miriam, was long gone, his wife had left him, again. She'd be back. The profit margins even now, for those with the right attitude and sleight of hand, were too good to abandon; he'd seen to that. He rolled onto his side, pushed himself up to a sitting position, and instantly he felt nauseous and giddy. His feet didn't touch the ground.

'Jesus,' he said aloud. What had they slipped him at the staff club? He'd throw up if he didn't put his head down right away. It was so dark. He eased himself down, realising that the bed was hard and cold against his bare skin; no sheets, no pillow. A table? He'd fallen asleep on the dining-room table? Damn it. He needed comfort, he needed his bed, and now he needed Dave to stop. His head was throbbing itself into something nasty.

He couldn't remember anything after he'd rolled out of the club, stumbled through the bamboo garden and down the hill towards the lake and the car park. Somehow, he'd made it home. In his car? Good Lord. Painkillers, water, buckets of it, bed, for Christ's sake.

Dave and the gang grew quieter. Maybe his wife had returned, after all, had snuck in under cover of his stupor. Maybe she'd come over and help him to bed. And in the morning, they'd make up, again.

'Deirdre? Is that you, sweetie?' He tried to inject a tone of contrition into his voice.

'Not Deirdre, sweetie.'

No. 'Is it you, Richard? Did you drive me home? Thank God.' He certainly had no memory of the drive. He pushed himself up onto his elbow, and then, very slowly, rose once more to a sitting position. The giddiness wasn't so bad this time.

'Richard, turn the lights on, will you. I need a pick-me-up. It's so bloody dark in here. I thought I saw a moon earlier.'

'The moon has retired for the night, sir. It's a brand new day and time's a-wasting.'

It wasn't Richard Scrimshaw, his golf partner. Then who, in his own home? One of Miriam's old boyfriends straying off-course?

'Who is it?' He pushed himself off the table and took a step forward. So far so good. Dave and the quartet grew louder again. 'Miriam isn't here, if that's who you're after.' Something tingled in his extremities, and his mouth grew dry. Where was the light switch? Which room was he in?

Then, bright light filled in every space, and his eyes closed involuntarily at the intense glare from banks of fluorescent tubes overhead. He covered his face with his hands and gradually opened his eyes, peering through his fingers. He turned around. He'd been lying on a table, all right, an old wooden one with turned legs, all chipped black paint and dented surfaces. To the left of the table, in one corner, were half a dozen music stands, crammed up together, leaning into each other, looking strangely huddled. Beyond the table, which had been placed in the centre of the small room, the top half of one wall was made of glass. Behind the glass, in an even smaller room by the look of it, were black consoles. A recording studio? A radio station? It had to be a student prank. They'd find out all about pranks once he called the Dean, the little bastards. He tried to blink some moisture into his burning eyes.

When he turned to face the door, a figure was standing directly in front of him. A man in dark overalls, wearing orange safety goggles, and black gloves. The man smiled at him; he smiled back. Automatic.

'Is there a problem?'

He managed to ask the question as the stranger took half a step towards him and punched him so hard in the stomach he instantly folded in half like some kind of hinged puppet. He groaned and coughed, trying to catch his breath. The man pulled him up and slammed him onto the table, stretching out his legs, making the pain in his stomach worse. His eyes were watering now, no need for more moisture. He gasped but no words would come. He was winded. He felt something flung across his shins and then pulled tight, very tight. His heels pressed uncomfortably into the hard surface. He tried to lift his head as another something landed on his chest and pinned his arms to his sides as it, too, tightened around his body and around the table. It pinched his chest hair. He was too slow. He could hear

2

something beneath the table, a ratcheting sound as the ropes, or cables, whatever they were, grew even tighter.

'I can't breathe.' He pushed the words out with what he thought was his last breath, and the strap loosened a little.

'Thanks for that info.' The man smiled down at him, and backhanded him across the cheek, hard. 'Not long now, sir.'

'Who are you? What's going on? You're not Miriam's boyfriend. Where are we?' His cheek stung where the man had hit him.

'Questions. Never many answers though, are there? There you go, another question, just like that.'

'If you're Charlotte's husband, you have to understand, it was a flirtation only. Nothing to go berserk about, I can assure you. Charlotte was very unhappy until I came along. I mean - '

'Poor Charlotte,' the man said, and slapped him again, harder.

'Hey.' He heard some anger enter his voice and felt bolder. 'This is a prank that's out of control. Who are you? Let me up. Now.' He mustered as much of his authoritative voice as he could, lying naked strapped to a table. 'Now. I demand you stop this, you - do you realise who I am?'

'A sensible question, at last.' The man pulled his goggles off and placed them on the carpeted floor, then began to rummage beneath the table. 'Who are you?'

'I'm Professor.' He thought better of it. A different strategy. 'I'm nobody.' He could bluff his way out. 'It's a case of mistaken identity. Look, this is a criminal offence you're committing. Offences.' This creep must have broken a dozen laws. Slipping him a mickey, kidnapping, holding him against his will, assault.

'I know exactly who you are, sir, but since you seem to want to remain incognito behind your honorary title, let's stick with Professor. Do you know who I am?'

He stared up at the man, and then noticed what he held in each hand. 'What are you - you're a medical man? Are they - ? ' He tried to think, but no thoughts would come. Everything felt soft.

'These little things?' He gazed at the scalpel in his left hand and its exact copy in his right. 'We're only just beginning, sir.' He placed the scalpels on the table beside the Professor, who wriggled and managed to move himself a centimetre away from them.

CHAPTER 2

'Easy. Easy, I say. Go right, don't stop, get around that heap, now swing it back. Floor it. Floor it, Gar. Flatten it, now.' Henry Pinkert, the urger in the passenger seat, tried to lean forward to emphasise his instructions, but the steepness of the hill we climbed, combined with Henry's low, spreading centre of gravity, held him firmly in place. To compensate, he grunted loudly after each shouted direction, as though the little hatchback would go faster with this generous donation of extra, heartfelt energy.

The grille appeared first, directly ahead on the crest when I thought we were home free. It came right for us, high and powerful. The grille glared at us, it shone like banks of Christmas lights and Guy Fawkes' sparklers, it pinged the sun at us from a thousand tiny points, every one a miniature halogen burst. It was the cleanest, shiniest, widest grille I've ever seen. It was buff, and it was menacing, and it grinned horribly.

Everything slowed down, and I thought it was all over before it had begun. I heard Henry shout 'Turn, turn. Jesus,' and I thought, 'Which way?' And before I could think again, I was turning, turning right across the narrow street, screeching everything that could screech, yelling something over and over. It might have been 'Oh dear,' but probably not. The wheels locked and we mounted the footpath the hard way, via the gutter. Henry and I bounced up and down together, perfectly synchronised as though we'd practised the move a thousand times. I stood on the brakes in front of a low, orange brick fence. The cat who owned the fence leapt off and ran down the driveway to the left, telling us in its own silent way that we might have considered that sensible car-friendly option ourselves.

'You fucking dickhead.' Henry had unbuckled his belt - he moved quickly for a big, slow suit in search of a steam iron - and pushed himself out of his seat. He yelled after the car's broad black boot where more chrome bumpers shone at us. 'You bastard.'

4

'Henry.' I got out of the car and joined him.

'Arsewipe,' Henry yelled, and actually shook his fist at the departing vehicle.

The black car glided down the hill, well under the speed limit, stately. It looked like a Buick or an Oldsmobile, something gigantic. The driver's bare arm slid out of the window and his hand gave us the middle finger salute. There was laughter, too. I turned away from the car in time to see the Nonna whose cat owned the fence shoot us a cursing stare from her front door and then slam it hard. Suburbia, who doesn't love it? And the cat was one of those marmalade jobs, all white and ginger stripes, just like Aunt Edie's old tom. What was his name?

'Thank Christ you missed the cat, Gar,' Henry said. 'Edie'd have a fit.' He stretched back, hands on hips, and groaned.

'That's Edie's cat?'

'Moved up here when Edie moved to the waiting room and I moved into Edie's.'

Henry referred to all retirement villages and nursing homes, however vigorous their residents, as waiting rooms.

'How is Edie? I haven't seen her since I got back.' I stared down the hill at our destination before we'd detoured, Edie's old house at 56A, now Henry's place of business. Our place of business.

'She's great. Living the high life. Bingo, mega yard sales, casino crawls, ladies club lunches, all singing, all dancing. I'll see you down there.'

Henry had no trouble travelling downhill. He was a few metres away when I thought to ask.

'Henry, why the hilltop approach?' The other end of the street ran off Hardgrave Road and you could see everything you needed to see to avoid shiny grilles, orange cats, Nonnas and brick fences. I'd visited Edie often enough with my mother, may she rest in peace, to know it was the only sane way to enter Whynot Street.

'Gotta keep you on your toes, Gar, now that you're my driver.' He laughed and kept walking.

The street looked much the same as the last time I'd visited Aunt Edie, except that a lot of the houses were newly renovated, the trees had grown and thickened, there were many more cars, and the council had thoughtfully installed two speed bumps. They'd help with the hillcrest head-ons, sure they would. I took a breath or two and felt some calm return.

'I'm not your driver, Henry,' I said quietly, re-entering the car. 'I'm a cook.'

I backed out in a wide arc, at last taking advantage of the smoother driveway entry as recommended by nine out of ten orange cats. 'No, I'm not a cook, not anymore,' I told the steering wheel. 'I eschew cooking.'

I revved the engine past appropriate and tracked Henry to his new digs, gliding into Edie's driveway and down the side of the house into the shade. Why not use the tradesmen's entrance and get a feel for the place before I found out what the hell I'd committed myself to a month before in a moment of maritime desperation way out in the great rolling Pacific?

CHAPTER 3

OPERATION BLUEWATER POLARIS #001

'You know a lot of people, Professor. Deirdre, your wife; Richard, your friend; Charlotte, poor Charlotte. Your lovely daughter, Miriam. Are you sure you don't know who I am?'

'No, I've never seen you before, and you're mistaken about me. You must stop this. Where are we? I have to go home. I have responsibilities, appointments.' Babbling. He was babbling. What else could he do?

'I'm glad you asked where we are.' He glanced around the room. 'We're in a recording studio of our university's music department. I spent so many happy hours here. My name is Guy, by the way. Guy Friendly. I'm a friendly guy, Professor.' The man laughed. 'Didn't do me much good in Iraq, though, or Afghanistan, being a pianist. Or friendly, for that matter.'

Friendly bent down again and came up with a razor. He removed the plastic safety cover and leaned over the table.

'No.' The Professor felt the razor gliding through his chest hair, first above the strap and then below it, around his nipples. His heart pounded in his ears.

'You're getting soft, Professor.' Friendly poked his chest with one gloved finger and flicked the shaved hair onto the floor. He turned the razor at an angle and pulled it along the Professor's ribcage. He yelled in pain as a thin red line of blood rose from the cut and spread across his skin.

'You've got the wrong man, I tell you.' Adrenalin pumped through his body, his head throbbed. His hands and feet were freezing. Dave Brubeck kept playing. The blood felt warm. 'I'm just an ordinary person.' He couldn't focus on anything but the pain.

'Anything but ordinary, sir. You're a decision-maker. An extraordinary decision-maker. Something we respect where I come from, but only when the right decision's made.'

'What? Why are you doing this? If it's money you want - everyone needs money, I can give you anything you want. I'm very wealthy. Did you hear me? I can write you a cheque now. We can just forget this ever happened.' He'd call the police the second he got out of this room. Now they'd believe the threatening phone calls were real. They couldn't ignore it now that he had proof - he was bleeding.

'I know you'd like that, but Professor, it isn't about money. Which just goes to show you how mad I must be. Mad as in angry, I mean, what else? Here's what it's about.' Friendly threw the razor across the room, grabbed the Professor's head in both hands and turned him roughly. 'It's about suffering, and disrespect, and revenge.'

The Professor could smell and feel Friendly's hot, minty breath on his face.

'I don't cause suffering, Mr Friendly. I don't. I promise you, you've got the wrong man.' Every word pushed against his fear. Panic filled every cell, panic like he'd never felt before. 'Come on. How much? I'll reimburse you whatever it is you've lost.'

'Shut up.'

From somewhere, a roll of silver duct tape appeared. Friendly tore off a strip and stuck it firmly over the Professor's mouth. He tried to speak, but only muffled sounds emerged.

'It's simple enough, Professor, revenge. Some might call it reparation, the polite ones. But really, unvarnished, it's revenge. Not many people do it, not really, not in our civilized society. We rationalize. Something I learned in Iraq, though - when people get pushed over a particular line - they act, and the law is irrelevant, the courts, jail terms, even justice. It's pure revenge, and it feels great. I highly recommend it. You know the biggest difference between us and them, those fundamentalists over there in the sandpits? They're prepared to die for their cause, for what they believe in. Would you be prepared to die for what you believe in? Oh wait, your belief system is the ESP model. Isn't that right? Expedience, self-interest, profit. No room for sacrifice there, except by others.'

The Professor began to shake, he couldn't help himself any longer, and then he felt warm urine spraying across his lower abdomen and thighs, beginning to pool between his legs.

'That's a shame.' Friendly bent down once more and came up with a towel. He threw it over the Professor's genitals and pushed the other half down between his legs to soak up the liquid. 'Don't want to leave too much of a mess for the cleaners. Not that they'll be here for a while, holidays and all.'

The Professor strained every muscle, and felt himself, heard himself trying to scream through the immovable tape, in the soundproof studio.

He suddenly realised that nobody else in the world knew where he was at this moment.

Friendly bent over him and pulled the tape aside. 'What's that, sir? Your non-verbals disturb me.'

'Why?' the Professor said, beginning to cry. 'I'm nobody. I'm sorry, whatever it is you think I've done.' He'd removed the tape. He'd listen. He'd realize he'd picked the wrong man. He tried to smile, his smile of trust. One of his best features, Charlotte had said.

'Glad you got that off your chest? I was going to leave you with a little mystery, I thought it would upset you more. Bit cruel, I know, but given your apparent complete ignorance,' Friendly's voice rose in anger, 'I'll give you the reason, Professor. And something else. You can't reimburse me for what I've lost.'

Friendly leaned in to the Professor's face. 'Two words. Jacinta Hurley.' He leaned back.

'Jacinta Hurley?' Not that. Not now. 'How do you know Jacinta Hurley? You aren't her husband. I know him. You're not him.' The Professor felt himself relax, just a little, a muscle here, a sinew there. At last. He'd wondered if it would catch him. Decision-maker, yes, he'd been the decision-maker then, but the others had voted with him. 'It was a unanimous vote. Everyone agreed.' But they weren't here now to unanimously save him.

'Unanimous? That's my understanding, too. Makes things easier.' Friendly re-taped the Professor's mouth. 'You're the first one, you know. I haven't done exactly this before - usually, it's mercy killing. I thought I'd start at the top, the figurehead top, get a bit of practice, and go from there. Plus, I'm all for instant gratification. Good plan?' He smiled down at the Professor and the Professor could see that the smile didn't reach his eyes.

Friendly picked up the scalpels again, one in each hand, waved them for a few seconds in time with 'Take Five' rolling through its second loop, and drove them simultaneously into the soft flesh just above the moaning man's kneecaps.

CHAPTER 4

'We offer a full service protective detail, Ms Harding.'

Henry had a punter, and he was lathering it on. Full service? What did that mean? Did you get fries with it, and a Margarita? I stood near the kitchen door waiting for a cue to enter.

'I'm the senior specialist, of course, and as CEO, I supervise all operations and assign the staff most appropriate to your needs. Following a full analysis of your situation, of course.'

'There's nothing complex about this, Mr Pinkert.'

'You'd be surprised how many people say that, Ms Harding. But as a former Homicide detective with 30 years experience in one of the country's most crime-ridden cities, I can assure you that nothing is ever as simple as it appears.'

Henry would be smiling benevolently as he spoke, trying to invoke a sense of trust and authority, a man who's seen it all. Hmm.

'One person, Mr Pinkert, that's all I need. Male, big, strong, and he should look as though he knows what he's doing. Do they wear uniforms, your people?'

If male, big, and strong weren't cues, I don't know cues. I walked into Edie's living-room, now Henry's conference room judging by the fat round table and its six heavy wooden chairs.

Ms Harding was a top shelf example of corporate panache. Shining blonde hair in undulating shoulder length curls, face perfectly made up, but a little pale - the chic, sunless look. Navy blue suit, crease-free, snug around the hips and breasts, but not blushingly so.

'Ah, Fletcher,' Henry said, staring at me staring at Ms Harding, urging me to be a professional something-or-other. Not a trawler cook. 'Ms Sarah Harding, Mr Garfield Fletcher, security expert and expedition leader.'

Expedition leader? Ms Harding offered me her hand. She had a firm grip, but it was cool and eager to withdraw after an obligatory two seconds. Fair enough.

'How tall are you, Mr Fletcher? Six? Six-one?'

Ms Harding wasn't curious about what kind of expedition leader I might be. She looked me up and down.

'Six-two,' I replied. 'Six-three in heels.' I smiled what I thought of as one of my beguiling, *Magnum, P.I.* smiles. Ms Harding dismissed me and turned to Henry.

'I'll need him tomorrow morning at 8.00, 167 Eagle, 13th floor.' She turned back to me. 'See you then, Mr Fletcher.'

'Ms Harding, the contract.' Henry tried to regain control of things.

'Bring it with you, Mr Fletcher. Our CFO will sign and issue a cheque to Pinkert's Protection and Investigation Systems and Services. That's the correct name isn't it? Anyway, it's neither here nor there. The whole thing's cosmetic, as I explained earlier, Mr Pinkert.' She paused. 'We're good for it, you know. Things are grim for some, but we have fat to burn. We run responsible investment and hedge funds.'

There was such a thing as a responsible hedge fund? You learn every day. Not that I had more than the faintest clue about hedge funds.

At the door, she turned back to us. 'Don't forget the uniform, Mr Fletcher. Appearances are everything in my business. And you may need a raincoat, judging by the sky. I guess we'll just have to play some indoor games over the weekend.'

'Pardon?' Henry said.

'Good morning, gentlemen.' She was gone.

I sat down at the conference table and watched Henry fidgeting with his worry beads.

'Henry?' I said.

He looked over at me, but didn't want to make eye contact.

'Henry, you still have trouble with a certain kind of woman, don't you?'

Henry blushed, or it could have been the heat, which was rising quickly as the severe weather system approached from the north. He removed his coat after the draining meeting with the woman who was a dead ringer for his ex-wife, Sylvia.

'And Henry? Expedition leader? Security expert?'

'Don't push it, Gar. You're the one who ran away from the sea and back to the land. You should be grateful we're cousins, and that you're Edie's favourite. Get my drift, sunshine?'

Henry's mother and my mother, both deceased, are Edie's sisters. Edie sold Henry this house and the one next door at a discount rate, but on the proviso that I was included as a silent partner. I own half the business, not that you'd notice from Henry's attitude.

'What's the pay rate, Henry? I'm a bit short at the moment.'

'Whatever you got slinging hash on the SS Minnow, Gar. Halve it.'

He went out to the bathroom and left the door open as he took a pee. Can urine sound angry, do you think, or was that just my sea salt imagination at work?

CHAPTER 5

'You moving into Belle's?'

Henry brought two black coffees into the conference room and set them on the big table.

'Thought I might.' It was that or the toothless, punchie, burnt-out no-hopers' hostel in Browning Street where men my age looked 20 years older and experienced life as one damned blackout after another. 'Redundancy payments for a ship's cook buy a ham roll, Henry, hold the ham.'

Henry grunted, sat down and started sipping. I went to the kitchen and brought back the sugar and milk. Ever since I went to sea, I've needed plenty of sugar and milk in my hot drinks. They're good for dehydration and freezing oceans. Could be helpful in new jobs, too.

'Yeah, well, hope you don't scare easily.'

'Why's that?'

'According to Edie, there's a ghost at number 54.'

'Ghost?'

'Belle, apparently. Not frightened of little old lady spectres, are you? Music at odd hours, lights on and off, on and off.'

'Belle? Are you kidding?' Belle, Edie's best old friend of 50 years, found one morning six months ago, dead in the front room, which was pretty much where she'd lived for the last three, frail years of her life. It was Belle's death that had knocked the wind out of Edie's sails, and Henry's real estate urgings had simply hastened her move to the retirement home

'Why not Belle? Everyone needs a hobby, Gar, even the dead.'

'Are you trying to fake me out before I even move in, Henry? Don't you want me next door?'

'What would make you say that, cousin. You'd be surprised at some of the stories I've heard at murder scenes. Spooky doings, Gar, after the events. Messages from the other side. Don't knock it.'

'I'm not knocking it, but is this why you came north again, Henry, to get over the breakdown? Or to rip Edie off with these houses?'

Henry sat up and glared. It was a pretty good one, too, and it would have worked on nine out of ten homicidal perps, but we've known each other all my life. Henry, 15 years older, and the mature side of 50, was beating me up long before I could even remember the bruises. But I was human kryptonite to Henry now: none of his punches were packing anymore. That didn't mean we couldn't still play regularly, even though he'd had a lot of trouble with his nerves since the divorce.

'Just remember, you're an equal beneficiary, junior.'

'Speaking of which, where's the petty cash?' I stood up.

'Petty cash? What do you want?'

'Groceries, Henry. The basics of life. Food. If you're not paying a salary, I'll need some walking around money. For the weekend, too, with Ms Corporate Appeal.'

Henry fished his wallet out of his pocket, and thumbed a few fifties.

'And another few - consider it an advance against next pay.'

'You think you'll last that long?' But he handed the notes over and I reached for the car keys.

'Hang on, where are you going with those?'

'To the shops, dear Henry, where else?'

'No, I'll drop you off. I'm going into town to get that cheque and contract from the hedge fund girl. You can't be too careful with those stock market types.'

'Exactly what am I being hired for, Henry?' I realised that I hadn't heard that part of the conversation other than the buzz phrases 'expedition leader' and 'security expert.' Food security?

'Check that, genius.' Henry threw a glance at the wall behind us where a couple of framed documents hung.

I hadn't taken any notice of the detail but as I got closer, I saw my name on a certificate of accreditation as an investigator and protective services provider. It was dated two weeks after I'd agreed to Henry's offer - under Edie's duress - of partnership; the ink still looked wet. Henry's name was on the other document as the registered proprietor of Pinkert Protection and Investigation Systems and Services.

'I must have done some cramming for this one, Henry,' I said, a little shocked to see my name up in, well, up anywhere.

'Yeah. You'll be getting a bill for the tuition fees, sunshine. Here, put this in your wallet.'

Henry handed me a small, laminated card. In the top left corner was a head shot of me that looked suspiciously like the photo on my driver's licence. I had a pony tail when that one was taken and now it was short back and sides and a few years older with a little bonus grey around the gills. The description was brief but accurate enough: hair - red-blond; eyes - green; height - 183 centimetres; complexion - fair.

'Where did you get this?' I asked.

'It's a Pinkert ID - your security and investigations officer authorisation.'

'Not that - the photo.'

'Networks, Gar - friends in Licensing.'

'Is this kosher? Look, my hair's different. It's obvious this photo is older than the date on your ID.'

Henry was so worried about my fake ID, he didn't even reply, and instead made for the door. My choices were limited, so I followed him.

Outside, there was no sunshine; a cyclonic depression was twirling its way down the coast. By tomorrow we could all be floating in our cabanas. It was grey and muggy and you could almost smell the grass sweating and waiting for the deluge. But for me the day couldn't have been better at that moment. I had money in my pocket, a job to look forward to, and as we backed out of Edie's yard, I gazed over at number 54, the new roof over my head. If Belle didn't mind sharing, then neither did I. Naturally, the moment didn't last.

CHAPTER 6

I organised delivery and walked home from the Boundary Street shops. Home, a place that didn't rock 24-7 and offer porthole views of rolling, spuming, ever-restless ocean, a place where I could cook, or not. Not, I decided, for today at least, strolling along the favourite street of my childhood.

At the top of the hill, I stopped at the Nonna's house to apologise, and knocked on her front door. The curtain beside the door moved a little and I pretended not to notice, waiting while the Nonna, Lucia Magiolo, decided to talk to me. After a minute, the door opened a crack and Mrs Magiolo stared up at me. She'd lost some height and I'd found it since our last close encounter, which was more years ago than is polite to mention in front of an older lady.

'What is it?' she asked. 'You've come to finish off the fence? Maybe the house next, eh?'

'Nonna Lucia, I'm sorry about that. It's me, Garfield. Garfield Fletcher. Edie's nephew.' I smiled, and received a frown in response. Another angle was needed. I squatted in front of her. 'Remember? I used to play with Gianni.'

Gianni Magiolo was Nonna's favourite grandson; he was always around the place when I was a kid, mainly because his parents worked shifts and childcare was a family affair; no-one else would make the grade. Gianni and I gravitated towards each other out of necessity: no-one else to play with - we were both only-children - and a shared love of Italian food. And I still loved the Nonna.

'Garfield?' She put her hand out and touched the top of my head. 'My little redhead, Garfie. Of course it's you. Where have you been?' She motioned for me to stand up.

'At sea.' In more ways than she could ever imagine, actually, but that didn't need scrutiny at the moment. 'I'm back now, though. I thought you might like some of these.'

I pulled a packet of Minties from the one grocery bag I'd carried home myself and held them out to her.

'Garfie, you remembered.' She took a few steps and hugged me around the waist. I hugged her back, and I think we both enjoyed the unexpected pleasure of an old affection. 'I'll just take one, to remind me - I can put it in a jar and smell the scent whenever I feel like it.'

'You don't like Minties anymore?' I had nothing else to offer.

'I love Minties, darling, I have diabetes. So.' She gestured a what-can-you-do with her hands.' Enjoy them for me, Garfie.'

She took one Mintie from the packet and put it in her pocket, scrunched the packet closed, grabbed my empty grocery bag and dropped it in. Then she did a neat twirl with her left wrist and the bag was magically knotted at the top, everything inside safe and shipshape, the two handles sticking up like a rabbit's ears. Lucia used to own a fruit and vegie shop. Her twirling of brown paper bags full of apples, peaches, bananas, potatoes and every other variety of edible was legendary in West End, and she was no less adroit with plastic grocery bags. For thirty years, from the fifties to the seventies, she had no peer. She handed me back the bag. I slipped my fingers through the rabbit's ears.

'Thanks, Nonna.'

She patted my hand. 'And tell Henry to mow the grass. Belle and Edie like it short.'

CHAPTER 7

OPERATION BLUEWATER POLARIS #002

He'd never liked the idea of women being hurt. There was nothing to be gained by it, in his opinion. Really, what was the point? They were smaller, far less muscular, weaker, generally speaking, mostly they did nothing too harmful in war. Although, he'd come across a few suicide bombers in Iraq who were female. Very harmful. Deluded, all of them, not only the women. Reason with them? Not for a second, especially not with detonators in their hands. But women overall? Unsurpassed.

Which was why it pained him so much, this particular duty; why he'd decided on an operational name in the first place: Bluewater Polaris. It gave him the illusion of distance. He could imagine that he was simply following orders, his own, to be sure, but the margin was enough to work with for now. It had even helped him come to terms with this grubby location he'd chosen; it was so dirty and sad, if a building could be sad. Was there anything more depressing than a closed-down ice-works in a sub-tropical city? It said a lot about pathetic business practice, an inability to sell cold stuff to hot people clamouring for relief. Or maybe they'd been victims, too, taken in by promises, greed, their own preference for ignorance in the face of unlikely windfalls.

It was a big old joint, Cool Cubes, at the far end of an industrial estate along the river, full of machinery and dust, most of it in darkness with occasional spackles of light fighting through the rusting walls. It had its own generators, though, in case of emergency; he'd confirmed that they hadn't been sold off yet. So when times were good and hot, and load-shedding occurred on the steamiest days, the ice-works kept icing away. Earlier in the day, he'd rigged the generator for one of the smaller freezer rooms and now, returning in the van via the seldom-used river road, he confirmed that no other vehicles were about before driving into the loading dock and closing the roller doors behind him. There were busybodies everywhere, maybe fewer of them now that the rain had begun in earnest.

He used a miner's helmet with a light attached so he could see ahead as he carried her into the darkness. She was limp still, thankfully; he didn't want to have to give her more sedation. There was a part of him that wanted her to wake up now, in his arms, and know what was happening, and to panic and feel her heart banging against her ribs and her terror rising and rising without pause. But this part fought with the part that told him to act like a gentleman the way he'd been taught.

What, though, would his teachers think of a woman like this one, who'd managed to achieve the unforgivable, and maintained the charade for so long? He hoped she'd remember what he'd whispered into her ear right before he gave her the needle: Jacinta Hurley. He'd spoken Jacinta's name lovingly, slowly, as the woman lay beneath his much heavier body on the kitchen floor in her apartment. It had been so easy to gain entry that he thought for a moment that the shoe was on the other foot, that he'd been set up somehow. It was amazing how a tradesman's getup, a clipboard, a big cardboard whitegoods box on a trolley and a request from the body corporate to replace the complex's faulty, fire hazard stoves, could work wonders. People were so trusting, and most of the time they were right to be that way. You didn't often encounter people like himself, so intent on his task.

He'd grabbed her as soon as she'd let him in - surprise was your biggest advantage, even against a weaker opponent - covered her mouth with his hand and pushed her down to the tiled floor. She stared up at him in absolute terror, no doubt expecting rape and probably torture. Did he look that bad? When he'd spoken Jacinta's name, she'd looked puzzled until the memory returned; then she'd gone limp and then totally rigid. By then he had the needle out, the cover off, and before he injected her, he added the coup de grace: Jacinta was with child, he said, feeling the words, offering them to her syllable by syllable. He liked the old-fashioned phrase. Had she known, this woman? Her eyes suddenly filled with tears - for the baby? For Jacinta? For herself - and he'd felt his own throat beginning to swell and prick. Then the needle went in, and her eyes closed, and that was that.

He'd loaded her into his prop, the stove box, a reinforced construction with a wooden base and hinges so that one side opened like a door and allowed him to easily position her inside. Off he went to the van, box on trolley, another working stiff doing a lady a favour and removing the packaging from her new appliance. No-one does that anymore. Let them wonder if it was the old stove snugly, conveniently inside.

Once he'd wrestled the box into the van, he closed the doors behind him, hauled her out and lay her on a mattress on the floor. He didn't want her expiring inside the airless box, not in this weather, not before she could experience the full majesty of her fate. She'd never know, but her demise was far less harrowing than that of Bluewater Polaris Number One. Who'd have thought the human body contained so much blood? He knew it did, of course, but even as a soldier, he hadn't seen as much as he'd left on the walls and floor in the recording studio. Things had gotten a little out of hand, but then, Polaris Number One had been the special, the first, the captain of his fate from the day he'd messed it up irretrievably for them all.

When he reached the freezer room, he placed her carefully on the floor. As he hauled open the door, gusts of icy air blew out into the dank warehouse space. The chill was almost overpowering. He hurried back to the van and retrieved the mattress, tossing it onto the freezer room floor. Then he lifted her again, one last time, and carried her into the almost frozen space. He let her down gently onto the mattress and rolled her over. He slapped her face a few times to rouse her, and she moaned once, twice, already beginning to shake. He removed and pocketed the one item he needed from her quivering body.

'I'll leave the lights on, dear, so you can see how it's going to be.'

She rolled her eyes open, blinked once, twice, closed them again.

He stood up and went outside, slamming the door shut. He checked the temperature gauge - not quite at maximum freeze, but he didn't want to blow the generator, and the temperature he'd set would be sufficient to get the job done. It would just take a little longer. He guessed that would be quite distressing for her, but she'd freely made the decision that led her here; so be it.

He leaned against the door and breathed deeply. Revenge was hard work, but rewarding in the end. What was that expression: a dish best eaten cold? Or was it served? Served cold? She was certainly going to be served cold to someone when they found her, if they ever did. He was sorry he couldn't watch the final breaths of this one, little white plumes in the chill air, and then nothing. But there were other, more pressing matters: number three, for instance, and the rest. He hummed a Christmas tune as he returned to the loading dock and rejoined his favourite monsoonal city.

CHAPTER 8

The groceries were delivered, and shortly afterwards Henry brought home the cheque clearance and the rain. The deluge seemed to arrive in an instant. One minute we had a muggy, cloud-covered, syrupy city-in-waiting, and the next, you could barely hear yourself think happy thoughts.

I managed to retrieve my luggage from the boot of Henry's car as the roaring sound of the downpour made its way towards us across rooftops and streets. I love that sound; it's scary and inviting. It's full of the energy of promise and provocation. You just don't know if you're going to be the one who wins or loses. Will your car float into the newly-created lagoon at the dip in the street? Will you be at the wheel, mouthing silent screams at the windscreen right before you go under three doors from home?

I stood on Belle's verandah thinking these thoughts when Henry walked out onto Edie's verandah and waved at me. He gestured a phone at his ear, so I went inside with the rest of the grocery bags and my luggage, and waited.

'We're all go,' he yelled when I picked up. The rain was louder than loud on our tin roofs.

'You still haven't told me what I'm going to, Henry,' I yelled back.

'Protective security, Gar, right up your alley. And don't forget the uniforms, you heard the lady. I store them in Belle's linen cupboard in the bathroom. There's plenty there so take what you want. This is a four-day job, tomorrow to Monday. Go to the 13th floor, 167 Eagle, at 8am. Aurora Investments and Securities. Okay?'

'I have a few questions.' More than a few, since I felt neither protective nor secure.

'Wait'll the rain eases, I don't want you dripping on the new carpet.'

'You don't have carpet.'

He hung up, so I grabbed the umbrella from the fake elephant's foot on the verandah and ran next door.

Henry had already begun his sundowners' session. He offered me a vodka and tonic on his way out to the back deck; I declined. I haven't had a drink since I used up my quota last decade. Not a pretty story, not worth the trouble of remembering, if I could remember.

'I seem to recall Ms Harding mentioned she wanted someone big and strong, who knows what he's doing. What's that all about, Henry?'

'Gar, it's a business. We know what we're doing, mate. Seems reasonable doesn't it?' Henry sipped at his drink and watched the rain falling and falling.

'You might convince a drunk at closing time.' I waited.

'It's nothing. Ms Harding said they've had a few abusive phone calls, idle threats, from some disgruntled investors. Little people who are angry. Small investors, those whinging Mums and Dads they're always interviewing on the news. All talk, no action, Gar.'

'Like us.'

Henry threw me a sour look.

'You've got to admit a uniform does not the protective security officer make, Henry. I'm a cook, former cook.'

'And before that, you were Army,' he said.

'As a cook.'

'And trained to kill, if I'm not mistaken about armies. And now you work here.' He waved his arm around. 'You're a partner. Pull your weight.'

'You can hire someone, a contractor. Get onto some of your mates in the trade. There's sure to be someone big and strong who actually knows what he's doing.' I stood up. 'I'll need to study some of the stuff behind that certificate you bought me before I'm prepared to do anything like this, Henry.'

He turned to face me. 'I can get you a gun, Gar. If it'll make you feel any safer. I've got a Glock, a couple of thirty-eights, a nice Czech .38 actually. Very comfortable in the hand. Never jams.' He smiled and sipped.

'I'm not frightened, Henry, but a gun is a bridge too far. You said yourself it was a babysitting detail. And I don't have a license.' Which was a redundant argument, from Henry's counterfeiting for idiots standpoint.

'Gar, it's you or no-one, and I can't get anyone else at such short notice. All my operatives are busy and I - you know, with my back the way it is, I'm restricted to being the desk jockey.'

'Since when?'

He ignored me and went on with the pitch. 'Plus, it's a small job. Most of the big firms wouldn't touch it, and we'd be looking at breach of contract now, anyway. It's a done deed, you understand. These finance people are sharks. Come on, pal. Babysitting. At a resort, too. You might meet someone.'

Babysitting sharks. I walked to the end of the deck and stared next door at Belle's. I looked down at Henry's little hatchback parked between the two houses, getting pounded by the rain, big, thick drops cleaning off the dust. Mud puddles were busy forming in the driveway.

'Blood's thicker than water, Gar, Edie always says. And it was your choice, remember? Partner?'

This muddy water might give the blood a run.

'Exactly how many operatives do you have on the books, Henry?' I had to be sure. I turned back to where he sat.

'Exactly how many would make you happy, cousin?' He met my gaze, maintained the smile, and didn't blink.

So there were none, or at least none living or real. No other certificates on the wall, no desks other than Henry's, one laptop - Henry's, on Henry's desk; no signs of recent habitation by staff members eagerly researching and organising protection and investigation. Henry's firm consisted of Henry and me, and Edie, the original generous benefactor. I was still waiting on Belle to make an appearance - a cameo partner to boost our numbers - but there was time enough for that.

'Babysitting, you say?'

'Nothing to it. Just look menacing, like when you're dicing and slicing your onions and garlic. Splash of Tabasco, Gar, and we're all go go go.'

Henry's last 'go' was lost in the increased volume as the monsoon proceeded to dump another gout of water on top of us. He stood up, drained his glass and pointed at the kitchen door.

'Come on, Gar, down the Taj, I'll spring for a curry. Early start tomorrow.'

'I haven't said yes.'

'And don't forget to exercise that scar rampant, mate. With that glaring out from your forehead, nobody's going to take you on.' He gave a laugh and slipped into breezy, devil-may-care mode.

That, of course, was Henry's ultimate bargaining chip, the scar that linked us forever and a day. It was the thing that allowed him to take it for granted that I'd follow in his wake. I didn't have to keep doing that, did I? My life was a meandering series of career path changes and travels on a whim, and Henry knew it. If I had a solid core at the heart of me, it had yet to manifest itself. Henry knew that, too.

'Here sport, you're the designated driver.' Henry threw the keys over his shoulder. I caught them on my fingertips. 'Try to miss the gutter this time.'

A career, someone said, is an uncontrollable lurch downhill. So what happens once you reach the gully at the bottom?

CHAPTER 9

One-six-seven Eagle Street was an unimpressive high-rise, no architectural splendour on display at all, but the rents were juicy because it was right on the riverfront and the eastern side had wonderful views of the bridge and the snaking waterway and all of their vehicular and marine traffic.

I should know; I'd worked in the building for a couple of years on and off, as a clerical type. That was just before the wanderings began and took me away from the country. I'd worked on a floor that was just above the level at which the fire brigade could save us with their ladders. During the infrequent fire drills, held when someone remembered, everyone was supposed to file down the stairwell and meet at a designated safety location across the road beneath the Moreton Bay fig. But several of us would hide in our cubicles and joke about becoming human incendiary devices, screaming and shining brightly as we passed each floor before flaming out in the muddy Styx below. This was long before the events of September 11, 2001 when such innocence from twenty-somethings was considered, well, perfectly excusable, sane enough, and yes, harmless.

I'd never been to the thirteenth floor until this day, but it seemed to me that there was a level of luxury present there that had never graced the baby-poo yellow industrial carpets of the ninth floor where I had pushed my pen and the patience of my supervisor. The place reminded me a little of my former dentist's rooms in Queen Street. Panelled wood everywhere; lush, plush, carefully brushed Berber carpet designed to hush the heaviest footfalls; expensive-looking wall hangings and tasteful landscapes - was that an original Sidney Nolan? There was some kind of contemporary sculpture in the reception area that resembled a large, somewhat out of square grey box. It was either marble or plastic, or tinfoil.

There was also an interesting absence of people, and noise. Ms Harding herself greeted me at the front desk and explained that most of the staff were on annual holidays, but the senior several were retreating to the resort to brainstorm and carefully plan their next moves.

'There may be some delay to our departure, Mr Fletcher,' she said, looking me up and down in my uniform. I'd thrown it on in half-darkness as the rain pounded and I discovered that most of the light bulbs in Belle's house had blown. No wonder she'd retreated to the front room.

'No problem,' I said. With a bit of luck, the entire trip would be cancelled and I could confront Henry about the business and my place in it. A proper career.

'Apparently, the transport has broken down - they're arranging another shuttle. You can wait in the staff lounge if you like. I'll get Delia to organise some coffee. This way.' She turned and walked off towards the riverside of the building where the light was brighter. Some compassionate clever-dick designer had decided that the plebs toiling in the darker boxes in the centre of the floor and beyond at least deserved a lovely view once or twice a day when they broke for morning tea and lunch.

I stood at the windows and watched the river for a while, idly measuring the moored and moving pleasure craft and calculating the potential spaciousness of their galleys. It's a sea cook's thing.

'Mr Fletcher?'

I turned to the voice and saw a woman about my age standing near the door. She held a tray with Starbuck's takeaway coffees and Shingle Inn cakes.

'Garfield,' I said. 'Shingle Inn? Good taste.'

'You know the area?'

'Used to work here - well, not here exactly. Down on the public sector floors.'

'Me too, years ago. I'm Delia Porter, temp, contractor, dog's body, whatever.'

'Nice to meet you, Delia,' I said.

She smiled and set the tray down on the coffee table in quite a graceful motion, I thought. Delia would do well at sea in rolling conditions. She was dark-haired and green-eyed, small-boned, quite a few centimetres shorter than me, and she was beach-phobic pale.

'You're the security person, Mr - Garfield?'

'Correct. Are you coming with us to this resort, Delia?'

'I'm it, so yes.' She looked outside at the empty office.

'It's like the *Marie Celeste* out there,' I said. 'Where are our fellow travellers?' There were a lot of empty desks, and by empty I mean cleaned off, the monitors shoved over to the sides, correspondence trays clear of paper, not a pen in sight, no sign of a casually discarded annual report.

'I'm not sure, but I seem to have replaced about 20 of them.' She placed a coffee and a cake packet in front of me and picked up the tray.

'Looking to get a permanent job here?'

'I doubt they'll be around far beyond Christmas, and I have other plans - this is a stopgap.'

'Well then, in that case, you obviously need a break. Won't you join me?'

'Other deliveries to make. The chiefs - '

'Chiefs?'

'Chief Financial Officer, Chief Operating Officer, Chief Executive Officer. Chiefliness rules here. Oh, and the Chairman of the Board. Chiefs and Chairs. They're behind the closed doors on the four corners. Plus Ms Harding, of course, Chief Wrangler, or something in Human Resources. She's in the middle office on the north face.'

'Ah,' I said, 'the north face,' not knowing what else to say. I was surprised I'd made it this far in the conversation.

But someone had a voice.

'Delia.' It was a very loud, male voice, and it seemed to be coming from the office behind me whose door was slightly ajar. 'Coffee, Delia,' the voice demanded. 'Now, love, while you still have a job. And bring the files I asked for half an hour ago.'

Delia lowered her eyes and I thought for a moment that she might cry. But it turned out she was made of sterner and more creative stuff.

She peered at the letters marked on the coffee cup lids and moved one to the other side of the tray, away from the rest.

The voice erupted again, and this time the Chief Screamer actually put his boofhead out the door, a blonde head with a flushed face squeezed out of a tight collar and striped tie. He was heavy-set and a little shorter than me, thick and pasty-looking.

'Make sure it isn't too bloody hot this time - I won't tell you again.' The head retreated and the door slammed.

I looked back to Delia. 'Graham Butler,' she said. 'CFO - pays the bills, or rather, tries not to pay them.'

'Would you like me to shoot him?' I asked her, smiling the Magnum smile. 'My cousin has guns, and I have a licence.' I wanted to grab him by that tie and pull it extremely tight before stapling his lips to his precious files.

'No need, but thanks Garfield. Appreciated.' Delia picked up the tray and walked out to reception.

I could follow her progress from where I sat because the staff lounge had clear glass walls and the blinds were open. She paused near the water cooler, put the tray down, removed the lid from the isolated coffee cup - the boofhead's - and poured some of it out into the cooler's slops' tray. She pulled a plastic cup from the dispenser, but instead of going to the cooler for water, she took it to the large fish tank on the other side of the coffee table and swooped out a measure of water. Hmm.

She poured the fish water into the coffee cup, replaced the lid, dropped the empty plastic cup into the wastepaper bin and retraced her steps, deftly grabbing a pile of files off a desk and slipping them under her arm on the way. She veered off to the boofhead's office as she neared the staff lounge again, giving me a little nod and a half-smile as she went past. I had a sudden urge to applaud the performance, and wondered what exactly Delia might do for an encore. It so happened, I had this whole, long, resort weekend to find out. Henry's folly might just turn into a worthwhile assignment, after all.

CHAPTER 10

'Men in suits. Who invented the suit, do you think? Someone who hated men, or someone who loved men?'

'I don't know. I - '

'Either way, men in suits look silly once you take them out of the high-rises, the eateries, the pubs, the clubs, the shopping precincts, the conference and training centres of any CBD you'd care to name. Even in the miniature CBDs in the suburbs, the SBDs, they don't seem quite right, do they? I mean look at this lot.'

I'd been staring out the bus window to avoid this lot, but I decided to follow instructions and so I turned and stared at the backs of the bobbing heads of Aurora Indigestibles and Synthetics, whatever it was called. I couldn't seem to keep the company name in my mind, even though I'd sat in its staff lounge for the entire day, prompting Delia to drop by at intervals and suggest I try out for a Beckett play. Instead, I tried my meditation breathing exercises, but once I'd achieved enlightenment, which coincided with Delia bringing more coffee and this time, Danishes, there were still six hours of the working day left.

The shuttle, as Ms Harding called it, was supposed to arrive at 9am, but there had been a mechanical or mental breakdown involving either the shuttle or the driver, or both. As moments crept by, I made several quiet phone calls to Henry, informing him each time that the job was over before it had begun. And each time, he insisted that I stay the course, sounding unjustifiably optimistic about the shuttle's eventual arrival.

'Anyway, Gar,' he said during our last communication, 'I can't afford a refund, so get with the program. Guard something while you're there. Look official, and don't call again, I'm busy.'

'Busy? With what?'

'Business. Making money, for us.' He hung up.

He was full of it, and most likely he'd be at the conference table doodling firearms.

I sat on - with occasional standing periods at the windows to watch the progress of a sloop or cruiser on the river - and observed the goings on in a high-class stock-broking, investment, hedge fund, securities operation. Delia came and went with files, entering and leaving the Chiefs' and Chairs' offices. She photocopied, sorted mail, filed, answered the phone - which rang infrequently for a place of business this large, but it could have been the seasonal shutdown; there were only weeks until Christmas. Did the financial sector and its members have seasons the way humans did? Who knew?

At 1pm, four doors opened almost simultaneously and one grey, two navy blue, and one deepest brown suit walked hurriedly towards the lifts, passing through the empty central core of the company like a group of spectres scared of themselves. They stood waiting for their lift as Delia came over to me, carrying yet another coffee and white packet. How did she manage to slip in and out without being seen? I should direct my certified observational skills away from boats on the water.

'Thanks, Delia, you didn't have to go to any trouble, you know.'

'No trouble. Garfield, those are four of your six protectees,' she said. 'They're on the edge of hysteria right now.' She looked over at them.

'Why's that?'

'My bet is they don't know whether to stay or leave. No sign of the Chairman, Philip Downer, or the CIA.'

'CIA?'

'Chief Investment Adviser. In this case, Melanie Rogers-Hilton. No relation.'

I raised my eyebrows.

'To the Hiltons,' she said. 'As in Paris, Nicky, some others I can't remember.'

'Oh. You'll have to forgive me. I've been at sea for years on and off, and I don't read papers or watch TV much.'

'Me neither.' Delia almost beamed. 'They're fabulous nobodies, anyway.'

'So, the hysteria?'

'These people sit in their offices all day texting and emailing each other. They go out to lunch as a group, they travel almost everywhere together. They're frightened of their own shadows. Their world is collapsing, Garfield, and they don't know what to do about it.'

'I thought this company was okay? Ms Harding told Henry - '

'You can't believe a thing they say. Just the unclassified stuff I've seen would send you grey if you had money with them now. Well, I'm using the term loosely - not so much money as figures written on bits of paper and spreadsheets and graphs. Ephemeral.'

'You mean they're broke?'

'Not absolutely sure, but there've been threats - from former employees and dudded investors, but they can't prove anything, yet. They handle almost a billion dollar's worth of investments, on paper. Most of it's worthless now, or will be, so they're juggling like drunks to stay in the game.'

Almost a billion. I had trouble picturing all the noughts.

'Anyway, I better go - more to do before the shuttle.'

She darted off into one of the recently vacated offices and I had my lunch. At 2.30pm, the four suits of the financial apocalypse returned silently to their offices, faces expressionless, and closed their doors. They remained cloistered, texting and emailing, I assumed, until Delia announced the shuttle's arrival at 4.45pm. She went by each office and gathered their bags onto a flatbed trolley. I helped her haul it into the lift and down to the basement where the bus and driver - newly repaired and drugged, or simply new, we weren't sure which - waited, idling exhaust fumes into the air-conditioning intake vents.

Things can only improve, I told myself, now that we're underway; I've always been hopeful, even in the rollingest of seas and in the face of the least promising of kitchen supplies. But I hadn't banked on the next fiasco, and it made me wonder what Henry Pinkert had been thinking the day he made certain decisions.

CHAPTER 11

The driver stayed in his seat, silent, and didn't offer to help with the baggage, but he popped the boot. Delia and I threw the suits' bags in and placed our own very carefully on top of the pile. The four arrived after another ten minutes, digital gadgets in hand, and settled themselves into the front two rows - one seat on either side. All of them except Sarah Harding, who nodded, stared me up and down as they boarded, but no-one spoke to me. One, a fellow with a crew cut and a big gut, raised his eyebrows, but thought better of lowering himself to an expressed thought, let alone an introduction.

Delia and I boarded last and sat on the bench seat at the rear, leaving a row between us and them, and off we drove into the Friday afternoon peak hour.

When we stopped at the on-ramp to the freeway, Ms Harding turned around to face everyone. 'I forgot to tell you that Philip and Melanie texted me a little while ago. They'll see us at the venue.' She smiled a smile of superior knowledge.

'How are they getting there, Sarah? Limo? Helicopter? None of this cattle class, rubbish transport for those two. Hope the shagging was worth it.' It was the blonde head on a suit who'd yelled at Delia and got fish poo for his efforts.

The bus took off with a jerk that encouraged Ms Harding back into her seat.

'Who did you say he is again?' I whispered to Delia.

'The CFO: Chief Finance Officer - Graham Butler. Turd in a tie.'

All of them appeared to be overly relieved by Ms Harding's revelation, despite Butler's outburst. It was as though the parents hadn't abandoned their chicks after all. They slumped comfortably in their seats and only moments before they'd been sitting up straight like kids in Miss Brighton the Basher's Year Four class. Now they started chattering as though Miss Brighton had had a sudden rush of blood to the head and fled to join Volunteers' Abroad, leaving the bullies in charge of the classroom.

'Why are they going away, if there's no money left?'

'Probably to plan a getaway and whatever they can get for themselves before they all go down in flames.'

'Seatbelts,' the driver yelled, looking back at us through the rearview mirror.

'Seatbelts, please,' said Butler, laughing his head off as he opened a hip flask and drained it. 'Oh, sorry, I should have kept some for our piss boy,' he told his colleagues.

Ms Harding stared ahead, but the other two, the one with the crew cut and a skeletal, grey haired hatchet-face, turned and smirked at each other.

Butler turned around to me and held the flask towards me. 'Get enough of it, do you, buddy?'

'Pardon?' I asked. Was he talking to me, or had he seen a reflection of himself in the rear window?

'Enough of it. Enough piss.' He couldn't seem to make eye contact; his gaze made it to just south of my collar. What did he have in that hip flask?

'I don't drink. Thanks anyway,' I said. Delia shifted uneasily beside me.

'This is rich,' Butler laughed. 'He doesn't get it. He doesn't even know, do you, you poor silly prick?'

'Know what, sir?' Sometimes it was best to revert to the tried and true formula of the hierarchy. I had three years in the Army to perfect that particular gambit before I woke up, smelled the gunpowder, and realised what I'd done to myself. Still, it came in handy with certain individuals, and I'd retained some other skills.

'Pinkert piss,' he said, still talking in riddles, still laughing. 'Superior to all other brands. Why don't you enlighten the man, Delia dear. Bored now.' He turned back to his friends, but not before the bus lurched to the right and he was flung against the side of the cabin. 'Steady on, driver, or we'll have to give you the flick and do it ourselves. How about some music?'

The driver appeared to ignore him, but after a few seconds, some kind of jazz music floated around the cabin. The noise was enough to allow me to quiz Delia without the suits overhearing.

'Delia, do you know what he's talking about?'

Delia did the eye lowering movement again. That was a worry. Was I about to get the fish poo treatment?

'Garfield, your uniform. Have you worn it, before today, I mean.'

'Uniform? It's Henry's idea. To look professional. Bit much, is it?' I thought I'd done well to combine Henry's black polo shirt with my black moleskins and black, all-purpose, galley-proof, deck-grippy, weather-impervious, idiot-repelling eight-hole Docs. Especially dressing in the dark courtesy of Belle's bulb-blown home. I suppose it also made me look a bit like a waiter in an up-market-slightly-down-and-dirty-bistro.

'The logo, Garfield, you know, the company name. Didn't you notice?'

The Pinkert logo. There was a Pinkert logo? I hadn't noticed anything in the gloom of Belle's bathroom. I followed Delia's gaze to the writing on the left breast pocket of my shirt and pulled the fabric out so I could see it. The word Pinkert sat in green letters above four words whose first letters were brighter than the rest. The whole formed Pinkert Protection and Investigation Systems and Services, but what you could readily read was this: Pinkert PISS.

'Mmm,' I said, because there wasn't much else to say, other than touchè, Mr Turd in a Tie.

'Don't worry, they've had their fun,' Delia said. 'They'll ignore us, they ignore everyone who earns less than several million a minute. Not that they're earning nowadays.' She smiled more brightly. 'On the plus side, you could read up on them, if you like, so you know who you're taking a bullet for.' She indicated her laptop.

'Bullet? I gave up bullets for Lent.'

'It's juicy reading, even just the headlines.' She turned on the laptop, called up a folder and handed it over.

In a few minutes as we sped along the freeway out of town, I'd scanned through a selection of newspaper articles that made me wonder why they weren't in a prison van instead of rollicking off to paradise delayed. Their participation in hedge funds and derivatives and other strangely-named investment vehicles - there was some kind of pyramid scheme called a Ponzi - and their connections with ruined Wall Street traders, had cost their clients their businesses, assorted assets, superannuation savings, retirement funds, charitable foundations, and family homes. Family homes. There had been suicides.

'Now you know why the threats,' Delia said.

'How bad are these threats?' I hadn't asked Henry for any real details. I didn't know if he even had any details beyond the superficial.

'Are you wearing your gun, or is it in the luggage?' she asked.

CHAPTER 12

By the time we reached the turn-off for the resort, it was dark and I missed the exit number. There was a large volume of traffic on the freeway, all of it turned blurry and slow by the incessant rain. If anything, it had become heavier during the drive, as though we were heading more deeply into it rather than away, as the weather bureau's radar had indicated in earlier reports. Things have a way of changing rapidly, though, and the wind had picked up, too. The van waggled around in the gusts, and at least one of our colleagues up front, the hatchet-faced man of silence, wasn't feeling terrific, judging by a couple of comments. He must have been used to limousine and Lexcen smoothness.

'What's the name of this place, Delia?' I asked.

'The resort? It's not really a resort, more of a lifestyle retreat. I think Philip Downer called it a resort so this lot wouldn't jack up. They think it's the lap of luxury, but if it's the same Apostles' Eyrie I know, then – ' She paused and smiled. 'Well, it can't come a minute too soon.' She let a slow smile develop and slide away.

'Why are you working for them? You dislike them, you don't respect them, not that they're worthy of it; they treat you like the help.'

'I am the help,' Delia said.

'You know what I mean - some decency and professionalism wouldn't go astray on their part - especially from the turd in a tie.'

'Haven't you ever had to do a job you didn't want to, but circumstances intervened?'

'Of course, all the time. But you - you could get a job anywhere.'

'How kind you are, Garfield. Have you noticed we're in a recession? The worker doesn't rule any more, if she ever did. Employers, even Aurora in its death throes, can be picky.'

'Then thank God for fish tanks,' I said.

'Here we go.' Delia seemed to sense that we were about to change course, and then we did, moving from the smooth macadam of the off-ramp and its adjoining arterial travelling beneath the freeway and into the hinterland. There was a brief stop at a T-intersection, then a left turn and we'd entered a deeper layer of darkness and a slightly rougher terrain. We'd crossed a line into rural; it certainly wasn't urban or suburban.

'Do you know where we are?' I asked Delia.

'Pretty much,' was all she said, not that any description would have helped me geographically. I'd never travelled a lot in this area.

'Driver, don't get us lost or we'll have to kill you and eat you to survive.' It was Butler again. He must have swallowed a few more hip flasks along the way.

The driver maintained his dignified silence but turned up the jazz. It was a very familiar piece of music, but I just couldn't dredge it out of the ethers. I decided to call Henry and tell him we were well underway, but when I tried to connect, the signal had died or temporarily disappeared.

'You won't get a call out here,' Delia said. 'Leave it for later. There'll be a landline at Apostles.'

She leaned back in the seat and relaxed, so I thought I'd do the same. The darkness and the drumming rain encouraged drowsiness and the narrower, rougher road somehow rocked the van in a quite restful way. I lulled myself with the thought that I could protect just as easily from a position of fairly alert inertness. And what would I be protecting them from down here, in here, over or up here? Wherever the here was that we were aiming for, its nastiest aggressors were likely to be mosquitoes and leeches, or a face-slapping palm frond.

Another change in road surface woke me, and then we were crossing a bridge, it seemed, given the regular ker-thumping as we drove over the bearers. I opened the window a crack and peered out into the night. There was welcome fresher air, rain and more rain, blank blackness except for the stray bit of headlight flare thrown out to the side of the van. There was a buzz and fizz of noise and a gurgling beneath it of something wilder, a creek or river rushing, about to flood. The foliage was very close.

'Delia?'

Delia turned her head and opened her eyes. 'Yes?'

'That was the bridge. Is it far away now?'

'Not too far. Another 20 minutes or so, if the road's okay.'

'When did you come here?'

She stretched and sat up.

'Years ago, before it expanded. It used to be a retreat centre for religious orders. You know why this crowd really ended up here?'

'Philip Downer's ironic idea of a bonding exercise? I've seen those things on the lifestyle shows. They do rope climbing, origami, flying-foxes, group hugs.'

Delia looked at me, sizing me up, I think, but for what I had no idea. Maybe she'd decided I was pure flake in motion. Just then, the van came to a sudden halt, jerking us all forward at whiplash speed. That woke us up.

'Fuck it, man, what do think you're doing?'

It was the silent one, hatchet-face. He practically ran from his seat to the door of the van.

'Open it,' he croaked, and the driver saw that something was wrong and pressed the release.

We heard hatchet-face vomiting out in the darkness. After a while, the driver moved from his seat - it was the first time I'd seen him stand - and went to the door. Then he looked back at me. He was tall and stooped and wore navy blue trousers and a short-sleeved white shirt with navy epaulets on the shoulders and a plain navy tie: the quintessential bus driver.

'Give us a hand,' he said, and saw my reaction. 'Nah, not the vomiter. Trouble on the track.' He stepped out into the rain and then I saw him lit up in the headlights, standing over a lump of something.

Delia stood and made her way forward past the others, who seemed happy to wait for the help to help. I followed her.

'It'll be all right, Garfield,' she said, peering out at the driver. 'It's perfectly safe.' She turned back to me.

'Safe? Of course it's safe.' I lowered my voice. 'But did that Chief get the fish poo treatment, too?' I asked her, glancing out at the vomiter bent over at the side of the track.

'Mr Leason? He'll be okay. Better hop to it. Dean's a bit impatient sometimes.'

'You know the driver?'

'In a manner of speaking. Not long now, Garfield.' She moved back and sat in the driver's seat, flicked the lights to high beam, and stared me out into the rain.

CHAPTER 13

Peter Leason decided to walk the rest of the way to the resort, which Delia assured him was only a kilometre up the road. Meanwhile, he'd take Delia's umbrella, thanks, and sit quietly on a rock until he felt better. She handed it over to him as I made my way up to the driver.

'And I'll be driving us home on Monday,' I heard him tell her, 'not that bastard with his jerks and brakes.'

'Is it?' I asked her, when she joined the driver and me on the track. 'A kilometre to the resort?'

She'd produced another umbrella from somewhere, and a torch, and came to stand with us. Better company than the two drunks in the van who simply sat and waited for things to reboot themselves. Ms Harding had opened her laptop as I walked past her, oblivious to her surroundings, or determined to appear so. Maybe she'd had enough of shepherding the rest of them.

'A kilometre? Who knows? Who cares?' She trained the torch on the lump in front of us. 'What's this?'

'Dunno,' said Dean the driver. 'Got a stick? Could be a bomb.' He pushed at it with his boot.

'Looks like it fell off the back of something,' I said. It was a rectangular box covered in hessian, drenched, bedraggled and muddy.

'Probably mud crabs on ice, for this lot,' Dean muttered. 'We can't leave it here. This is the only road in and out, and I don't want any debris when I'm leaving. Shit like this causes accidents.'

Anything out here could cause accidents.

Dean leaned down and pulled at the hessian, but it was wrapped tightly around the box and secured with thick rope. 'Got a knife?'

I handed him the pocket-knife I always carry on my key-ring in case an apple is in urgent need of peeling. He took a look at it, rolled his eyes, and handed it back to me, so I made up for my blade's lack of bestial power by kicking the box.

'It's metal,' I said, and checked out the ends, which had convenient handles protruding from the wrapping. 'Looks like something from Army surplus, or a caterer's storeroom.' You didn't need fancy packaging behind the scenes in a restaurant, or a galley. Durability was the gold standard, and metal like this could protect, withstand, stabilise, seal, and preserve, if it was packed professionally.

'Maybe the chef's arrived early and doesn't know he's lost it.' Delia looked up and down the road as though trying to catch the recent vibrations of others passing through.

'The other end, mate,' Dean said to me. 'Time's a-wasting.'

He grabbed a handle, and I grabbed the other. He nodded and we lifted together. It was a heavy box, and could very well have been full of mud crabs on ice.

'There's a chef?' I asked Delia as we grunted our way back to the van.

'Apparently, Mr Downer, Aurora's Chairman, organised everything. He likes adventure style getaways.'

'As long as they're catered,' I said. Dean snorted.

We reached the back of the van and opened the boot, but realised the box wouldn't fit. So we slid it into the cabin and pushed it down the aisle, positioning it beneath the rear bench seat Delia and I shared.

'What is it?' Ms Harding asked as the other two watched us slide it along.

'Not sure yet,' I said. 'We'll take it with us, in case someone claims it.'

'Very good, Pinkert piss,' Butler said to me, 'put a mystery box in the shuttle with us and hope it doesn't explode. Hahaha - pissweak protection, now with bonus stupidity.'

'There's no danger, sir,' I said, grinding my teeth. Could there be something dangerous inside? Dean didn't seem to think so. And who would come all this way to plant it in the middle of the road in the middle of a cyclonic weather system? A broke investor, who also happens to understand and have access to incendiary equipment? Shouldn't it have exploded by now, since we were almost eight hours late?

'Shut up, Graham.' It was Ms Harding.

'What? What did you say?' said the turd in a tie.

'I said, shut up, Graham.' Ms Harding folded her laptop and stood her ground, although she was seated, but her back was straight. Then she turned to me. 'I apologise, Mr Fletcher. Mr Butler here is tired, and emotional, and ignorant.'

Butler stared at her, opened his mouth, and closed it. Then he said, 'Good one, Sarah, keep us in line, dear. You won't be doing it for much longer.' He leaned back, facing the road ahead as Dean jerked us into motion again.

Ms Harding glared at the crew-cut, who looked at her, shook his head slightly and turned to the window. He opened it, raised his hand and waved at the vomiter, Leason, who disappeared into the darkness the second we passed him.

I said to Delia, 'Does that bloke have a torch?'

Delia, the fish poo poisoner, raised her eyebrows. 'I'm sure his night vision is excellent, Garfield.'

Just then, a very heavy downpour caught up with us; Dean turned the wipers to frantic and slowed to a crawl.

'You can go back if you like, and walk with Mr Leason.' Delia smiled her Mona Lisa smile.

I thought about that for a moment, but not two. 'I think my role is with the group, Delia, don't you?'

She nodded. 'I couldn't agree more. You never know what could be up ahead, or down below.'

She tapped at the mystery box with the heel of her boot. It sounded both hollow and full. I leaned down and touched it. It felt very cold in one spot, and merely cold in another. Versatility, another gold standard in box design. I felt for my pocket knife hanging off my key-ring and rubbed its smooth handle. It offered no comfort whatsoever.

CHAPTER 14

We didn't know we'd arrived until Dean did a loop and pulled up beside a solid, dark mass.

'Here we are,' said Ms Harding, too brightly.

'Here we are where?' the crew cut asked. 'Where, Sarah?'

'This is it, isn't it, driver?' Sarah hesitated.

'Yeah.' Dean turned off the wipers, the lights and the engine and all we could hear was the rain, not on the van's roof, but above us and behind and in front of us. There was a covered walkway from the front entrance out to the driveway.

'This is it, David,' she said to the crew cut. 'The Apostles' Eyrie.'

Ms Harding stood up and took a step towards the van's door, but then looked back at me. 'Mr Fletcher, if you'd be so good as to check things out. I have a set of keys.' She fumbled in her handbag as I made my way to the front of the cabin, and came up with a keyring you could have used in weightlifting exercises. 'This one, I believe, is the front door.' She singled one key out, and gestured with it in the direction of the large building. 'If that's the front door.'

'Why is everything so dark?' the turd in a tie asked. It was a good question.

'Was someone supposed to meet us?' I asked, taking the keys.

'The chef?' Delia suggested. 'We've already met the mud crabs. Almost.'

'Maybe the kitchen's a way off. He won't know we've arrived, not with all the noise from the rain.' Ms Harding sat down again and for a moment everyone remained where they were, uninterested in movement, until Dean popped the boot.

'Everybody out,' he said. 'I've got another job.'

Delia moved first, gliding up from the rear seat past the executives to stand behind me. 'It's all right, Garfield, you're safe,' she whispered. For some reason, I believed her and stepped out into the humid night.

At the door, I realised there were no security lights waiting to be tripped by our movements either close in or at the van where the rest of the gang had begun to empty the boot and Dean the driver was wrestling the mud crab box down the steps. I fished out my keyring, found the small halogen torch I always keep with me and turned it on the door lock.

Inside, it was cooler and darker and the rain's noise receded. I reached for the light switch and flicked it, but nothing happened. I flicked it a few more times, to prove the definition of insanity, and sure enough, I got the same result. 'No power,' I called to the group. 'I'll see if there's a generator.' A place like this in the middle of nowhere would surely have back-up power, unless we really were roughing it courtesy of Philip Downer.

I made my way down a long corridor towards the rear of the building, passing a number of open and closed doors on either side. I checked a couple of the rooms and tried a few light switches along the way, just in case it was a simple matter of blown bulbs like Belle's place. But there were too many gone. Then, near the end of the corridor, I heard music. I stopped, trying to discern a direction.

'Anybody there?' I called. 'It's the Aurora group. We're late.'

The music continued and grew slightly louder as I opened the door at the end of the corridor. It was the kitchen. Even in the dim glow of my torchlight, I sensed that it was a large space. I played the torch around and the light disappeared into the darkness. The music came from further away near the rear wall and behind a large column in the middle of the room, around which were a cluster of ovens and benches.

'Hello, chef?' I called. No answer except the music, catchy and jazzy. It sounded like 1930s' stuff, Benny Goodman, Woody Herman. Someone had good taste. 'We've got your mud crabs.'

Why did I feel uneasy in this strange building full of nothing in the middle of nowhere on a moonless, monsoonal night in the rainforest? Five other people were less than a hundred feet away, and I was, after all, a Pinkert Protective and Investigative Services and Systems Officer. I was tall, I wore a uniform, I curled my toes inside my idiot-repelling boots and listened.

I moved closer to the music's source, passing the ovens and benches. On one bench was a chopping board on which sat a loaf of bread waiting to be sliced by the bread knife lying beside it. I picked up the knife and proceeded to the back door. The music was just outside, along with a scrabbling noise, and, I now realised, the sound of footsteps, slow and deliberate, heavy.

I wanted to run very fast back to driver Dean and beg him to take me with him so I could run very fast back to sea. But that would have been both sensible and unmanly, so instead I stood near the door, put my torch in my pocket, raised the bread knife in my right hand, and turned the doorknob very slowly. I pulled the door open and plunged out onto the verandah. There was a scream - was it me? - and I ran into a dark figure, knocking it down. As we fell, I felt a sharp pain in the centre of my chest, I couldn't breathe, and then there was nothingness.

CHAPTER 15

A white light, strong and bright, shone at me. I raised my hand and something grabbed it around the wrist.

'Garfield?'

'Yes?'

'Are you all right?'

'Am I?'

'Come on, you can sit up.'

'Aaaah - wait. I think I've been stabbed.' I felt my chest - it was merely damp from the rain, but something had hit me.

'Stabbed with a torch, Gar. I think you were winded. Come on.'

'Delia?' It was Delia. She set the torch down and my eyes adjusted to the dimness and her shape above me. Who knew torches could feel so knife-like when you fell on them? My bread knife had disappeared.

'I came around the side to find the generators. After you left, I remembered from when I was here years ago. They were always having problems then. Even the kids learned how to boot them up.'

I stood up and looked for the music. A boom-box sat on a chair near the back door. 'What's this all about?' I reached over and turned it off.

'Maybe the chef's gone looking for the generator,' Delia suggested. 'Maybe he was getting things organised and playing some music and the lights went out.'

'So I guess we'd better find it, the generator, before the gang cuts up rough.'

'They're arguing the toss with Dean. They want him to wait in case they don't like the place. Actually, they already hate the place. I think they want to go home right now.'

'What about the other people, Downer and the woman? What's her name?'

'Melanie Rogers-Hilton. They probably left it until tomorrow - the weather might improve. Come on, the generators are down this way - they have their own shed.'

I huddled under Delia's umbrella and we walked slowly through the slush to the corner of the building where a brick shed with a red tin roof and a green door sat snugly on a thick concrete slab.

'In here,' Delia said, pointing with her bruising torch. The door wasn't locked.

There was no sign of the chef, but inside the shed was dry and the generators, all three of them, looked well cared for, by torchlight anyway.

'Here we go - lights and points on this one; hot water on this one.' She pushed a lever on the wall above the generators and then pressed the red buttons on two of them; they kicked over instantly. 'That one's a backup for the backups, I think,' she said, pointing to the third machine.

'Thank God for you, Delia,' I said.

'Don't thank me yet. Let's see if they've worked.'

Inside the building, a number of lights were already on and the place looked far more welcoming. We heard the chatter and footsteps of the Auroras and waited for them to find us in the kitchen.

Dean had left them the minute they emptied their things from the van's boot. They weren't a happy trio, and Mr Leason was still dragging the chain somewhere out on the track.

'Delia,' said the turd in a tie, Graham Butler, 'thank God. Where are Downer and Hilton? At it again in one of the dorm rooms?'

Butler appeared to be in his early forties, but he spoke like an undergraduate with a testosterone imbalance. He didn't wait for an answer.

'Where's the toaster, Delia? And where's the fucking chef?' he asked. He'd busied himself finding another bread knife and was slicing the bread we'd seen earlier.

'I'm sure it'll be in a cupboard somewhere, Mr Butler.' Delia placed her torch and umbrella near the back door and quietly watched the room.

'I'm starving. How about the rest of you?' Butler looked over at David, the crew cut, and Sarah Harding, who was wiping her luggage with a scrunched-up tea towel. She didn't acknowledge that he'd spoken and simply went on wiping.

'No, thanks, Graham,' said David. 'I think I'll find myself a room. Plenty of time to look around tomorrow, and eat, when the rest of them get here.' He turned to me. 'The lights - they're likely to stay on now?'

'Yes,' I said. I had no idea what the lights would do but I sounded confident. 'In that case,' he said, 'you can get out there and find our COO.'

'Your coo?' They'd lost their pigeon somewhere?

'Peter Leason, Garfield,' Delia said quietly, coming over to me. 'The one who said he'd walk? He's designated as the Chief Operating Officer, the COO.'

'Designated?' said Butler. 'Delia, Mr Leason is the Chief Operating Officer, just as I'm the Chief Finance Officer, and you're the Chief Dog's Body, in the absence of a better one. Any butter, love? Some foie gras?'

'You could try the fridge, sir,' I said, forgetting my vow of silence in the face of ignorance.

Butler glared at me and gripped his knife harder. I was taller than him, but he was rounder and thicker, and I'd bet my cook's redundancy pay that he'd play dirty, like a tight-head prop out to collapse the scrum, and possibly win.

'Bring the mud crabs in before you leave,' the crew cut said to me. 'Graham, take it easy on the booze.' He picked up his bags and made for the door. 'We've got a tough weekend ahead of us, remember.'

'Someone has,' Butler said. He raised the knife and stabbed it into the wooden cutting board. It stood there for a second or two and then keeled over and clattered onto the floor. He left it there, picked up the slices and went in search of a toaster.

Sarah Harding looked up briefly when the knife fell, then picked up her bags and slipped out of the room ahead of us. Butler, opening and closing cupboards, didn't seem to notice that he was about to be left to his own company.

'I'll give you a hand, Garfield,' Delia said, far too brightly, and pushed me towards the door.

In the corridor, she dropped the smile. 'Be careful of Graham Butler, Garfield.'

'He doesn't worry me,' I said. 'I learned a few things in the Army, you know.' Delia couldn't know I was trying to make up for the lack of substance behind my certificate in investigation and protection.

'He doesn't play by the rules. He's more of a guerilla than an army guy. He'd come at you from behind. I've seen him deck one of the brokers in the office.'

'Deck?'

'It was when things were really unravelling. Just after the Madoff arrest.'

Madoff, Bernard Madoff, the Wall Street whiz and former pillar of the financial sector, who'd taken hundreds of investors for at least 70 billion dollars. I'd read some of the headlines on Delia's laptop: 'Biggest Swindle Ever,' one said, above a picture of the benign-looking Madoff with his lipless, muppet smile. There were others, but one of the saddest pictured an elderly man and woman sitting on a bed; the caption: 'Couple ponders final years on skid row.' They were both ill, in their eighties, and had been defrauded, by Madoff, of their million-dollar life savings investment meant to pay their nursing home bills. Meanwhile, around the same time, Mr Madoff, under house arrest in his beautiful Manhattan apartment, had posted a million dollars worth of his family jewellery off to relatives to save it from confiscation.

'This lot had investments with Madoff in some roundabout setup, and they were into hedge funds and other phoney stuff. No one understands the hedge funds, and everybody wants to get rich with them. But they're like a house of cards.

'The guy he punched out - nobody ever knew what he'd done because Butler had him frog-marched out of the office by security. But I think he told Graham that he'd blown the whistle on Aurora. He hasn't been seen since, and the crap's really hit the fan in the last few weeks. Nobody knows how many local investors are going to be broke, or homeless. Or both. That's why we've been getting nasty phone calls, and letters with white powder in them - we had to evacuate the building and get the hazardous chemicals team for one of those last month.'

We reached the front of the building, grabbed our bags and put them inside the front door, then returned to pick up the mystery box.

'I hope the ice has lasted,' Delia said. 'Otherwise, it'll stink as much as this firm does.' Was there an extra edge in Delia's voice?

We lifted the box together on her count. Delia was strong, or refused to let on that she was suffering at her end. It was one heavy motherload.

'It doesn't seem like much of the firm is left,' I said as we hefted the box down the hall. 'And what's with all the Chiefs? Where are the indians.'

'Well, that's what happens when you start king-hitting them - the indians, I mean. The titles are largely meaningless now. They're using them as boosters to impress clients, and the more gullible staff. But they're all but gone, too.'

We pushed through the door into an empty kitchen. There was a walk-in cooler in the far corner, so we put the box in there. I noticed that Butler had dropped a couple of pieces of bread on the floor near the back door, which was open. The rain continued to pour beyond the verandah.

'Must have gone looking for the chef,' Delia said. 'I'll wait for you, Garfield.'

'Wait?'

'Peter Leason? He's possibly the least objectionable of the bunch, but that's not saying much. They're all thieves. Dave's the boss, David Oliver - the one who asked you to look for Leason? Crew cut, crew brain, CEO. Multiple divorces. Alienated kids. The usual.'

'There's a recommendation.' I'd forgotten about Leason momentarily. I could walk out along the track for a bit, wait a while and then turn around and come back. He was a grown-up, he'd find his way. Maybe he and the mystery chef and Butler could start a boy scout fire with a couple of handy twigs and Butler's $300 silk tie. On the other hand, Leason could have slipped down a gully and broken something, or been bitten by a snake, and

I was his contracted protector, at least for another few days, hedge fund or no hedge fund. I had a laminated licence to prove it.

'You could walk out along the track for a half mile or so,' Delia said, 'and then come back. He'll turn up, one way or another. What do you think?'

I stared at her and tried not to think. Who was this woman - my new soulmate?

'Garfield?'

CHAPTER 16

Beyond the few lights shining in the Apostles' Eyrie was the simplicity of darkness and water, in great abundance. It was like being at sea again, though without the ocean's pitch and roll. I didn't have to wonder about Delia's mind-reading skills, nor concern myself with the whereabouts of the chef or Graham Butler. My attention was fully focussed on the steps ahead of me, steps I tried to take with safety using Delia's torch.

The track was muddy and full of puddles but it was obviously a track, for the moment, anyway, and if Peter Leason had stuck to it, he should have made his destination by now. Maybe he was sicker than we, or he, had thought, and had taken a longer break. Or the almost complete darkness may have disoriented him into the scrub, a date with the local creepy-crawlies and a fractured limb. Either way, here I was, investigating and protecting, as instructed, and moving beyond the hundred-metre minimum.

I called out his name a few times before realising that the rain dampened my voice into nothingness almost as soon as I spoke. I waggled the torch around in the hope that he'd see it and not be terrified that it was a tiny alien craft piloted by drunks. When boredom set in, I tried to cheer myself up by doing a few devil-may-care Gene Kelly steps along the track, Delia's red umbrella held high overhead, until I stepped into a pothole and remembered both the possibility of an immobilising injury, and somehow ending up on a web video captured from a movement-sensitive handycam strapped to a nearby tree fern. It happens.

Trudging seemed to be the least worst option, although I've always thought that a dose of *Singin' In The Rain* can cure the most horrible of ills. That, or a Strauss waltz, *The Blue Danube*, or *Tales from the Vienna Woods*. I attribute my eclectic musical taste to the spotty education provided by Nonna Lucia when Gianni and I would pester her for entertainment options on rainy days in West End. She taught us both to waltz in her tiny lounge-room to scratchy LPs she must have brought from Italy; and she took us to see Gene and Donald and Debbie whenever *Singin'* had a reprise screening at the Rialto up on Hardgrave Road. Perhaps Delia would agree to a dance session tomorrow if the Eyrie boasted a recreation room. Who knew what other music the boombox at the kitchen door might offer?

But in keeping with the reality of the evening, I trudged along the side of the track, stepping carefully around puddles and slick, sliding mud lumps, risking the palm-frond slap. The torch's beam, when I played it into the foliage, disappeared quickly and thoroughly. We may have been only a couple of hours from the magnificently lit city, but I might as well be navigating the mysterious tropical forests of the dwarf planet Pluto.

I stopped to get my bearings and checked the time. I'd been walking for over half an hour and there was no sign of Leason. Not that a sign would be easily detected. The loudness of the downpour obscured other noises, such as weakened or distant cries for help. The darkness covered up movement, and the rain created so much noise in the leaves and branches and twigs that anything and nothing might be significant. If he wasn't in plain sight, a morning search would have to do. I decided on another 15 minutes on the track. Surely Leason couldn't have been so stupid as to attempt an overland trek through the undergrowth. Even funny-money stockbrokers had to have a few practical brains to call their own, didn't they?

I saw something at the side of the track as I made the next turn and did a torch sweep from left to right. It looked like a clump of dead palm fronds - maybe I wanted it to be palm fronds - no longer green, but light brown and creamy in parts. There was a swatch of red on top of it - leaves from a poinsettia? I moved closer and kept the torch trained on the bundle. When part of it moved, I stopped.

'Hello,' I said. 'Mr Leason?' No answer from the fronds.

I took another few steps and stared down at the deceased rainforest foliage. Nothing but palm fronds and poinsettia flowers. Nature was playing with me; it was time to go home and say goodnight to the folks. I turned and went to take a step, but my right foot had tangled itself in something. Wait-a-while? Did it grow here? I shook my foot and tried stepping again, but the pesky thing was latched fast to my ankle, or rather my idiot-repelling boot. I dropped the umbrella, reached for my keyring and apple-peeling pocketknife, and as I flicked it open and leaned down, something muddy lunged out of the mud and gripped my other ankle with the strength of a trapeze artist working without a net. From somewhere down there came a hoarse noise that sounded like 'help.'

CHAPTER 17

'Fell,' he said, coughing up phlegm and mud. 'Fell down.'

He released his grip on my ankles and slid half a metre down the slope in the darkness beside the track. It would be easy to lose your footing and go all the way, although how far all the way was I couldn't tell. As he slid, I bent quickly and grabbed his hand and pulled hard. We grunted and fumbled until I had enough of him over the edge of the slope so that he could pull one leg and then the other onto the flat.

He rolled onto his back, panting and coughing, oblivious of the rain pouring onto his face, cleaning the mud away, sending more of it into his hair and ears. I grabbed the umbrella and held it over him. He didn't look very much like a Chief of anything at the moment, but he did look familiar with his grey hair darkened and streaked by the mud, and I couldn't think why, or where I might have seen him before. Something about his face was different, too, and then I saw the line of blood trickling from both nostrils. His nose had been rearranged; the hatchety aquiline was gone, replaced by a slightly flattened, crooked version. He must have reminded me of so many of the army boxers I'd sparred with when we all had too little sense to know any better.

'Mr Leason,' I said, 'do you feel like you've broken anything?' Reassurance, that's what he needed. 'Your arms and legs look okay.' Which was simply to say that there was no obvious compound fracture to make an arm or leg look like a discarded marionette. 'Would you like to give them a flex?'

He looked up at me, focussing and re-focussing until the question sank in, and then gave the smallest of stretches of arms and legs before a slight shake of his head. I helped him to sit up and propped him against a boulder, trying to keep the umbrella over us, although we were both so wet by now it was all but irrelevant.

'Nose,' he said. 'Broken?' He felt along the line of his nose very carefully with thumb and forefinger and realised that it had indeed lost its way. 'Fuck.'

'What happened, Mr Leason? Did you get disoriented in the darkness and fall?' I hadn't seen him drinking with Butler beyond a symbolic gulp at the beginning of proceedings, but he could have some non-prescription medications of his own on board. Who knew how they were coping with the imminent death of their company and livelihoods?

'Tried to kill me,' he said, and leaned forward.

'Who tried to kill you?' I asked. A feisty python? An aggressive fern?

'You,' he said, and lunged away from me. He didn't get far, though, because his legs were still jelly-like from the shock of whatever had happened to him. He slipped in a puddle and went down. I joined him with the umbrella and tried to hold it over him. It seemed to be the least I could do, but he tried to scrabble away from me on his hands and knees.

'Mr Leason, it's me, Garfield Fletcher,' I said. 'I was hired to look after you. Remember?' I stayed where I was, and hoped he'd begin to think more clearly very soon.

He pushed himself to his feet and stared at me, eyes wide open, nose bleeding, one arm up in front of him in a defensive gesture. His shirt was torn in several places, his tie had turned into a thin scarf tangled around his neck, and he'd lost a shoe. He had no idea how vulnerable and pathetic he looked, but I had to give him credit for trying to be a worthy foe.

'It's all right,' I said, 'you're safe now. I'm here. It's okay. Your CEO sent me out to find you.'

He blinked a few times. 'Dave?'

'Yes, Dave. Dave Oliver.' Crew cut, crew brain.

'Some bastard tried to kill me. I thought you were the van driver. It was the van that came at me.'

'The van? Are you sure?'

'Sure, of course I'm sure. He came back after the first go - he reversed and tried again. Twice.' He'd started to shake.

'Could you see the driver?' I asked.

'It was our driver. Who else could it be? If it wasn't you.' He kept his distance from me, still in two minds about my status as either killer or protector. 'I had nowhere to go but over the side. Jesus.' He fumbled in his pants pocket and pulled out his mobile phone. 'He tried to kill me.'

'It doesn't work here,' I said, but I pulled mine out as well, and checked for a signal. Nothing.

'The police. There must be police around here,' he said. 'We're not that far away.' He shook the phone, stared at its screen and snapped it shut.

'I'm the only police you've got at the moment, sir,' I said, and if that statement didn't scare the rest of Mr Leason's wits right out of his ears, I could feel mine leaking out of my idiot-repelling boots and dissolving into the mud.

CHAPTER 18

Delia was waiting, as she'd promised, when we returned. I'd walked ahead of Leason and encouraged him to follow; he was still wary of me. It took us twice as long to get back as I'd taken to walk out. The COO was a wreck and the rain seemed to get heavier for a while. When she saw us coming along the driveway from her perch near the front door, Delia waved to me and then disappeared inside.

By the time we'd reached the covered walkway, she'd returned carrying towels and bottles of water. Leason collapsed onto the cast iron garden bench near the door and remained so still for so long I thought he may have entered a catatonic state. Meanwhile, I towelled off as much of the night and its content as I could without actually departing for the showers and fresh clothes. It seemed that my place was with Leason, the traumatised, so I took the opportunity to explain to Delia what had happened to her Chief OO. She listened carefully, but asked me no questions, and kept her eyes on Leason.

'Mr Leason,' she said eventually, and very gently, after we waited and waited for a sign of life. 'Mr Leason, I have some water for you.' She held the open bottle in front of him, but still he didn't move, simply staring down at his lap. She put the bottle down and unfolded a towel, placing it gently around his shoulders. Then she took his right hand, and clamped it around the bottle. 'Drink,' she said, 'you'll feel better.'

He looked up then, and the right side of his mouth turned up in a smile.

'Thank you,' he said, and held the bottle to his lips. Some of the water made it into his mouth and some ran down his throat and neck. 'Why?' he said, handing the bottle back to Delia.

'Dehydration,' Delia said, 'is strongly correlated with shock and stressful experiences.' She placed the bottle beside him on the bench.

'Why me?' he said. 'Why would he want to hurt me? I don't even know his name.' He shook his head, and then a light went on somewhere inside. 'You know him, Delia. You hired the shuttle. Who is he, for God's sake?'

Delia straightened up and took a step back. 'The original shuttle was cancelled, Mr Leason, remember? This one was a replacement. I'd have to call the company and see what they know.'

'Then do it, girl,' Leason said. Some level of anger was rising in the COO, but he was attacking the wrong person. 'No. Call the police first. No, wait. The shuttle company, then the police. You can tell them the name.' He sighed loudly.

'I'm sorry, Mr Leason,' Delia replied, her voice even and low, 'I've already tried the landline here. It's out. The line's down.' She reached down and picked up the spare towels. 'Perhaps you'd like to take a shower.'

Leason looked up at her. 'Water,' he said. 'More water. You can't get away from it.' He slowly stood up. 'Why not?'

He was like a balloon, blowing up one minute, and deflating the next. The effort of logic required to decide who to call first had winded him.

'Thank you for coming to find me.' He put his hand out towards me. I took it and we shook. Winded him, and made him more polite, momentarily.

'That's all right, sir,' I said. I couldn't shake the thought, looking at him under the now-operational security lights, that I'd seen him before, or someone very like him.

He shuffled off into the foyer, holding his towel to his broken, bleeding nose.

'Up the stairs, turn right, your bags are in room 102,' Delia called after him. 'The shower's down the hall from your room - all lit up.' She turned to me. 'You might want to do the same, Garfield. Big day tomorrow.'

'Tomorrow I think we'll be leaving here, Delia, even if we have to walk out.'

'Leaving? Why?'

'Someone - Dean, presumably - tried to kill Leason. You heard him.'

'You've only got one side of the story, Garfield,' Delia said. 'Besides, the others won't want to leave now that they've settled in - well, except for Butler. He's still out looking for the chef, presumably.'

'You told Leason you didn't know Dean, but you do, don't you?'

'No, I don't know him.'

'When we stopped to pick up that box, you said he was a bit impatient. And that you knew him, in a manner of speaking. What does that mean, Delia? You've known him since 5pm today, and you're fast at friendship, even with an entire bus between him and you? Because I didn't know he was impatient, and I've known him since 5, too.'

'It is a manner of speaking, Garfield. Don't make too much of it. I barely know Dean. I've seen him a couple of times when I've done contracts for other companies. They tend to use the same few service providers.' Her voice was reasonable and calm. I should follow her example.

'Okay,' I said. The night, and Leason, were making me paranoid, too.

'I just can't imagine him doing what Leason says he did. Maybe he reversed to look for him, and Leason had already slipped off into the darkness.'

'That's not quite how Leason tells it. He says Dean reversed and chased him down the track until he got the bright idea to throw himself into the bushes. He broke his nose when he smacked into a tree, but at least it stopped him from falling further.'

'Hmm,' she said. 'I suppose we could give them both the benefit of the doubt.'

'I suppose we could, except that Leason says Dean - if it was Dean in the van - came back and revved the motor as though he was waiting for the race to start all over again.'

'Or he could have been revving to indicate where he was, so Leason could come out and get a lift back here.'

'You'd make a great lawyer, Delia,' I said. 'Everything you say sounds somehow plausible. And yet.' I paused and gazed at her, but she was giving nothing away.

'Shower time, buddy,' she said, smiling. 'Come on, I've found the laundry as well. We can get the wet clothes into the washer and dryer.' She took off at speed, leaving me at the front door.

I looked out at the night. I could go out and find the turd in a tie, and the chef, or I could look for high ground where I might get a mobile signal. Or, I could shower and go to bed, and dream the dreams of a seagoing cook flailing around on unfamiliar terra infirma, hoping to wake before the nightmare emerged.

CHAPTER 19

OPERATION BLUEWATER POLARIS #002A

Of course he knew that no operation ever went entirely to plan. That was why plans were made: to be reviewed, revised, discarded when necessary, but made anyway. They were like weather reports: no-one actually believed them, but they were a comforting lie and guide to the unpredictable, and uncertainty was the bane of every mortal's life, wasn't it? Wasn't that why they were so terrified of death, the most absolute of certainties, but treated as though it was anything but definite? Everyone secretly fantasised that they might live forever and yet not age nor grow ill and infirm.

There weren't too many who genuinely liked the idea of not knowing what was around the corner, not in his experience. A couple, maybe, over the years, fellow soldiers who might win bravery medals, because they were in love with the unpredictable, the spontaneous, even as they polished their boots and deified routine, and therefore they were both fearless and stupid. He believed he possessed the dual personality, but he didn't act on it, not often. He preferred to know where he was going, and he preferred to be in control. Though ready for and expecting it, he could do without the unpredictable. Had he been in charge the day Jacinta - but he wasn't, couldn't have been anywhere near it. He was in charge now, though, and he meant to see it through to its predictable, certain, satisfying end.

Then the delay occurred, and he thought they might cancel altogether, and he'd have to return to individual surveillance and removal. But the driver showed up and it was on again. He'd followed them all the way, killing the lights and relying on his night goggles once they'd reached the point of no return into the rainforest. He'd been here several nights before and knew the road well enough. It was a strange place for a knees-up, but there was no accounting for taste.

When they slowed, he slowed; when they stopped because of the obstacle, he stopped a couple of hundred feet back, hidden by the darkness and rain and noise, and their complete lack of suspicion. He couldn't believe his eyes when they drove off, leaving one man behind. He'd started up the car and was ready to go on, thinking they were all aboard, but then he noticed the man at the side of the track. Although it was hard to tell at this distance, the fellow didn't look particularly worried, so the decision must have been his to take. He sat on a rock holding an umbrella over his head as the van rattled off into the night. Then he leaned over and vomitted.

He hadn't bargained on such an easy target, and it threw him momentarily. He figured he should confirm who the fellow was, for archival and recording purposes. He took out his file and turned to the photographs. It was hard to tell at this distance and in the darkness, even with the goggles, but the long, narrow face made it pretty obvious. The hair was different, and there was something about his features – but it was him, yes.

He could do it now, or he could wait for a break in the weather - unlikely. Or he could give him a fighting chance - something Jacinta hadn't been granted - and wait for him to recover his equilibrium. He'd always enjoyed night manoeuvres; why not enjoy a little frightenin' and a-huntin'. It would keep him sharp for the rest. The plan revised, he poured himself a coffee and ate a bagel, and then another. He'd wait for the fellow to move. There was all the time in the world, he thought, until he saw the headlights directly ahead of him on the track. He tore the night vision goggles off immediately, but the intensified effect of the headlights left him momentarily blinded and blinking rapidly.

He could still see his mark step out into the road, a silhouette in front of the lights, and wave his arms about, but the vehicle seemed to speed up, not slow down. The arm waver leapt to one side and fell on his face. The vehicle kept coming and was almost on top of him as he threw his Jeep's gearshift into reverse and floored it. The headlights stopped moving - the driver must have stood on the brakes - and then reversed away from him. He held the goggles up and, turning to one side to avoid the van's headlights, he could see that the man behind on the ground thought the driver was coming back for him, that he just hadn't seen him in time. Once again he stepped into the roadway, waving, waving. Some people just wouldn't learn. He knew enough from working in war zones to recognise deliberate intent when he saw it, even if he could only judge the driver by his vehicle's movements.

This time the waving man flew through the air like an acrobat to save himself. It was amazing what adrenalin could do for you in suddenly extreme conditions. He disappeared into the undergrowth and the vehicle began another forward run towards the Jeep, this time with the horn blaring. He continued reversing and pulled the goggles on securely, straining to see behind him; he'd seen a walking trail, he was certain of it, not far back. As long as he kept his gaze away from direct contact with the headlights, he could just about manage.

He sensed the white indicator picket for the trail almost before he saw it, and turned the Jeep to the right, sliding across the slushy track and into the narrower trail, knocking down a line of wooden bollards on the way through. He braked and pulled off the goggles, jumped out of the car and hurried into the thick undergrowth beside the path.

He waited. Minutes went by, but the vehicle that had almost wiped him out, didn't drive past, and this was the only road in and out. Could he be so fortunate and unfortunate that someone else wanted the world to be rid of these no-hopers, too? And who might this person of excellent taste be, he wondered? He might have to go. It was nothing personal, but there was only room for one of them in this exercise. And he - as he'd known since the horrible day he'd read Jacinta's final text messages, a year to the day since she'd sent them to him - was that one, that one and only.

CHAPTER 20

'How are you feeling, Mr Leason?' I asked. Leason looked greyer than before as he emerged from the showers, and thinner in his T-shirt and board shorts, both of them billowing around him. His eyes would be badly bruised by morning; the broken nose was red and blue-black in patches already.

'Aren't you going out to search for the driver and bring him in? Make an arrest?' He looked at me and then, 'What's your name again?'

'Fletcher, Garfield Fletcher, sir.' Army habits die hard, I'll admit, but I was getting sick of hearing myself add 'sir' to conversations with people who hadn't earned it.

'The driver. You work with him, don't you?'

'No, I've never met him before today.'

'He's a psychopath, a killer.' Leason shook his head and then winced; the nose would be throbbing in waves across his face and up into his eye sockets and forehead. There was still mud up there in his hair, but I hesitated to point it out. It reminded me of my earlier impression of familiarity.

'Have we met before?' I asked him. 'In the last couple of years?' Why not take the simple approach?

'I doubt it,' he replied, but paid more attention to me. 'Why do you ask?'

'It's nothing, just, before when your hair was darker with the mud, and there's something about your face that seems familiar.'

'I can assure you we haven't met,' Leason said, and walked off towards his room, or so I thought.

After I'd showered, I felt hungry and realised I hadn't eaten a thing since Delia had brought me lunch. No wonder Butler had been scavenging in the kitchen. So I went down to have a scavenge for myself, and there was

Leason doing exactly the same. He was busy at a benchtop arranging cheese, olives and crackers on a plate; he'd found the patè and added several slices of well-slathered bread to the mess. I decided on self-protection and didn't mention my previous occupation in case the chef had gone bush forever. I don't cook for the ungrateful, which was one reason why I spent so much time at sea: sailors are generally very thankful for those who nourish them.

When Leason looked up and saw me, he picked up his plate and the bottle of red beside it and hurried towards the door without a word.

'Goodnight, Mr Leason,' I said to his departing back. 'It might be worthwhile if you write a statement about what happened tonight - for the police.'

He grunted or coughed a reply that may have been 'okay,' and disappeared into the hallway. I decided to work before I ate, and took my saturated boots over to the alcove in the far corner of the very spacious kitchen where one of my favourite pieces of cooking equipment stood. It would be the quickest and least damaging way to dry my boots, if it was in working order and had the requisite combustibles handy.

It can take up to two years to get the hang of a wood stove, but once you do, you wouldn't cook on anything else. This one was big, black, beautiful cast iron from its feet to its flue. Quality workmanship. It had been recently used, judging by the ashes in the burner, and there were kindling, paper, kerosene and firewood stacked neatly beside it. Someone here enjoyed the challenge of the fire, too.

I took a lifter from the lattice holder at the side and lifted the circular lid nearest the front so I could build a mound of paper and kindling in the burner. I sprinkled it with a little kerosene for added zest. That was Aunt Edie's contribution to the job, get it started quickly, and the best way to do that was with something flammable, like kero. I struck a match, threw it in, and up it went. Flames licked around the open lid, but they quickly subsided as the kindling took its responsibilities to heart and the kero burned off. After a few minutes, it was time for some wood. I replaced the lid, opened the front hatch and pushed a couple of smaller pieces in on top of the kindling; the trick is to do it so you don't tamp the flames down too much. You need just the right amount and size of wood pieces, and whoever had split these logs was well aware of the need for a variety of sizes from light and slender to thick and hardy.

I closed everything up, worked the dampers experimentally - every stove is different - and waited for the heat to move into the oven by making myself a cheese and olive sandwich and a strong coffee. It was instant, but I could look for something of quality tomorrow. I might even be tempted to cook the Auroras breakfast, if I could forget who they were for half an hour. I'd do it for Delia; she could use some waiting on, and a thoughtful lunch deserved a breakfast in return.

I went to the stove to check out my handiwork and opened the oven door. The space inside was hot enough, so I placed a few flattish pieces of firewood on the open door and sat my boots on top of them. The dry heat coming from the oven would do the trick in no time, but it was a job that required observation. That's the thing about wood stoves, they're as unpredictable as people. And it helps to turn your boots every so often to prevent cracking and uneven evaporation.

The cheese and olive sandwich was going down very well - although a swipe of hot English mustard and a swirl of tomato relish would have helped - when I heard the kitchen door that leads out to the hallway swing open. I couldn't be seen where I was in the far corner way beyond the big pillar in the middle of the room, so I thought I'd wait and see who it was that needed a near-to-midnight snack.

There was the unmistakable sound of a mobile phone being turned on, and numbers being stabbed.

'Hello?' said the voice. 'Hello, are you there? Hello - shit.'

Footsteps moved towards the back door. I stepped out of the shadows and walked around the pillar.

'Where are you off to?' I asked, not expecting to surprise her, not very much anyway.

'Fuck,' she said, simultaneously turning and dropping the mobile onto the lino floor. 'What the bloody hell are you doing here?'

CHAPTER 21

'Delia,' I said, 'it's just me.' I hadn't heard that tone in Delia's voice before. She'd been the soul of neutrality and composure all day. Now she sounded scared, and angry.

'God, you gave me a fright.' She bent to pick up the phone, whose back cover had spun to a stop at my bare feet.

'Who were you expecting? Leason's psychopathic killer driver?' I leaned down and picked up the cover.

Delia stared at me. 'What makes you say that?' Now she looked horrified.

I gave her the cover and noticed that her hands were shaking.

'I didn't. Leason's words. He thinks there's a loony out there, and it's Dean the driver.'

'He's no loony,' she said, trying to fit the cover back on. 'Leason wouldn't have a clue. He's the bloody loony.' She stared at the two pieces of phone as though they were about to explode in her face.

'May I,' I offered, and reached out to take the phone and cover from her. She let me have them without protest. I fitted them together and handed it back to her.

'Thanks.'

'Remember, you said these don't work here,' I said.

'You never know - they may have installed another tower.'

She didn't sound very convincing, but I let it go.

'Why do you say Leason wouldn't have a clue?'

'He just wouldn't, that's all.' She sighed heavily and looked for a chair. There were none in sight, so she jumped up onto the bench and slumped forward, staring at the floor, kicking her heels against the cupboard door. 'These people live in another world, and they never see what's really going on around them.'

'So what's going on, Delia?' If Delia knew Dean and if Dean had gone postal on her, she obviously hadn't been expecting it. Perhaps he was supposed to be as calm and collected as she had been before the Leason incident. 'Should we be locking this place down?'

She raised her head. 'This place?' She gave out a little laugh. 'This place is a rabbit warren, Garfield. There's no security. Why should there be? It's in the middle of nowhere and it was originally built for religious orders to come and meditate and practice random acts of kindness on each other, for Christ's sake.'

'But they've turned it into a resort since then, haven't they?' Whoever they were; Henry had done no research on the place, or none that he was willing to share with me.

'There was still no real need for extra security beyond door locks and insect screens. You saw the generator shed - it was open to the world. Who the hell would come here with malicious intent? It's a holiday haven.' Now she sounded sarcastic, but still with a big twist of fear.

'Well,' I said, 'going back to my question. What's going on? Who's Dean?'

'It doesn't matter who he is,' she said. 'It's what he is.'

'A psychopathic killer driver? What do you mean?'

'You read some of those articles on my laptop?'

'Sure - the Madoff thing, the shonky investments here. People out of their homes, businesses gone. Makes me glad I've got nothing to lose.'

'Neither has Dean - anymore.' Delia slid off the bench and went to stand at the open back door.

He could have been behind any of the headlines I'd read: 'Hundreds of backers face total ruin,' 'Family fortunes at risk,' 'Investors tell of mounting losses.'

'He invested with Aurora?'

'He and his brother, Max.' Delia turned to face me. Her eyes were glittering with tears.

'Delia?' I went over to her and touched her arm. 'What is it?'

'They invested everything. The profits from the sale of their business, their life savings. Philip Downer, the chairman of Aurora's board? He convinced them they'd be millionaires. Early retirement, big returns. The whole deal.'

'Too good to be true.' I'd read that in one of the articles. An investment analyst who blew the whistle on Madoff years ago had become suspicious of the big returns he was getting for his investors; he knew it was all too good to be true. But the authorities ignored his warnings until it was too late.

'Downer took his clients out for slap-up dinners at his private club, and golf days - very exclusive membership. Dean and Max felt like millionaires before they even invested their money. They were lambs to the slaughter.'

It's amazing how greed can blind you to so much. I wondered if I would have taken the bait. Anything was possible.

'We've got to find him, Garfield.'

'Delia, we'll only find him if he decides to come to us. And who knows how well he knows this area?'

'He knows it like the back of his hand,' Delia said flatly.

'He does? What, he came here as child, too, like you did?'

'No. This was the only place he could get work when he and Max lost everything. Doing maintenance. He knew the owner - former owner. Another victim. This joint closed a couple of months ago. Everyone lost their jobs.'

'Let me guess - expansion courtesy of Aurora's flaky investments.'

'Yes, derivative bundling, or something, but there was no real money involved. That isn't all, Garfield. If Dean really did attack Leason, there's another reason for it. I just never thought he'd do anything like this.'

She stopped and I waited. We listened to the rain, as heavy as ever. If Dean was still out there, he could have drowned by now.

'Max. Max, um, he was more fragile than Dean. Dean always looked after him, even when they were little. That's what he told me. He loved him so much; he adored him. That's why they went into business together. Dean knew Max needed the support that he wouldn't get from strangers.'

'That's fair enough,' I said. Henry had offered me a job, and I owed Henry my life, although I doubted that I could kill for him. But if that was the case, then what the hell was I doing working as one of his protective services agents?

'Max killed himself three weeks ago.' Delia leaned against me and I put my arm around her shoulders. There wasn't much of her.

We didn't speak, but stood together, waiting. For what, I didn't know, but I did know that if Dean had gone Old Testament on us, and really was intent on plucking eyes for eyes, I needed to do something very soon. For the life of me, I couldn't think what that might be.

CHAPTER 22

Apparently, I was in way over my head. I'd have to rely on my army training, the small amount of it that wasn't lost to years of soft-shoe shuffling around kitchens, and other assorted occupations. There was no apparently about it: I was in way over, rainforest over, psychopathic killer driver over, ignorant stockbrokers over. And I was the closest thing to the police that they all had, at least until tomorrow when we could hike out across the bridge and find the nearest house with a phone intact, or the nearest mobile tower. Henry hadn't counted on this when he got me my certificate of accreditation.

'We need a perimeter,' I told Delia, who looked at me blankly. 'But we don't have one, because this place is so open to the world. So, we'll do the next best thing.' Which wasn't much at all, but it was all I could think of at the moment.

'Yes?' Delia said, a bit too eagerly. Did she believe I had answers to anything?

'I'll check this building and lock whatever's lockable, especially on the ground floor. We won't alarm the others, not at this stage. Leason's terrified enough to stay in his room for the rest of the night, and crew brain - '

'Oliver.'

'Mr Oliver is dead to the world on Butler's whisky flasks. And Ms Harding - she went straight to her room, so I guess she'll stay there.'

'It'll give her a chance to stick pins into her voodoo doll of Butler,' Delia said. 'I'll come with you, if that's all right.'

'Sure.' I closed the kitchen door and locked it. It had a slide bolt as well, so that was something slightly more impenetrable than a number 1 skeleton key. You'd have to do a bit of kicking to get through the old hardwood door. Or, I noticed, simply put your hand through the open window beside the doorframe and slide the bolt back. I pulled the window closed; it was a casement that had been painted and repainted so many times that it took a strong commitment to closure to secure the hook and then do the same with the rest of the casements along the back wall.

'Okay,' I said, 'that's about all we can do in here.' Now, any psychopath would have to rouse themselves to the challenge of cracking glass and then putting a hand through.

We went along the corridors and locked or closed firmly as many windows as were lockable or closeable in the multitude of small rooms. Several of them were offices and there were a couple of small meeting rooms with conference tables and a few chairs. I suspect most of them used to be monastic cells. For extra insurance, we locked any doors to the rooms that happened to have keys in their locks. As Delia secured the main entrance, which had been left open since our arrival, I tried not to think of the fact that we could be locking Dean in with us. It was a U-shaped building three storeys high; if Dean was lurking anywhere, he'd be on a floor where we weren't.

'I think I'll check the upper floors; you never know, the chef could be asleep up there in a marijuana stupor.' I gave Delia the reassuring TV-detective smile, but I don't think it worked as well without the moustache, and Hawaii, and good weather. And Magnum.

'I'll come,' Delia said.

'You don't want to be alone.'

'Do you mind?' she asked.

'Not at all.' I didn't want to be alone either, especially if there was something nasty upstairs. If Delia really knew Dean well enough, she might be able to prevent further bloodshed. Mine.

Then I remembered the other important part of the plan.

'I'll have to check the generator shed and see if there's a key for the door. We'll be sitting ducks in the dark if Dean decides to pull the pin on the power.'

'Really, Garfield, this isn't Dean. He isn't like this. He isn't. You believe me, don't you?'

'I believe that you believe that's the case. I won't be long. Maybe you can keep an eye out from the verandah.'

Delia nodded and we retraced our progress along the corridors and through to the kitchen again and unlocked the door. I rolled up my jeans, grabbed Delia's umbrella and torch and went down to the shed. The cool rainwater was refreshing on my bare feet; it probably would have been a lovely place to spend time in less dangerous circumstances. If we'd left our jobs on the boat a month sooner, I could have brought Rita here; we could have taken up meditation, planned something together.

Why was I thinking of Rita all of a sudden? It must have been all the water; the place looked oceanic in the darkness, but there was no point anymore to wondering about Rita. Focus on now, I told myself. Focus on coming and going without harm.

The shed was the way we'd left it, the generators humming along happily in competition with the rain. I looked around the doorframe and beyond for a key. There were no keys on handy hooks, nor any keys - even the wrong ones - lying casually on the narrow shelves around three of the walls. Where would a groundskeeper place a spare key to the generator shed? Not in the generator shed.

I stood outside the shed and trained the torch along the inside wall of the U until I saw it: a rectangular box attached to the brick wall. This important receptacle wasn't locked either. I pulled the door open and there was the key, sitting beneath the fuse box's surge protector. I took it back to the shed and inserted it in the lock; hand in glove. I locked the door and dropped the key in my shirt pocket feeling somewhat superior.

As I turned to face the building and make my way back to Delia, or rather Delia's dark outline on the verandah, I looked around at the U. I hadn't taken any notice of it the first time out here, and as I glanced up at the windows, I saw a light go on in one of the top floor rooms. Timing is everything, unfortunately.

Was it Dean? The chef? Escaped mud crabs? Dean, the chef, and escaped mud crabs having a friendly picnic out of the weather? It was one thing to airily say I'd check the upper floors when I didn't know that anyone was up there, and was fairly certain noone was there at all. Now that I was the closest thing in the vicinity to the police, and there was definitely someone up there, I had no choice, did I?

CHAPTER 23

'Delia,' I said, as we stood on the verandah, 'I think it'd be better if you stay down here while I check the other floors.'

'No way,' Delia said.

'I really think you'll be safer.' I unrolled my jeans and felt more manly.

'Down here, on my own, surrounded by kitchen knives.' She went inside and I followed, locking the door behind me. Now we could all feel like rats trapped in a cage.

I remembered my boots and went over to the wood stove. The fire had begun to burn down, but there was still plenty of heat coming through the oven. My boots were dried to a nice finish. I felt inside - not a trace of dampness - put them on the floor and closed up the oven door.

'Any luck with the mobile connection?' I asked.

'Not yet. You're right, we won't get anything here. There's a hill you can reach through one of the rainforest trails - we might get a signal up there.'

'Not in the dark.' Indoors with lighting was worrying enough.

'Well, let's go upstairs,' Delia said, 'I'm tired and I want to get five minutes sleep before these buggers get up and start their whinging.'

'You really think Dean won't hurt you?' I asked. 'How can you be so sure, Delia? You can't be taking risks with this situation.' I suspect a police officer, or even an actually accredited protective and investigative systems and services agent, would have been more forceful.

'Trust me, Garfield.'

'You sully people's coffee with fish tank water.'

'I melt chocolate laxatives and spread them on their muffins, too. Come on.' She walked off through the swing door into the hallway.

I debated whether or not to tell her that a light was on upstairs; it could easily be a malfunction of the connections between the building and the generators. The signals could be crossed and doing any old thing they wanted to, especially with all the humidity and water around. Who was I trying to kid?

'Delia, I saw a light go on upstairs on the top floor when I was out at the generators.'

'The top floor?' She furrowed her brow. 'That area's been closed off for some time. They were still renovating, but they ran out of cashflow when the investment earnings disappeared.' She took off up the stairs.

'Wait,' I called, knowing perfectly well that Delia would wait for no-one. I followed her two steps at a time, and caught her as she reached the stairwell up to the top floor.

'Let me,' I said, moving around her and taking the lead.

'He's less likely to stab me,' she said.

'We'll see about that,' I replied, which didn't seem to come out quite right.

When we reached the top floor, I had to reorient myself to work out what part of the building I'd seen from the generator shed. I went to the nearest window and looked down at the middle of the U. The generator shed was at the pointy end of the U's left-hand stem and I'd seen the light appear in the approximate middle of the right-hand stem.

'This side,' I told Delia, and we set off slowly and quietly down the hallway.

When we reached the turn at the bottom end of the U, I snuck a look around the corner. The hallway was empty as far as I could see; there were little pilot lights at intervals along the skirting boards. It was like a theatre aisle with no seats on offer, only small rooms on either side. Each room had a transom window and it was easy to spot the one that was lit up with dim but demonic flare.

Delia came to stand beside me and I pointed out the transom light. She nodded, and we moved silently down the hallway, praying for heavier rain to mask any squeaks or rattles we might make. But we didn't have to worry; as we got closer, I could hear noises inside the lit room. Things were being thrown around, it seemed, creating a combination of soft, muffled, and sharper sounds, and muttering. Dean talked to himself; that wasn't a sign you wanted to observe in the vengeful. I put my hand up, gesturing at Delia to wait where she was, a couple of metres from the door. The sounds changed to something that sounded like someone being suffocated. I took several steps forward until I could kneel down and peer in through the keyhole like some pervert in an old-time movie.

Once my eyes had adjusted to the light and to squinting through a tiny hole, and I could see what was going on in there, I felt a strange sensation rush through me and almost buckle my legs. I leaned back and Delia came over to kneel beside me. She raised her eyebrows in a question, 'What?' and

I pointed at the keyhole. She peered in and then looked back at me, her eyebrows raised even higher. We helped each other up, backed off, walked around the corner and made it to the top of the stairs before we had to sit down and let out the sheer relief. We laughed until we heard a door open and then we took off down the stairs and back to the kitchen.

CHAPTER 24

'Did you suspect?' I asked Delia, once we'd reacquired some level of sanity. Not finding Dean in the upstairs room waiting to disembowel us with his trusty handyman's tool kit had caused a cathartic release of tension: uncontrolled, unconcerned laughter.

'Not for a minute,' Delia replied, and laughed again. 'I thought they hated each other's guts.'

'There's nothing like a stock market crash to bring the troops together.'

'Together. If they were any closer together they'd be behind each other.'

As we laughed again like naughty kids at the penny-dreadful scene we'd witnessed through the keyhole, the kitchen door swung open and one of the show's stars marched in. Delia immediately assumed her Office Delia demeanour, but this time with a big pinch of bravado.

'Mr Butler, how may we assist you?' she asked, smiling.

'It was you, in the hallway,' he shouted, glaring hard at me and then Delia. Shameless.

'It was you, upstairs,' Delia said. 'We thought it was Dean the driver, come back for Mr Leason. But it was you, and Ms Harding, and strangulation - ' Equally shameless.

'How dare you invade our privacy, and what the fuck are you talking about, anyway?' The beginnings of bluster.

Butler took a step towards me while maintaining eye contact with Delia. I suppose he thought it was menacing, but he looked almost comical standing there in his Batman boxer shorts, bare-chested. He was round and pale and soft, like a shapeless hill of mashed potatoes with a head. He'd been far more impressive as the turd in a tie.

'Oh, you were - otherwise engaged when Mr Fletcher brought Mr Leason home,' Delia said. Home.

'And?'

'Mr Leason claims the driver, Dean, tried to run him down.' I stepped towards Butler until the invasion of his personal space became too much and he leaned back towards the kitchen bench.

'Leason's full of shit,' he said. 'He's got a drug for every occasion - can't take the stress anymore. He's probably hallucinating. Gutless wonder.'

Unlike you, I thought, noting his lack of muscular development. At least I had the benefit of months at sea, eating the food I cooked myself, which meant, of course, that I ate very little. Cooks don't enjoy their own work so much; I think it has something to do with familiarity brulèeing contempt.

'So you think he's exaggerating?' I asked Butler.

'Could be. Or he could be reaping his reward at last.' Butler turned to leave, and then remembered why he'd come down here. 'Don't come up to the top floor again, either of you. Ms Harding and I are working on our operational plan.'

Without the shadow of a smile, either.

'What do you mean by reaping his reward?' I asked.

'Most of the threatening calls we've had have been for him,' Butler said. 'What was that?'

From somewhere outside came a booming sound.

'That noise, was it thunder?' Butler asked.

'Could be a storm front moving in,' Delia suggested.

'This weekend's about as good as Downer's last adventure getaway, only much bloody hotter,' Butler said.

There was another boom, and then a third. As though they were cues to action, Butler slid away from the bench and went to the pantry. He loaded up on crackers, then went to the fridge and took out cheese and dips. On his way out, he stopped at the wine rack and grabbed two bottles of red. 'At least Downer got the snacks organised,' he said as he shouldered his way through the door.

'That wasn't thunder, was it, Garfield?' Delia asked.

'I don't think so. Did Dean come into any military ordnance recently, Delia? Are you close enough to him to know that?'

'He wouldn't do that.'

'Do what?'

'Blow us up.' She sighed and pushed herself up onto the kitchen bench.

'And you know this because you confine yourself to fish tanks and laxatives as your weapons of choice, so how could any friend of yours contemplate lethal weapons? Is that the logic?'

Delia decided that silence would be the stern reply to that one. She stayed where she was, tapping her heels against the cupboard.

'So, is Leason the main target?' If he was, it might make things easier with only one target to guard against mischief.

'Wishful thinking - they're all as culpable as each other. Butler's trying to fob his mistakes off to Leason. And the threatening calls have been democratically distributed around the chair and chiefs. Fairness rules, Gar.' She nudged out a quick smile, but she wasn't happy.

I'd thought as much about the Auroras. I unlocked the kitchen door and stepped out into the fresher air.

The rain kept coming, but there was no lightning and no more thunder, or ordnance. If a storm front was on its way, it was Dean made, but what was he up to? Was it a test run before he moved closer to us? Or had he blown himself up by accident, a bitter, screwed-over investor inexperienced in destruction and mayhem, but determined to avenge his brother's death? I could imagine wanting to bump this soulless gang off myself in the face of such a tragedy, but I didn't know if I could turn fantasy into reality. It seemed that Dean was well on his way.

CHAPTER 25

OPERATION BLUEWATER POLARIS - STAT. TARGET #001B

All in all, Guy Friendly preferred the desert to the rainforest. In the desert, he'd felt a sense of freedom unlike any other. Liberation is what it was: from things, objects, animals, the overwhelming accessorising that something like a rainforest seemed to have to offer whether you wanted it or not. In the desert, there was absence, there were gaps, only sand and rock, the odd oasis with its careful, reticent, desert fertility. And it was dry, oh, how eye-achingly dry it was out there, how unforgivingly, grittily beige. He loved it, and yet, here he was, in the midst of a green profusion of life so abundant and keen, sometimes he could barely breathe. But he had no choice; it was this, or check out; maybe it would be this, and check out. After Jacinta, and the baby, what was the point, other than revenge. The word made him smile; revenge, a dish best eaten any way you pleased. It was ironic, given Jacinta's circumstances. He thought he might prefer his revenge heated, then. He was sure that at least one of the Eyrie's facilities could accommodate his requirements.

He waited a long time for the van driver to reappear. Eventually, it seemed that the fellow was intent on other activities, so Guy would get on with his schedule. No-one was going anywhere, after all. He'd driven out of the walking trail and followed the main track back to the bridge. It was a simple matter of rigging it and blowing it, although he hadn't bargained on so much water. The creek's current was dangerously fast and furious and the water would be lapping the sides of the bridge within half an hour. Since it was likely to go under anyway in the next couple of hours, was it gilding the lily to get rid of it? He couldn't afford to take the risk; the monsoon could be weakening.

He grabbed his bag of tricks and left the Jeep's dry cabin for the rainy blackness, pulling the hood of his waterproof slicker over his head. It wasn't much, but it was something. He pulled on his night-vision goggles and scanned the area for movement beyond the jumpy vibrations of branches and shrubs and leaves bending and shaking to the rain's unrelenting beat. Nothing. He pulled the goggles down to hang around his neck and proceeded to the bridge, shimmying down the bank about half a metre before he met water. It was all too easy, wasn't it? They were a bunch of sitting ducks, only unlike ducks, this lot couldn't fly away from trouble, not now. Jacinta hadn't been able to fly her way out of trouble, either. All she'd needed was for one of them to have remembered. And if any one of them had expressed so much as a peep of remorse for any of it, he might have taken a different path. Might have.

He forced his mind back to the task at hand, pulled out the plastic explosive and moulded a piece around a set of likely-looking bolts. He did the same on the other side, and then moved into the middle of the bridge to plant some extra insurance. He'd hoped to be able to accomplish something more elaborate beneath the structure, but that wasn't an option any more. He attached the detonator wire and carefully rolled it back from the middle of the bridge and from each side, moving to the Jeep to attach the wires to the detonators. He'd always erred on the side of caution, never trusting one multi-wired detonator when three individuals could improve the odds so significantly, and reduce his stress levels.

There was no time like the present, he thought, his thumb and forefinger poised on the first switch, but then he stopped. There was something nearby, a noise out of rhythm with the other noises that had already established themselves. He placed the detonator in beside the other two near the front tyre and out of the rain, and slowly pulled up his night-vision goggles. He scanned the immediate area in a broad arc, across and back, and again. He moved around the Jeep, scanning as he went. The movement, when it came, was 30 feet or so off the passenger side. A mere shadow rising from its hiding place and taking a step, but it was human, he was certain. And then it was gone. The van driver? The vomiting man making a break for freedom from his colleagues? He pulled off the goggles, and shoved them beneath the Jeep - they were too cumbersome when running and leaping might be required.

Friendly hunched down and moved quickly to the shoulder of the track, practising his sensei's first and most important rule: be like water. Flexibility is everything. He became one with the forest, slipping beneath the drooping fronds of a large tree fern, stopping to listen, moving in the direction of the aberrant noise. He crossed an open patch, rounded a boulder slick with moss and water and suddenly he was on top of the man, who reared up at him and caught him on the temple with a fist wrapped around what could only have been a rock. He staggered back, cursing himself, and fell against the mossy boulder as the man threw several rocks at him before taking off into the blackness. No gun, then. Friendly straightened up and thought for a split second about returning for the night-vision goggles, but knew equally quickly that he'd lose the man. He took off, splashing through puddles and mud, pushing aside branches and fronds, narrowly missing the trip of a strangler vine.

They were travelling slightly downhill, he thought. He stopped for a moment and listened; the man continued running ahead of him. Friendly took off again; they seemed to be on some kind of path. It had become a channel for the rainwater and resembled a small creek. Why didn't the fellow take to the bush and give himself an even chance? But then, he couldn't know that the wrath of god was running him down.

The path widened and its sides steepened as more water poured along under his feet. It was doing a good impression of a creek now. The sense of running downhill became more apparent and he slowed to feel the current. There was no way the man could climb out of here; he was trapped. Friendly kept following the noises until he sensed movement beside him. The side of the newly-formed creek was collapsing and when he turned he saw a wall of water coming for him. He looked ahead and saw his quarry standing still and watching him. Who was trapped?

Friendly ran for the other side of the creek as its opposite collapsed into the water wall. His momentum propelled him halfway up and he grabbed for a clump of strangler vines. The surging water knocked his feet out from under him and he clung to the vines, twisting his head to locate the man. He thought he saw his outline just as the water and mud reached him. Then no-one, blackness again, rumbling mega-tons passing by. It was one way to get the job done.

He made his way back to the bridge through a changing landscape. The flash flooding had created new channels and paths; more debris littered the way, and he was glad to find the main track largely intact. He hurried over to the Jeep and reached under it for the detonators. They appeared to be intact. He remembered, this time, to wear his ear muffs.

The first explosion shifted the bridge's left side, dislodging bearers and the two nearside pylons. The ground beneath him shook for seconds. He waited for the last chunk of wood to land and settle before setting off the second bomb. This time the entire bridge moved sideways. It was impassable. The third explosion, in the middle, was the icing, but that was all right by Friendly. Waste not, want not. He flung the detonators into the shrubbery as the bridge began to float - in large, jagged pieces - down the creek. He backed up the Jeep and drove slowly, very slowly - who knew what other lunatics might be out here? - towards the hide he'd built near the Apostles' Eyrie. After the delay with the van man, there was no time to lose in securing his next target.

CHAPTER 26

My mother, Victoria, God rest her sweet soul, and Nonna Lucia, had several things in common. They were both great cooks, they only ever wanted the best futures for their children and grandchildren, and they both believed in the overnight solution. Everything will look better in the morning, Mum would tell me at bedtime when I'd had a particularly trying time failing trigonometry. The gravy is always better the next day, the Nonna would explain in her cosy little kitchen. They believed in making considered decisions based in adequate sleep and mature spaghetti sauce.

I had next to no sleep and the Eyrie's kitchen could never approximate the Nonna's gravy, even with a Michelin chef in residence, but we'd all staggered, in our different ways, through the dark hours and here was the morning. I had to do something about Dean, but first I needed reinforcements.

I'd made tea and toast and was lacing up my boots when Delia arrived.

'They've been and gone,' she said. 'I heard them rustling around when I was meditating.'

'They've hiked out?' This wasn't good, but if I moved quickly, I could catch them and shepherd them back until I could work out if Leason was delusional or not.

'No, I mean they're over at the new conference centre, planning their financial escapes to the Cayman Islands and Switzerland.' She went to the fridge and brought out the milk.

'Which is where?'

'From the main entrance, you go down the driveway to the left, join up with a walking path, and you come out to a clearing about a hundred and fifty yards away. It's the newest building here, finished just before the fall.'

'The kettle's still hot,' I said, more relieved than I cared to admit. 'Cuppa?' Apparently, the Auroras, even Leason, weren't worried about having me, their security blanket, in the same building as them.

'Thanks.' She found some cereal in the pantry while I poured her tea.

When we'd settled at the table, I thought I'd try again.

'Delia, if I'm going to do my job properly, I really need you to be honest with me.'

I munched on my raisin toast and watched her fill her cereal bowl to the rim with rice bubbles. Then she sent in a thin stream of milk and the ricies rose to the occasion, bobbing up and up. Finally, she sprinkled sugar over the lot and delicately began to work her way in from the side with her spoon.

'I don't know any more than what I've told you, Garfield,' she said, focussing on the bowl. 'Dean isn't the type to kill anyone. He isn't.'

'Then I'll take your word for it,' I said. 'And I won't need to arm myself when I hike up the hill to get a mobile signal.'

'I'll come with you,' she said. 'We should go while the troops are pre-occupied. They might want to leave later on, but I can't imagine them wanting to hike in the rain.'

The rain. There it was. I glanced out the open windows and noted that the scene hadn't changed. It may have been morning, but the sky was dark and low; it would probably feel like twilight for the entire day. Delia was right; they'd stick around until another vehicle arrived to ferry them out. Which reminded me.

'When are Philip Downer and Melanie Rogers-Hilton due to arrive, Delia. Is there a schedule?'

'No idea. They were supposed to be here yesterday. So was the chef, unless he's here and avoiding everyone so he doesn't have to cook. If he hasn't been paid in advance, he might think he'll get dudded, like everyone else.'

No wonder Henry had gone to the trouble of having our cheque cleared. 'We'd better go before they get here, then. They'll leave us behind if we're not back.'

We had to go out the front to get to the track that led to the hill climb. This track went in the opposite direction to the one for the conference centre. The path wasn't straight, but went back and forth up the face of the hill.

'Did you remember your mobile?' I asked Delia.

She drew if from her jeans pocket like a six-shooter.

'Did you?' she asked.

I raised my eyebrows in response, but patted my top pocket to be sure.

'Garfield, I have to know. Why are you doing this? You don't seem the type.'

Here was my opportunity to confess, to tell Delia that I had no idea what a Pinkert PISS boy did, and furthermore, I had no idea what I was doing with my life since Rita and I split. I glanced sideways at her as we hiked along the path. Maybe if I shared, so would Delia; I knew she was being extra careful with what she revealed about Dean.

'I was a cook, at sea,' I said. 'I had a relationship that didn't work out, with a deckhand.' Was that enough? No. 'She left me.'

'Why?' Delia asked. 'You seem like a very nice person.'

'Thanks, the acting lessons have paid off,' I said, but I couldn't quite manage the Magnum grin. 'I was cooking the crew's dinner when she went overboard in a rough sea. At first no-one noticed because she was down the back. When they did notice, she was nowhere to be seen. And it was already dark.'

'That's terrible.' Delia stopped walking and we stood facing each other under cover of the rain slickers we'd found in the Eyrie's hall closet. 'What happened? Did you find her? What's her name?'

'Rita. Well, it was Rita, then. We called for help with the search. There were planes, helicopters, all the shipping in the area was on alert. After three days, we were sure that was it. We were in mild temperatures, but there were sharks, and exposure. We didn't know if she'd hurt herself when she fell.' I hadn't discussed Rita with anyone since that time and I was surprised at how I began to feel breathless and light-headed. 'Towards dusk on the third day, the first mate started sounding the horn. By the time I got to the deck, she was near the boat. I jumped in with a couple of others and we brought her in.'

'Thank God,' Delia said. 'She was alive.' I nodded. She took a step or two, and then stopped again. 'So where is she now? Back in the city?'

'She decided to change her entire life. She said that by the end of the second day lost, she'd decided to take off her life vest and let herself go. She'd seen a couple of fins not far away.'

'But she didn't do it.'

'She said after she'd decided she could go, she wanted to hang around for a little while and see how freedom felt.'

'Freedom?'

'From the world, this dimension, she called it. After the rescue, she said that bumming around the world on boats wasn't part of her life anymore, and neither was I.' I'd said it, aloud, to someone else.

'That's rough, Garfield.' Delia reached out and patted my arm. 'I'm sorry.'

'She went to India. She lives in an ashram in Goa. Her name is Indira Rahnee Devi.' The whole Eastern mystic package.

'She's happy?'

'Blissful.' So I'd heard from third parties.

'So Garfield, that's Rita's story. But what's yours?'

There was more to Delia than reception and photocopying duties implied. 'What's mine? Apart from living in a house with a ghost and hardly any light bulbs, my story is come on, Delia, let's do this and get ourselves out of this flytrap.' Action was the answer. Work is the antidote to almost everything, including moping over lost loves and a lack of choice about where one rests one's head at night.

'Nice segue, Garfield,' Delia said, as we resumed walking. 'But you can't get out of it that easily.'

Up ahead on a turn in the path, I saw what looked like another obstacle and cursed under my breath. It was a brown bundle of something, but it wasn't square like the box of mud crabs.

'Wait here, Delia,' I said. I took slow steps towards it, waiting for movement, anything. There was a twitch at the edge of the brown and a hand came up from beneath some leaves.

'Come on,' I called back to Delia, and she ran forward. She was on top of the body before I could stop her, pulling at him, rolling him over.

'Dad,' she yelled. 'Daddy? Daddy?'

Daddy?

CHAPTER 27

Daddy was in no condition to walk, but somehow, between us, and after several stops and staggers, we got him down the path and into the sick bay on the ground floor. He was a mess. There was no part of him that wasn't wet and muddy; his white shirt and navy trousers had turned dark brown. He was covered in bruises and abrasions, and his torn clothes looked as though a hobo had been wearing them for two years straight and then got caught in a tsunami, an earthquake and a cyclone. He was mute with fatigue and, I thought, looking into his tired, red eyes when we found him, fear. When he'd realised we were there with him on the path, and that Delia was right beside him holding his hand, he whispered, 'Thank God it's you.' Who else would it be, but one or more of us?

Delia fussed with blankets and got the first aid kit out and open.

'Where does it hurt, Dad?' she asked.

Dean lay there inert and staring up at the ceiling. Then he registered Delia's question and said, 'Everywhere, sweetie.' He lifted his head, thought better of it, and lay back on the pillows.

Delia found some swabs in the kit, opened one and began wiping Dean's face clean of mud and leaf litter.

'You look like you've been in a river or something,' Delia said.

'Mudslide,' Dean answered. 'Flash flood.' Then his eyes grew even more fearful. 'Anyone come here?'

'Who?' Delia asked.

'A man, in a hood.'

'Who was he? The chef?'

'Too dark - couldn't see his face.' He paused to get some more breath into his lungs. 'Tried to kill me.'

'What?' I said. 'Who tried to kill you?' Leason's story was that Dean was the predator out there. Perhaps he had an accomplice waiting in the wings. The chef?'

'He was near the bridge. I drove the van up and saw his Jeep. Same one.' Delia kept wiping his face, but soon enough he pushed her hand away. 'Enough,' he said.

'What do you mean, the same one?' I asked.

'Same one as before.' He closed his eyes and Delia gave me a look that said 'enough' as well. She pulled the blanket up to her father's chest and he hooked his fingers over the top of it and clung to it.

Delia pointed to the door, told her father she'd be back in a minute, and herded me out with her. In the foyer, I waited for her to explain, but patience is something I'm still learning.

'Who's your father's other accomplice, Delia?' I asked.

'Other accomplice?' She looked surprised.

'Besides you. Was it Dean in the van trying to run Leason down, or this other guy?'

'There's no other guy - not with Dad. Or me.' Delia walked to the front door and looked out.

'Those bastards are coming,' she said, and darted towards the sick bay. 'Come back in here. I don't want them knowing about Dad.'

Bastards; it sounded like a good collective noun for stockbrokers, given my recent reading about their exploits. As I waited behind the sick bay door with Delia for them to pass by - footsteps proceeded up the staircase and Butler called out 'Leason, where are you, you lazy fuck' - other equally appropriate collectives occurred to me.

'A slime of stockbrokers would do,' I whispered to Delia, trying to coax up a little lightness. 'Or a deception of stockbrokers.' It must have been the tension. 'How about a manipulation of stockbrokers, a - '

'An arrogance, Garfield, a fraudulence, a revulsion of stockbrokers.' Delia's whisper was full of vehemence. 'A pustulence, a corruption, a rapacity, a miasma of stockbrokers. God, I hate those bastards.'

'Please, stop beating around the bush, Delia, I prefer straight talkers. You're a human thesaurus.'

'Poet, actually,' she said.

Then we heard her father moan and rushed back to him.

'What is it, Dad? Where does it hurt?'

'Ribs, Delia. Broken.'

He squirmed under the blanket trying to get comfortable and his face turned almost as white as the sheet he lay on. I grabbed the nearest receptacle, a wastepaper bin, and handed it to Delia. He could be vomiting soon.

'We'll have to immobilise where they're cracked if we can,' I said. 'See if you can find some bandages or tape.' I turned to Dean. 'I'll get you some water for the painkillers.' Delia took the cue and started unpacking the first aid kit. I could check the kitchen cupboards as well.

Immediately outside the sick bay it was quiet again, but the voices I could hear upstairs sounded as though they were moving along the hallway. At least they were within earshot, which meant I was fulfilling the terms of my contract to provide proximate security.

I pushed through the kitchen door and was met by a heatwave. Someone - the chef? - must have cranked up the wood stove. Maybe he was cooking the mud crabs. Whatever it was, the smell was unfamiliar, but then, I'm only a basic cook, former cook. I worked my way around the cupboards, checking likely drawers for aspirin. I found some in the drawer near the sink, which was near the wood stove. Stabbed onto a meathook hanging from the rail that ran above the stove was a sheet of yellow paper, A4 size. The word SURPRISE! was scrawled across the top of the page in black marker and underneath was a pair of eyes, eyebrows raised, the startled-looking pupils staring down at the wood stove. The drawing looked familiar, in the way that graffiti looks familiar: we know we could easily do that, too, so there.

The chef must have intended the Auroras to discover the tasty morsels contained within when they broke for morning tea or lunch. I might as well help them out and remove it to the bench. People unfamiliar with wood stoves often find themselves with burnt fingers and hands. I grabbed the thickest mitt I could find and unhooked the oven door.

When I leaned down to see what was inside, I'm certain I turned as pale as Dean. I sat down hard on the floor, and knew I'd be hyperventilating in seconds if I couldn't find a paper bag. I'd seen some in the aspirin drawer and reached over to pull it out and onto the floor beside me. I took out a bag, shook it open very easily with my shaking, quaking hands and put it over my nose and mouth. I pushed myself back from the open stove door until the waves of heat diminished a little and I concentrated on breathing evenly while staring anywhere except at the oven.

I knew it would have to come out, and quickly, before it burned to a crisp. I couldn't leave it for Delia to discover, or any of the others for that matter. After a few minutes, I pushed myself up to my knees and wobbled across the floor to the stove. I picked up the mitt I'd dropped and reached up to get another one from the sink. It was pure willpower that forced me to my feet and made my hands reach in and pull the roasting dish out. I carried it to the stainless steel bench beside the sink and placed it carefully. The fat in the bottom of the dish spat a bit, but that was the least of it. The head was so darkly roasted that I couldn't tell who it was, and the wrinkling and shrinkage had distorted the features even further.

CHAPTER 28

The tea and toast didn't want to stay down, but they'd gone too far to come back up. I took a step to the right and leaned over the sink, but all I did was cough and dry retch. I turned on the tap and splashed water on my face and over my head, but I needed more, of something. I went to the fridge and opened the door. The cool air was wonderful; then I saw the note: another sheet of A4 paper, folded in half and placed tent-style over a plate. The word above the startled eyes was LOOK! and the eyes stared down at the plate. I didn't want to LOOK! nor did I want to know what COLD CUTS, written beneath the eyes, meant.

There was no-one else; I couldn't allow Delia to find this mess. I carefully picked up the plate, tent cover still hiding what I presumed were the cold cuts, and walked it to the sink. I placed it beside the roasting dish, and went over to the wood stove to close the dampers and cut the fire as soon as possible. It wouldn't get rid of the heat quickly, but eventually the kitchen would cool down, and we needed as much cool as we could get our hands on.

I heard them coming and didn't know what to do. I'd lay odds the course I didn't take for my certificate of accreditation would not have included this scenario. I threw a tea towel over the roasting dish and went back to the fridge to check that there were no other surprises in there.

Water. I needed water for Dean and his painkillers. I pulled out a bottle of spring water for him, and one each for Delia and me. I went over to lean against the bench - my legs felt rubbery - opened my water and drank it down as the Auroras came through the swing door from the hallway.

'Ah, the chef's been hard at work,' David Oliver told the others. 'Something smells - exotic, I'd have to say. Out of the box.' He laughed at his own joke. After what I'd found in the oven, I wondered what exactly might be in the mud crab crate, but that was back-burner stuff for the moment.

'What's for morning tea, PISS boy?' Butler came over to the fridge as he spoke, and opened the door. I almost wished I could have turned back time a few minutes, so Butler could enjoy that moment of surprise. It wouldn't be long now, anyway.

'Mr Fletcher,' said Ms Harding, 'you don't look very well. Are you all right?'

'He's fine, Sarah,' said Butler. 'Can we get this show on the road. I've had it up to here with latecomers and no-shows.' He slammed the fridge door shut and looked around the room.

'Who's a no-show?' I asked. I couldn't help but picture the head in the dish, but it was too far gone to identify. No hair, black around the edges and the pointy bits; the eye sockets completely sunken, and the skin generally roasted to a dark, dark brown and wrinkling badly. Any longer in there and it would have looked like a barbecued cantaloupe. It had to be one of them, didn't it, one of the Auroras? It surely wasn't a stray monk, left over from the Eyrie's earlier incarnation, and now ready to be a scare tactic courtesy of - who, exactly? Could Dean be foxing; did he have the time and chutzpah to sneak in, rev up the stove, and place the head and plate, and then run back into the rainforest and lie doggo until we found him? He wasn't that good an actor.

'Philip and Melanie, for starters,' said Oliver. 'The blasted chef's arrived late, but we'll forgive him for that. At least we'll have lunch.'

'I don't think the chef's been here,' I said. But how could I be certain? Maybe this was the chef's work; maybe the chef made threatening calls, too. He could be like Dean, one of the duped investors who lost everything. He mightn't get any money back, but he'd already gotten the satisfaction of a head well done, whoever it might be. I didn't think it was a woman's head, but I couldn't work out why I thought that.

'So it's you that's cooking, is it, Fletcher? A man of at least two talents, or maybe only one if we're all axed to death in our beds.' Butler couldn't help himself.

I could imagine someone wanting to run him down, just as Dean had tried with Leason. Leason. Where was he? Had they been looking for him upstairs? Had they found him, still sluggish and recovering in bed from his nightmare? I took a deep breath and let it out as slowly as my racing heart would allow.

'I have to talk to you all about something that's - happened.' What should I do? Simply unveil the roasting dish and let them have it? They were adults like me; why should they be spared when I hadn't been?

Before I could continue, Delia walked in, looking as though she was about to shout at me for taking so long with Dean's water. Then she checked herself when she saw the three of them.

'Delia,' David Oliver said, 'I need those reports we were discussing yesterday. Did you make sure they came with us?'

Delia looked at Oliver as though he was a complete stranger.

'Pardon?' she said.

'Reports, Delia, the last quarter?' As Oliver spoke, he wandered around the kitchen, opening cupboards, until he ended up at the sink. I realised that I was on the other side of the room. Naturally, I'd want to be as far away from the horror as possible, and my body had taken its own decision and moved me away. 'Lunch?' he asked no-one in particular.

'Wait,' I said, but it was too late. He pulled the tea towel up and away with a flourish like a matador, and then looked down at the dish. I took a couple of jelly-like steps as I saw recognition dawning on his face. He dropped the tea towel and stood mutely staring at the head as I came to stand beside him. The others moved closer.

'What is it, David?' Sarah Harding asked. 'Overdone?' But she wasn't close enough yet.

Delia kept her distance. She seemed to sense the worst and didn't want a bar of it.

'Oh my sweet Jesus.' Butler stood gaping as Harding put her hand to her mouth and staggered back.

David Oliver, still mute, noticed the plate beside the roasting dish, and saw the invitation. He put out a trembling hand and touched the paper. Butler reached across and pulled the paper away. The two of them stared at the plate, and then at the roasted head. Now I could see what was missing.

'Is that - what - I don't - ' Butler turned to Oliver and the two of them turned to me. They were silent for what seemed a long time.

'Is this - what is this?' Oliver asked at last.

'I haven't seen it,' I said, coming over to them. 'I just took it out of the fridge and you came in.'

I got closer and checked out the plate. Beneath the plastic wrap tightly clinging to the plate, was a pale, pinkish shell of an ear with a diamond stud in the lobe. The diamond was pale blue, and set on a gold base shaped like, well, a graph. The ear was surrounded by drops of water on the plate and condensation had begun to accumulate on the plastic wrap above it.

'Do you recognise it?' I asked them.

They both looked too horrified to begin to think about who might have lost an ear. The head in the dish was missing an ear, its left ear. Simultaneously, Butler and Oliver raised their left hands to their ears. They both had the same style of ear-ring, but their diamonds were white, not blue.

'Are you in some kind of club?' Delia asked them.

'Club?' Oliver said, still mesmerised by the ear on the plate. 'Oh. No. They're mementoes of a trip we all went on - to the Antarctic. It's supposed to represent an iceberg - an iceberg shape. You know?' It still looked like a graph to me. He gestured with his hand and then stopped, his gaze moving from the ear to the head and back. He licked his lips.

Delia turned from him to Sarah Harding. 'Ms Harding? You're not a member?' Delia. Sharp as ever.

Ms Harding's ears were free of enhancements.

'Yes,' she said, 'I'm a member.' She said 'member' as though it was the most contemptible word in the language. 'I don't - ' she began, and then looked up. She caught Butler's eye. He was trying to communicate with her entirely through the magic of his grinding teeth - you could see them working away at the side of his jaw - and his furrowed brow. I'd had enough.

'Who else has one of these ear-rings?' I asked Oliver.

'Leason, he has one. But it - '

I cut him off. 'And did you see Leason when you were upstairs before?'

'His door was locked,' Butler said.

Everyone was silent for a moment. 'I'll be right back,' I said. 'Mr Oliver, make sure the back door is locked, and close the windows. Mr Butler, go and lock the front door please.'

I took off through the kitchen door and out to the hallway, past the sick bay - Dean would have to wait a while - and up the staircase. I pounded with both fists on Leason's door, worked the handle, pounded again. I yelled up at the transom window. Something stirred inside, and then it occurred to me that it could be the person responsible for the head and the ear. I stood back from the door and reached for my key-ring and my apple-peeling knife.

CHAPTER 29

Why did I take this job? Why do I think I still owe Henry, just because he saved my life? He couldn't save my parents, and neither could I. Not that I hold any of it against him; if it hadn't been for Henry, I'd be in the grave with them, a job lot. If it hadn't been for Henry, I'd be safely at sea, mourning Rita by making my extra special marine goulash, the kind she loved before she saw whatever light beckoned on the outrageous open ocean, and took her off to her own sweet nirvana. If it hadn't been for me, I'd be holding Henry's .38 Special instead of my apple peeler, and feeling more like a master of the Apostles' Eyrie.

The door handle turned slowly, slowly. I stood to the side of the door and a body length back.

'What the fuck do you want?'

I took a very deep breath and held it for a few seconds. I automatically checked Leason's ears. Redundant, I know, but there you are; the energy flows where the focus goes, and ears were it for now.

'You're okay. Good,' I said, relaxing. Leason looked no better after a few hours sleep. He needed a shave, and he looked even more familiar with the growth around his jaw, but I couldn't pinpoint the memory.

'You woke me up to ask me that?' he said, and turned back into his room. 'Prat.' Leason's earlier expressions of gratitude had been an aberration, it seemed.

I'm a bit rusty on the unarmed combat routines I learned in the Army four hundred years ago, and deliberately so. I have no desire to pursue a life of violence, but right then, at the 'prat' moment, I thought of the people Leason's crowd had divested of their money, their homes, their futures, and I could have given him a fright, one way and another. Instead, I used shock, and a soupçon of awe.

'There's been an incident, sir,' I said, and waited for Leason to turn back to me. 'A human head has been discovered in the kitchen's wood stove, and an ear, in the refrigerator.' I watched Leason raise his left hand to his ear; it had a diamond stud like the others. 'I suggest you join us downstairs so we can decide what to do about our safety.'

'What? What do you mean, our safety? Whose head is it?' His eyes grew bigger and he blinked faster.

'Well, we thought it might be yours, but we were mistaken. See you down there. You'll need to take a look, in case you can identify it. And, Mr Leason, I can't protect you if I don't know where you are, or you're out of sight.'

I walked away from him, and heard him scuttle back inside the room and then rush out to follow me down. He caught up with me and I saw that he had his sneakers in one hand, and a pill bottle in the other.

'This isn't some joke, is it? They're always doing these stupid things. They think they're pranksters. Punk'd, that's it, that's the word. They think they're TV reality stars on a getaway adventure. It's Philip's doing, isn't it?'

'Unless he's a murderer, I don't think so.' On the other hand, no-one had seen Philip Downer, or Melanie Hilton-Rogers. I'd assumed the head was real, and the ear. But what did I know about roasted heads, other than the ones on suckling pigs? What did I know about ears, except for Brian Thorpe's ear, torn almost clean off in an under-14s rugby ruck when I was at school? And what did I know about these people, other than their belief that greed was the only worthwhile human motivator?

It sounded as though Leason was hyperventilating beside me as we strode down the corridor to the kitchen. I pushed the swing door and a wave of wood stove heat hit us; it was taking its time to disperse, and those gathered were sweating heavily. Delia had disappeared, and taken Sarah Harding with her, apparently. Butler and Oliver stood on the opposite side of the kitchen from the sink. The head was covered again by the tea towel.

'Leason.' Oliver, ran his hand over the top of his stubbled head. 'You're all right.'

'Hardly. Is this a Downer gag? I thought we had more serious things to worry about, Dave.'

'A set-up? Oh. No, I don't think so.' Oliver motioned for Leason to follow him; they stood near the sink as Oliver drew the tea towel back. Leason gasped and took a step sideways.

'Who?' was all he could manage.

'We don't know,' I said. 'There's the ear.' I pulled the sheet of paper off the plate. There was the ear, pale, pinkish, but with definite signs of greying around the edges.

'Jesus, Mary and Joseph,' Leason said, and for a second I was back in Nonna Lucia's kitchen right before dinner-time. She'd say her own version of the prayer of grace before meals. Hers always began with the holy family rather than the lord above. He seemed too distant to her, but the family, they'd gone through the mill, especially the boy. 'Jesus, Mary and Joseph,' she'd say, and Gianni would take up the rest, 'bless us and these thy gifts, which of thy bounty, we are about to receive, Amen.' It wouldn't have mattered if Jesus, Mary, Joseph and every cherubim and seraphim in the heavens had blessed or cursed the Nonna's table; it was always top drawer. No wonder I ended up cooking.

'Come on, sit over here.' It was Butler, showing some skim milk of human kindness. Leason tottered the distance and sat at the table. I followed him over and sat opposite.

'Mr Leason, you don't recognise the head? Or the ear?' It was highly likely that the two went together, but I couldn't be totally definitive at this stage.

Leason glanced over at the sink and shook his head. 'It has to be one of us, doesn't it?' His hand went up to his ear and he stroked the diamond iceberg stud. His hands were shaking.

'Who else is there, besides the people here, who'd have an ear-ring like that?' That should narrow it down. 'It's a memento?'

'They're from the Antarctic expedition,' Butler said. 'Dave told you before.'

'Philip, and, ah - Melanie,' Leason said. 'They have them. Six.'

'You're sure?' If that was the case, then there were only two other heads to choose from.

'Of course I'm sure,' Leason said. 'It's an exclusive group. You don't forget the members. Six.' He slumped back in the chair and stared over at Butler, who was leaning against the fridge. 'That one,' he said, 'it's blue. Philip, he has a blue one.'

'Okay. Did you inform the police about the threats your company's received?' It wasn't much, but it was a place to start.

'Most of them couldn't be traced. They were made from phone booths, or pre-paid mobiles with dodgy paperwork. Or we got letters in some cases.' David Oliver was running his hand over his stubbled head again. He clearly wanted to come up with something, anything. I know I would have thanked him for it.

'What are you going to do for us, piss boy?' Butler. It was reassuring to know that the turd in a tie hadn't revised his manners. 'The police couldn't have cared less, Dave, you know that. They were glad we were being harassed.'

'Why would that be, Mr Butler?' I asked.

'Because everyone wants what we've got,' Butler replied. 'Why else?'

'And what is it that you have, exactly?' It was a cheapish shot, I know, but I'd had it with them, and now, by association, Delia and I, and Delia's father, could be targets, too.

Butler opened his mouth to answer, but then seemed to think better of it. Instead, Dave Oliver, the CEO, if I'd remembered their useless titles correctly, intervened.

'What matters now is our safety,' he said, and looked around the kitchen. 'We need to have everyone accounted for. And Pete's right. Philip has a blue diamond - that's what I was about to say when you charged off upstairs, Fletcher.'

As he continued scanning the kitchen, Dean shuffled through the door, his face as pale as Leason's white T-shirt, followed closely by Delia.

'You,' Leason said, standing quickly and moving back from the table. 'You're the driver. You're the one. You tried to kill me. He did the head, the ear. Phil's ear.' Leason looked as though he might keel over. 'It's him.'

Dean stared at Leason as though seeing him for the first time ever. 'Who are - oh, yes, I did.' Then he threw a sideways glance towards the sink; Delia must have explained what was going on. 'Not the head. No. I'm an agitator, not a murderer. I'd rather have you alive and worrying.'

'Which is what's happening now,' Leason said. His voice had risen several notes, and sounded dangerously close to hysterical.

'Where's Sarah Harding?' I asked. 'Did she go with you, Delia?'

'She walked past the sick bay. She was going towards the front door.'

'Not upstairs?'

'No, the front door, I heard it open.'

'This man is a murderer,' Leason said. 'You have to arrest him, Fletcher. You're the law here.'

'This man is my father,' Delia said, and the four men, crew-cut Oliver, turd-in-a-tie Butler, hatchet-faced Leason, and Dean Porter, the mad van driver, turned to face her as though they were a precision marching band on a tea break. 'And he wouldn't hurt a fly.'

'But,' Dean said, struggling to the kitchen table and sinking down in the seat Leason had vacated, 'I know who would, and he's out there.'

CHAPTER 30

The front door was still open. Ms Harding had taken off in a hurry, but where would she go? I grabbed a slicker, locked the door behind me, went out to the covered walkway and scanned the surroundings, but saw no movement other than the rain, no colours other than green and dun. There was mud everywhere, the paths were strewn with palm fronds and leaf litter, and even though the sky had lightened, there was no telling if or when there would be a break in the weather. Whatever had frightened Sarah Harding into leaving had more punch than the head in the dish and the ear on the plate; surely she would have preferred to stay in relative safety with the rest of us. I tried the oldest trick in the book.

'Sarah,' I yelled. 'Sarah Harding.' You never knew when there might be another Sarah lurking in the rainforest. 'Sarah. Sarah Harding. Come back to the Eyrie.'

I waited. The rain fell; the noise wasn't deafening, but I realised soon enough that Sarah Harding, or any other Sarah, would have to be standing no more than 50 yards away, or less, to hear my voice carry through the water noise. She was long gone, so I took an educated guess. She was too smart to try for the road out; it was a long way on foot, there was no guarantee that she'd be able to flag a vehicle down, and she'd probably figure that sitting ducks took the main road and could pay the price in the roasting dish.

The second time up the hill to the peak where mobile coverage might be available was more challenging, but I went a lot higher a lot faster and kept scanning the forest on either side of the narrow path for untoward activity. After about 20 minutes, a different water sound emerged and merged with the rainwater. A waterfall? If there was a river at the bottom of it, or even a substantial creek, perhaps we could follow it to a safer place. People liked to build their homes near attractive water views, and there was an abundance of beauty in this area, much of it courtesy of the river and creek system that sustained the rainforest plants and animals.

I continued up to the top of the hill, pulled out my mobile and dialled Henry's number. There was no sign of Sarah Harding. If Henry could alert the police, they'd probably be able to send in a helicopter, or at the very least, a fast car, to get us out and then search for the man Dean had seen near the bridge. Unless, of course, Dean really was the one, and the man at the bridge in the Jeep was either a figment of his imagination, or real and part of the plan to both decapitate and scare the Auroras to death.

The phone rang and rang and then I heard Henry's voice.

'Henry,' I said, 'it's Gar.'

Henry kept talking; it was his answering machine message and his voice managed to be both mellow and robotic simultaneously. 'Hello,' urbane, flatliner Henry began. 'You've reached Pinkert Protection and Investigation Systems and Services.' He said it, but he couldn't work it out. Pinkert PISS. 'This is Henry Pinkert, Chief Executive Officer and Senior Investigator. We value your enquiry, so please leave a message and I or one of my highly experienced colleagues will return your call within 24 hours. In an emergency, please dial triple-0 and ask for the police. Please leave your message after the tone.'

Twenty-four hours? What sort of service were we running? A pissweak one, by the sound of things. In 24 hours, the entire world could be nuked back to the ice age.

'Henry,' I said again, 'pick up, it's Gar. We have an emergency here. There's a head in a roasting dish and an ear on a plate, and someone's trying to kill our clients.' I stopped and listened. Was he there, laughing his head off at my attempt to get out of the contract and come home to Belle? 'Henry, this isn't a joke. I'm serious. We need help, now. Call the police as soon as you get this message. I'm going to call them now.' What else could I say? 'Henry. Are you there? Where the fuck are you?'

I hung up and dialled triple-0. Triple-0 was engaged. I tried again, and again, but the third time was no luckier. The fourth time, an operator answered; the connection was scratchy and tinny.

'Hello,' I said. 'Hello. My name is Garfield Fletcher. I'm at the Apostles' Eyrie. It's in the hinterland - '

'Sorry, sir - repeat - location.' Her voice was breaking up. ' - street reference -'

'The Apostles' Eyrie,' I said, louder, 'there's no street.' I was concentrating so hard I thought my eyeballs would combust, which was probably why I didn't hear whoever it was that arrived behind me.

CHAPTER 31

There was scuffling, and then nothing. How many times did Magnum get knocked out? Or Miss Marple? Did she suffer for her occupation? I felt the trickle of raindrops on my face; I heard the roll of thunder, and the fall of gravel; I grabbed up a handful of mud and held it tight in my hand as I opened my eyes. I heard myself groan but I felt no pain, only a fuzziness around the edges as though I'd been lightly anaesthetised.

I had a sudden and strong sense of danger, of a precipice. I drew back, the way babies draw back from the edges of things if they know what's good for them, and bumped against a thickness of something.

As the fuzziness cleared further, I saw where I'd been placed. Placed - that was the only word that came to mind, considering the precision required. I was on a ledge some yards down from where I'd been standing, I assumed, when my conversation with the triple-0 operator was terminated. The ledge was narrow, probably a metre and a half; beside me there was a reassurance of soil, rock and tree roots. Beneath me was an almost sheer drop to the creek, 50 yards at least, and I knew the view out to the national park would be spectacular from here, but it was cloaked in mist right now.

Someone - Sarah Harding? Dean's madman? Another? - had lowered me down here, very carefully. Someone strong, someone with access to ropes and harnesses. It didn't seem likely that Ms Harding could have managed it, but with a helper? Why couldn't all of this be an inside job? Who better to prey on the Auroras than one of their own, and none of them seemed overly fond of each other.

Whoever it was, the someone, had fitted me with an abseiling harness and hooked me to a stout rope, which they'd dropped down on top of me once the job was done. I sat up, leaned against a comforting rock, and coiled the rope. If it was long enough to bring me down here, it was long enough to raise me up again, unless it had been cut. I was neither bruised nor bleeding. I had no broken bones, I was alive and not waiting down below for a chalk artist to outline my pulpy, mangled body.

Whoever it was didn't want me to die. A cheering thought, replaced almost immediately by the perennial question: why? Nine out of ten 'whys' never receive an answer. I'm sure I read that statistic somewhere reputable. I thought I'd try out a different word and then several others, and hope to increase my odds of success.

'Help,' I yelled, 'help. I'm down here on a ledge. Come and look over - I'm down here.' I ran the risk of calling back the someone who'd put me here, to change their minds and finish me off, but my life wasn't about choices at the moment.

'Help. It's Garfield Fletcher. I'm with the Aurora Investments group.' Wait. Did I want to be associated with a crowd who'd received threats of physical violence, and had just been treated to roast head and cold cut of ear for lunch? 'Help. I'm trapped on a ledge. I have a rope.'

Was there rustling up above, or was it the raindrops falling on my head? Was the ledge about to go south, a victim of waterlogging?

'Hello,' I called, 'who is it?'

A hand came over the ledge, and then Sarah Harding's face stared down at me. She looked terrified.

'Ms Harding,' I said, 'thank God.'

'I saw you,' she said, 'I saw you on your mobile.'

My mobile. I felt in my pockets and looked around the ledge. It was gone.

'Who did this?' I asked her. 'Did you see them?'

'A man - in a rain jacket - with a hood.' She removed herself from my view.

'Ms Harding? Where are you?' I couldn't risk having her leave. I could scream for days, and there was no telling if Delia or any of the others, with their own worries, would come looking for me. I didn't know who was working with whom, or if any of them could have orchestrated the entire weekend as a trauma experiment, complete with rubber heads and ears, taking some kind of stockbroker revenge on their business partners. Henry had let me walk into this without vetting a thing about it.

'I'm here, Mr Fletcher. I'm afraid of heights.'

'You have to help me get back up there,' I said. 'I'll throw you the rope.'

'I feel dizzy,' she said. 'I can't come any closer.'

'It's all right, you don't have to. Just grab the rope when I throw it up. Loop it around a tree or a rock and tie it as tight as you can.' There was silence up above. 'Did you hear me?'

'Yes. Everything's slippery.'

I grabbed the coils in my right hand and held the other end near the harness with my left. I didn't want to fling myself out over the ledge with the momentum of the rope which was fairly thick.

'I'm throwing now,' I yelled, and heaved the coils up in a slight arc towards the top of the cliff.

'I've got it,' she said, 'I've got it.' Her tone sounded edgy; there was no time to waste.

'Tie it around something. Is there a tree, or a rock?' Why hadn't I been more observant of my surroundings? Because I was rusty, because I'd been cooking in confined, rocking spaces for far too long; because I'd been consumed with the outcome rather than the moment at hand. I should have followed Rita to the ashram.

'Yes, there's a tree,' she said.

I heard her moving around and muttering to herself, but the words were lost in the rain.

'Tie it tight,' I said, so I don't end up as Garfield McSplatter.

After a couple of minutes, I saw Sarah Harding's hand waving at me.

'It's done, Mr Fletcher,' she said as her hand waved like the Queen's on the balcony at Buckingham Palace.

A life of service. I could do that, I thought, no worries, no cliff faces, no poorly tied ropes, no plunging to my agonising death on the boulders below, left alive long enough to experience the full gamut of torturous pain and fear before expiring. Just waving, simply waving. Calm down.

'Okay. I'm climbing.' I checked that the rope was securely tied to the harness and not about to unravel like a magic trick courtesy of the dark presence who'd put me here.

There were a couple of useful footholds in between some exposed tree roots, but the soil was soft and crumbly after all the rain. I dug my idiot-repelling right boot in above a healthy-looking root half a yard up and tested my weight against the rope, pulling hard on it. It held well enough. There wasn't much room for error if I slipped and the rope went with me. There wasn't any room for error. What kind of stockbroker had any facility with knots?

Trust, climbing is all about trust. And confidence. I pulled myself up by the rope with both hands, and took a step with my left foot, this time relying on a rock jutting out from the wall. I found a handhold - another rock, to the left of the rope and grabbed it, hauling myself up and driving my right foot into the soil above another root. I was Spiderman, but without the handy webby, sticky stuff. I wasn't Spiderman, I clung to the wall and gripped the rope with white knuckle fever. It was humid and steamy and the rain, though lighter, made everything treacherous. I'd managed to angle myself sideways, so I turned my head and looked along the wall just below to find another foothold; I didn't have the upper body strength to do it all with my arms and shoulders. Note to self: join gym immediately on escape from Stockbroker Survivor, but first beat Henry to a pulp so a before and after strength assessment can be executed. Executed. I liked the sound of that word when it was so closely connected with Henry.

'Are you all right, Mr Fletcher?' Ms Harding's voice, from somewhere beyond the edge. 'I'm praying for you.'

What do you say to that? 'Thanks,' I yelled, slip-sliding to the next foothold, straining at the rope, wishing for my army fitness.

There was a patron saint of climbers, there had to be. There were saints for every day of the year and then some. Nonna Lucia would tell us horrible stories about martyrs torn limb from limb by straining horses, or sliced into small pieces, or flung into burning pits or freezing lakes. Hatred ran deep in opposing religious circles. I tried to distract myself with the Nonna's stories as I simultaneously focussed on the dirt in front of me and the vines and roots and rocks to the left and right of me. It seemed to help, imagining other poor wretches sent to their doom without a second chance. All I had to worry about was the drop and squelch.

I risked a move that required some stretching to the right: a V-shaped handhold provided by a rock, and a divot in the wall for my boot. I swung over, using the rope like Tarzan's vines, and made the handhold. I missed the divot and the jerking caused my left foot to skid away from its resting spot. I hung there for a moment, breathing heavily, my left hand wrapped around the rope, my right bleeding from the sharpness of the jutting rock. I felt like Jesus without the footrest.

'Are you all right, Mr Fletcher? Stay calm - don't panic.'

Perhaps that was the extent of Ms Harding's human resources advice manual. Was that what she told devastated, soon-to-be-homeless clients when they came looking for their investments? The thought sent a surge of anger and probably the last blast of adrenalin through me. I cursed and scrabbled with my legs and managed to drive my boots into the wall of soil. It was now or never. Never was unappealing in so many ways.

'You can do it, Mr Fletcher. You have to do it.'

Yes, I did, I had to survive. I couldn't imagine what my parents would say as they greeted me at arrivals in the other dimension. Actually, I could. 'We gave you life, we raised you, we fed you, we died in that burning car so you could perish on a mountainside like some no-hoping waster who couldn't even climb a few pathetic steps up a gentle slope?' The loving welcome would come later.

'No,' I yelled at my parents.

'Mr Fletcher?'

I took a deep breath, uncoiled the rope from around my left hand, grabbed it with both hands, and pulled myself upwards as I drove my boots into the wall as hard as I could, stepping and driving the last few yards, trying to remember my yelling, terrorising drill sergeant all those years ago. There was no room for hesitation now; momentum was pretty much all I had on my side.

When I reached the top, I saw Ms Harding, lying on her stomach as close as she could force herself to come to the edge, both arms stretched out, her hands waiting for me to grab them. I let go of the rope with my right hand and reached out; she grabbed my wrist in both hands and pulled. She was stronger than I would have given her credit for with such a slight frame. Her effort gave me enough thrust to take another step up and hurl myself over the top. I collapsed next to her and we both panted and gasped, speechless as the rain sprinkled down on us.

CHAPTER 32

'The man you saw, did you recognise anything about him? Could he have come into your offices?'

Ms Harding and I sat on the wet ground, leaning against the tree to which my rope was still tied. She'd done an excellent job of it, informing me that she'd been a Girl Guide and knew every knot in the book. The small mercies are the ones that save you in the end.

'It was impossible to tell,' she said. 'I heard something behind me and I ran into the bushes. I had no idea it was you, and I didn't know what you wanted. I was trying to get a mobile signal. I didn't want to go back until I had a chance to try, so I decided to wait and see what you did.' The memory prompted her to take out her mobile and try some numbers as we talked.

'I came up to find you, and to get a signal.'

'Well,' she said. 'When I saw you on your mobile, I was about to come over to you - I suppose I thought two phones would be better than one. Until I saw this mystery man. He came from the other side of the track.' She waved back into the rainforest. 'I don't know if he'd already seen me.' She stopped and took some deep breaths. 'I was terrified. I though he'd hear me gasping. And then, when he got closer to you, I thought you must know him and you were both out searching.'

'Who did you think it was?'

'I don't know. The chef who hasn't turned up yet? Your boss, Mr Pinkert? One of the others - he had a hood and I would have sworn he was wearing a balaclava. But in this heat, who'd do that?'

Someone who wanted to keep their identity to themselves. Someone who was going to commit uncivilised acts and wanted to get away with it. Not Mr Pinkert. No.

'Did you see what he did to me?' I still felt a bit light in the head, but I put it down to the climb, and fear, and panic.

'He took something out of his pocket and he put one arm around you, and whatever he had in his other hand he put up to your face. He was so quick, and you went down pretty fast.'

'It must have been some kind of sedative, or anaesthetic.' I rubbed my face and smelled my hand, but the rain and dirt and mud had washed away any residual scent. Whatever it was, it hadn't seemed to cause any permanent damage. I couldn't taste it on my breath, either.

'Then he put that harness on you and attached the rope to the tree, but he seemed to do most of the heavy lifting himself. It wasn't like he needed the tree, it was a safety thing, probably so he didn't go over with you.'

'Why would he send me over at all? Why wouldn't he just - you know, be done with it?' He could have killed me, but he didn't. Why? There was the question with the 90% failure rate again.

'He was very careful.' She turned to look directly at me. 'I was praying then, too, Mr Fletcher. At first, I thought he was setting it up to make it look as though you'd had an abseiling accident.'

I hadn't thought of that. Maybe he was, and changed his mind. Or maybe it was something else entirely.

'Thank you for your prayers,' I said. The Nonna used to say the rosary every day. Sometimes, she managed to entice me to say a few Hail Marys with her before I'd slip out while her eyes were closed and she was busy with the Glory Be and announcing the title of the next decade. She was a DJ of the worshipping set.

'I've found it very helpful since - ' She stopped in mid-sentence and turned to where the stranger had been. 'Anyway, we should go back, shouldn't we?' She pushed herself up and stood beside me.

'Yes,' I said, standing with her. 'Look, Ms Harding, thank you. I owe you my life. If you hadn't been here, I don't know what would have happened. The rope wasn't long enough to go down, and I couldn't have climbed up without someone anchoring it. I owe you.'

Somewhere nearby, a peacock shrieked and Sarah Harding flinched.

'It's all right, Mr Fletcher,' she said, 'you don't owe me. And don't get me wrong. I'm not into organised religion or anything.'

'What you believe is your business.' The Nonna's insistence on the holy trinity, and the miraculous powers of various angels and saints had little effect on me. They were stories, mostly enjoyable, even with the gory martyrdoms, but stories, that was all.

'No, it's just that - something happened on one of our getaway adventures, as Philip calls them, and it led me to, well, God. No. Trying to get to God.'

'That's great for you.' What had happened to her? Had she seen a vision in the icebergs? The holy mother in a nice warm parka and heated rosary beads?

'I haven't been very successful.' She collected herself and started off down the track as I untied the rope from the rock, unclipped it from my harness and wound it up. I decided to bring it and the harness with me. Perhaps the police could lift prints or DNA, something. I trotted to catch up with her.

'What would you say,' I said, 'if I suggested that all of this is a set-up?'

'What do you mean? Just to scare us?' She was busy scanning the rainforest, glancing left and right, and stopping to look behind us every ten metres or so.

'Whoever did this to me was doing it for the fear factor. Just like the head, and the ear. We'll know once we've checked them.'

'The head?'

'It's the only way to be sure,' I said.

If this was a Philip Downer gagfest, the joke could be reversed. It was just as likely that Downer had paid Dean the driver to menace Leason as a gesture of hilarity. Dean could have been HandyCamming it for the office Christmas party. The head was either genuine or false, and I was ready to pray with Ms Harding that it was as fake as the certificate of accreditation that had brought me here. The diamond, though, that looked real.

'Phil's capable of pretty much anything, Mr Fletcher,' Ms Harding said, and picked up her pace down the slope.

CHAPTER 33

When we walked through the front door - someone had left it unlocked - of the Eyrie's main building, I saw Delia at the top of the stairs, but as soon as she saw us she walked away and out of sight down the hall. I heard her voice briefly as she entered one of the rooms and a male voice replying, but I couldn't make out what they'd said. Presumably, Dean was resting more comfortably in one of the monk's cells with his fractures and abrasions.

Ms Harding took herself off to her room. We were both wet and muddy from our mobile phone and abseiling adventures. She'd tried several times to get a signal before we left the hill, but there was either nothing or static. No voices from the rest of the world, including her five-year old son, Evan, staying with his grandmother for the weekend. That failure seemed to upset her more than the stranger in the bush, or anything else about this weekend. It was the only number she could be bothered identifying for me; her son was the reason she'd run off. All she wanted was to talk to him. Surely there was another useful hill in this place where we wouldn't be stalked by potential killers, or - I still hoped it was the case - practical jokers, and where a signal could be found.

There really was only one way to determine if we were in mortal danger. I'd felt nauseous thinking about it since I'd survived the ledge test and flopped like a sick fish onto the ground beside Ms Harding. First, though, I procrastinated by going to my room and carefully removing the harness, trying not to touch the parts I thought my stalker would have handled. I wrapped it up in a sheet with the rope. I did the same with my clothes - you never know what forensics can detect, and he had bear-hugged me, according to Ms Harding - brushed off my boots, and took a shower.

When I came downstairs I checked that the front door was still locked, as we'd left it when we came in, and continued on to the kitchen. Oliver and Leason sat at the table drinking red wine and facing away from the head and the ear, which were in the same places, side by side on the sink. It looked as though the Auroras had found it difficult to move, somehow mesmerised by their proximity to the body parts.

Everything was a little cooler now that the wood stove's fire with its dry heat had burned itself out, but the humidity had returned. I could feel my skin prickling with sweat after the coolness of the shower and fresh clothes. My boots were damp, but I could live with that; I had no intention of putting them anywhere near that stove again, not after its recent inhabitant.

'I have to check the head and the ear,' I told them. There was no point in gilding the situation with these hard-nosed people.

'What?' Leason sat up straighter, drained his glass and refilled it.

'The body parts - they could be fake. The special effects guys in movies can do wonders with this kind of thing, and there's still a possibility that this whole situation could all be a prank, as Mr Leason suggested earlier. What do you think now, Mr Leason, still a prank?'

'There are no other people around except for that driver. I'll bet my bonuses he's the one. And if he was hired by Philip - .'

Leason paused and took another gulp. He was one of those drinkers who swallowed booze as though it was spring water. His earlier abstinence had been a temporary aberration.

'Yes?' I said, pushing an encouraging tone into the question.

'Philip will do anything to stitch people up. It's just his way of letting off steam. He likes to be in charge.'

'Perhaps he should be a bit more careful about who he targets.' What if it was Philip Downer who'd lowered me over the cliff? He sounded like a no-harm, no-foul smart-arse who cared not at all about people's feelings, or the real consequences.

I went to the drawers near the sink and pulled them open one at a time. When I met Downer, I might just deck him, and let Henry get me out of trouble with his talent for making problems go away by knowing more about the skeletons in their closets than his clients ever could.

'If you gentlemen want to leave while I'm doing this, you should go now,' I said. I found a Wusthof carving knife, one of my favourites, in the second drawer. They're beautifully weighted and the blade will last forever with the right treatment. You can get an edge on a Wusthof that kitchen geeks fantasise about.

'Leave?' Oliver stood up and came over to the sink. 'Bring these things to the table. We'll watch. We need to know so we can decide what to do next.'

He swayed as he stood beside me. There was only one bottle on the table, but I suspected others had bitten the dust while I was out acting as the butt of Downer's latest joke. I clung to the prank theory like a shipwreck victim clings to inferior quality flotsam. He knows that, sooner or later, it's going to get water-logged and sink.

'All right.' I handed him the plate with the ear, and the bread board, and picked up the roasting dish, wishing I had longer arms for this particular job.

Leason stood, took his glass and the rest of the bottle of wine and moved to lean against the benches on the opposite side of the kitchen.

'What about fingerprints?' he asked, waving his glass at Oliver's plate. 'Bet you haven't thought of that, Hercules Perette.'

I hadn't thought of that, but I was certain the prankster, or killer, had. There would be no incriminating evidence unless this person wanted some to turn up. I'd found a pack of disposable latex gloves in the top drawer and pulled a pair of them on, one yellow, one pink. They were more for self-protection from actually touching the objects I was about to carve.

'I don't think it's going to matter,' I said, removing the plastic wrap from the ear. 'It's Hercule Poirot, not Hercules Perette, by the way.' Edie's favourite detective. I wondered if she knew about Henry's instant detective recipe: just add monsoon water and stir.

'What?' Leason tried to push himself up onto the bench, but his arms didn't seem to have the strength to do it. Instead, he slowly slid down to the floor and watched me, but he couldn't see the items on the table, which was probably just as well.

The ear had thawed out in the time Ms Harding and I had been gone. There were drops of water clinging to the plastic wrap and from beneath the ear, a liquid substance, part water, part something pink, had pooled. If it wasn't real, it deserved a medal for trying. The diamond stud hung in there, but it looked as though the hole had dilated with the thawing. Then I saw that someone had made a half-hearted attempt to rip it off - the hole was more of a gash now that it was back to room temperature - and then changed his mind in favour of chopping off the whole ear.

'Wait.'

'What is it, Mr Oliver?' I held the Wusthof a few centimetres from the plate.

'What about the police? Isn't this evidence?'

'Yes, it's evidence, if it's real.' And even if it wasn't. There must be something in the criminal code about frightening people with pretend body parts, and lowering them over cliffs when they're unconscious.

'Then we can't destroy evidence.' He stared at me, but he was frowning and seemed to be fighting with himself. He wanted to know for sure, too.

'We have no choice,' I said, and gave them both the short version of what happened to me up on the hill. Oliver was silent.

'That doesn't sound like Philip,' Leason said from his spot on the floor. Now he'd taken to swigging straight from the bottle. 'He's more of a hands-off kind of bloke. He directs other people to do his dirty work, unless it's about the market. That's all his own work.' He sounded contemptuous, and then he swigged again and raised the bottle in a toast, smiling up at me like a little boy waiting for a pat.

'Whoever it is, we need to know a lot more than we know now.' I held the top of the ear between my right thumb and forefinger - it felt real enough - and sliced into the softest part, the lobe, above the ear-ring. The Wusthof slid through easily; I picked up the piece I'd cut and inspected the cross-section. There was nothing much to see - pinkish, whitish, creamish flesh tending to a greyish tinge, and a little ooze of dark pink. There were things that looked like blood vessels.

'Satisfied?' Oliver asked. He sat down at the end of the table. He showed no signs of wanting to get closer to the pieces.

'Not quite,' I said.

I undid the ear-ring, and then placed the lobe back on the plate with the rest of the ear. I went back to the drawer and took out another pair of latex gloves. I handed them to Oliver.

'I need you to look carefully at this and tell me if you think it's genuine.' I waited for him to think about it, then he slowly pulled on the gloves and took the ear-ring from me. He stared at it for a long time sitting on the palm of his hand before he picked it up and held it closer to his face. He turned it this way and that, and then decided a comparison test was needed. He put the ear-ring down and raised his hands to his left ear; they'd begun to shake and it took him some time to undo his own little memento. He put it on the table next to the other one. By now, curiosity had gotten the better of Leason; he stood behind Oliver and stared at the table.

'They're the same,' he said, and felt at his own ear. 'Except for the colour.'

Oliver picked up the now less mysterious stud and reached for his wine glass. He tried scratching the glass with the diamond.

'Does that really work?' Leason asked.

'I don't know,' Oliver replied, redoubling his efforts. Faint white marks appeared on the surface as he scratched away. 'Apparently.'

He did the same with his own ear-ring and produced the same marks. Forensically, we were batting one hundred. Such definitive evidence as this from a bunch of amateurs; who'd have thought?

'Look,' I said, 'they seem to match, and I think the ear belongs to that head, but - ' I reached over and lifted the head out of the roasting dish. It left behind a gravy of brownish congealed lumps. The smell wasn't bad. It was like pork, overcooked pork with a hint of burnt edges. I set it down on the bread board and when I took my hands away, it slowly keeled over.

Oliver leaned down and inspected the neck area.

'There's bone,' he said, 'and gristle. Looks like vertebrae to me. Looks like the same shape as my footy X-rays.'

'Are you going to slice it' Leason stared at me, already impressed by my ear surgery.

'I don't know,' I said. Slicing the ear had felt very strange. I half expected the head to cry out in pain, or at least admonish me. As a cook, I was used to cutting up and serving up all kinds of animals; the flesh of every palatable mammal, bird and marine creature was familiar and reassuring. But this? There had to be another way.

I righted the head and stared at the face. The sunken eyelids concealed what lay beneath, a blessing in itself. The nose had half collapsed, making the head look as though it belonged to an ex- and not very successful boxer. I pressed at the skin on the concave cheeks; it felt soft underneath, but the surface was almost crackly. The ear still attached felt hard and brittle; it would probably break right off with a bit of pulling, like a chicken wing. This meat was overdone. A sudden vision of my father, Martin's face replaced the roasted head; he was in the upturned car and he stared at me as Henry pulled me out by my legs. I reached out for him, but as always in this image, he didn't move or reach out for me. He simply mouthed 'I love you,' as the flames obscured his face.

'Fletcher. Fletcher?'

I took a deep breath and did what my meditation instructor had tried to teach me: it's a thought like other thoughts, Garfield; it's a transitory thought, like all thoughts; it's a memory from the past and you live in the now; acknowledge it, let it float away, and return to your breathing.

'Fletcher.'

It was Oliver. He sounded angry.

'Yes,' I said, breathing deeply. I noticed that I still held the head in both hands, a thumb pressed deeply into each cheek. This action loosened something; as we stared at the head, the lips slowly parted and the mouth opened. There was something shiny inside.

'Oh, Jesus.' Oliver sat back and his body seemed to collapse into the seat.

'It's - isn't it?' Leason said. He walked himself back to the bench and slid back to the floor.

I sat the head on the bread board and opened the mouth a little more. I could feel the sharp edges of the upper and lower teeth. The shiny thing was a gold filling in one of the lower front teeth. But there was something else. I pushed my forefinger into the mouth and carefully pulled out another piece of jewellery.

'It's the same,' said Oliver. 'But why are there two?'

'One's Philip's.' Leason stared up at us, restating the obvious.

'And the other one?' Was it a spare?

'It has to be Melanie's,' Leason said. 'Doesn't it, Dave?'

Leason and Oliver grew paler.

'Melanie's? You mean Melanie Rogers-Hilton.' I looked around the kitchen. We had no security, not really. The back door was open again, and the windows, too.

'Where's Graham Butler?' I asked. Delia, Dean and Sarah were upstairs - easy to round up.

'He went to look for Sarah,' Oliver said.

'Sarah came back with me,' I said, and I wondered how I would bring myself to return to the great outdoors. I took a deep breath and held it for a long time.

CHAPTER 34

OPERATION BLUEWATER POLARIS #003

Some people, for all their education and smarts, were just plain stupid. Common sense was the thing that mattered to Guy Friendly's father, and it mattered to him, too. You can have all the intelligence in the world, he'd say, but if you've got no common sense, then you've got nothing. You might as well give it away, give your life to someone else worthwhile.

His father had prided himself on his common sense, not that it had helped much in the end. He'd died screaming in pain, blown up in his own sparkling kitchen courtesy of a gas leak. Guy Friendly didn't like to think about it, but he'd always remember arriving on the scene, the last gasping yell, cut short as his father's heart stopped so abruptly it left them both staring in surprise at each other. Then he wondered if Jacinta had been staring out at the ocean, up at the sky, waiting for him, hoping for his face to appear in front of her, his kind eyes and calm voice to reassure her, his strong arms to gather her up and take her home. He felt the old familiar feeling, the lump in his throat, the prickling in his eyes, the churning in his gut.

No, there was no time for weakening now. He followed his target through the bush, parallelling his movements along the trail up to the hill where, earlier, he'd performed his expert abseiling-by-proxy feat. You had to be adaptable in this game; when the unexpected cropped up, you either changed the rules, or you lost the rubber.

This fool was drunk, he was certain. There could be no other explanation for the meandering, staggering walk, the muttered obscenities as the gradient steepened, the stupidity of trying his mobile long before he'd reached the summit. How long did he think the battery would last?

How long could Guy Friendly last? His patience knew no bounds; he'd taken his time about planning this project, but this fellow, the sooner he was put to bed, the better it would be for everyone. He was truly a waste of space, and a killer. It was time; he didn't want to have to deal with any of the others for the moment, so the sooner he immobilised this one, the better.

On the other hand, Graham Butler was such a boorish creature, he felt like having some fun, too. Jacinta wouldn't have approved, but then, who was he to say now what she'd think, after what had happened. If she could tell him, it might be: Gather them up, one by one, take them down, bring me my peace. He had to interpret as best he could, and this was his interpretation of her text messages. Why else had she used the last of her energy, her hands freezing by the second, every small movement agonising, to send their names, and what they'd done. She wanted him to do something, and she knew what he could do. Jacinta would approve, she would.

'Hey!' He yelled in the staggerer's direction.

Brown-eyed Graham Harold Butler, 41, twice divorced, overweight and unfit, mostly loving owner of Oscar, Golden Retriever, whom he forgot to feed from time to time, turned his head towards Guy Friendly. Butler listened, waited, muttered something, and then carried on. He would assume it was a peacock, or some other bird whose calls occasionally sounded human.

Friendly watched, binoculars steady, and speculated on whom it might be this time as Butler dialled another number. The ex-wife perhaps, cocooned from the global economic disaster by Butler's astute injections but, more importantly, withdrawals of funds, from a variety of investments that would turn out to be worthless in the longer term.

Friendly had done his homework; he had no intention of removing anyone from the earth unless he knew exactly who they were, that they had shown no remorse, and that they had continued blithely with their lives after taking the innocent life of another. What took the biscuit with this bunch was their brazen wearing of those diamond iceberg studs. At least the Harding woman had the sense to keep hers tucked away. Not that that was a saving grace. And as for the van driver, if his intentions were similar to Friendly's, then more power to him. But if there was any chance of identification, or of interference, then game over. He'd already had to face that issue with Henry Pinkert's security man.

'Butler,' Guy Friendly called.

Butler turned again as the lasso looped over his head and was drawn tight around his neck. Friendly jerked on the rope and his quarry fell with a loud scream, his phone lost in the undergrowth. He moved quickly through the brush, keeping the rope taut, until he stood above Butler lying awkwardly where he'd fallen, hands bunched into fists grasping uselessly at the rope, his left leg at a strange angle.

'Oh, dear,' Friendly said, glancing first at the leg, and then at Butler's stricken face. 'I didn't mean for that to happen. But, I guess it's a start.' He leaned down, ruffled Butler's hair, and tore the diamond stud from his ear lobe. 'That's better,' he said, as Butler yelled and the blood began to flow.

CHAPTER 35

'Someone's trying to kill you people,' I said. I'd closed the back door again, and the windows. He wasn't just trying, he'd been successful, but there was no need to emphasise the point.

'But not you,' Leason shifted around on the floor.

'Apparently.' I couldn't figure it out, either. Why hadn't our stalker simply flung me over the cliff? I'd be out of his way, one less active body to worry about. And I was their protector. What did he expect me to do, be grateful for my life, and then stand back while he wreaked havoc? But where I'd stood had made no difference so far.

'What are we going to do? We can't just sit here and wait for him to shoot us all,' said Oliver. 'And someone has to go and bring Graham back.'

He stared at me, but I wasn't ready to move in that direction yet.

'If he wanted to kill you like that, shoot you, you'd all be dead by now.' He was into fear and terror and every other synonym for horrified distress. 'He would have done it when we arrived. Or he could have waited until we came into this building and then blown it up. He's stalking you. He wants you to know he's out there.'

'Stop, you're cheering me up,' Oliver said. 'What are we going to do with these?' He forced himself to glance at the head and the ear. 'They're evidence - the police can probably catch him with this - they can do tests. And the bodies must be somewhere.'

'We'll put them in the cooler.' I stood up and went to the drawers to get the plastic wrap. Somehow, I didn't think the head and the ear would tell anyone more than the most basic stuff: he was a very angry man intent on - yes, revenge, that had to be it. But revenge for what? Could the loss of money inspire this reaction? Perhaps someone had died, like Dean's brother, Max. But this person was far more lethal than Dean.

Oliver held the roasting dish while I stretched the film over the head, and put an extra layer over the ear on its plate. Leason forced himself to his feet and we formed a little procession behind him to the cooler door. When he opened it and stood back, Oliver and I went in and found some room for our specimens on one of the shelves next to the ice-cream.

'Didn't you put the box from the road in here?' Oliver looked around the cooler. I followed his gaze and, sure enough, the box was gone.

'Now what? He's stealing our mud crabs as well?' Leason leaned in and checked the shelves.

I didn't think they were mud crabs anymore, nor that the chef had anything to do with the box. I didn't expect the chef to turn up and help us, but I'd left Henry a message. That was the best we could manage? There had to be more.

'We have to get out of here,' I said. I didn't mean to say it aloud.

Leason rolled his eyes. 'You're a genius as well,' he said.

'Excuse me,' I said, and left them in the kitchen. They'd be safe enough, or as safe as our stalker wanted them to be for the moment. Maybe he was busy with other things.

I turned left at the top of the stairs and walked the hallway until I heard murmuring behind one of the doors. I knocked and waited.

'Who is it?' Delia.

'Garfield. Delia, can I speak with you please?'

After some further murmurings, Delia opened the door and invited me in.

'How are you, Dean?' I asked. Dean was ashen-faced, or what I imagined ashen-faced to be, not a very tactful term in light of what was in the kitchen cooler, I suppose, but I was tired and I needed help.

'Been better,' Dean said in his usual effusive manner. 'What's happening?'

'The head and the ear are real. We put them in the freezer for the police. Oliver and Leason say the diamond studs belong to Philip Downer and Melanie Rogers-Hilton. Did you meet them, Delia?'

'Yes, I saw them the other day in the office. They were finalising the arrangements for this trip. They were supposed to be here before us.'

Parts of Downer had arrived before us. 'Did they get any direct threats, you know, just for them?'

'Aurora's been haemorrhaging for a while now. A lot of people are really angry.' Delia sounded uncomfortable discussing threats in front of her father, the threatening van driver.

'Why don't we leave your father in peace,' I said, and gestured towards the door. 'I need some advice.'

'You can't offend me,' Dean said. 'I'm glad the bastards are dead. I'd do them in myself if I could.' He leaned forward, groaned in pain, and lay back on the pillow.

'No, you wouldn't, Dad,' Delia said, and ushered me out to the hallway.

'That's the thing,' I said, as we made our way downstairs and into the foyer. 'Most people wouldn't, even if they'd like to have a go. They suck it up and hope the authorities will do the right thing for them. All your father wanted to do was annoy the hell out of them and spoil their holiday.'

'Sometimes, just making a threat gives you enough satisfaction,' Delia said.

'Or giving people like Butler bonus fish poo with their cappucinos.'

Delia blushed.

'Don't worry about it,' I said, 'I've filed it in my folder of fun things to do when I'm bored on my next job.' I opened the front door and we went out to sit on the bench with its view of the driveway and the path down to the conference centre. The rain was misty now, but the sky had grown dark again. There was more on the way.

'So what advice do you think I can give you, Garfield, apart from party tricks with laxative muffins?'

'You and Dean sussed this place out, and you were here when you were younger.'

Delia nodded.

'Is there a map, or could you draw me a map of the buildings and tell me what they're for? We're going to have to get out of here, but we might have to lock ourselves in somewhere for a while.'

'Lucky you're a professional, Garfield,' Delia said. She didn't sound sarcastic.

'I did three years in the Army and learned to be a cook,' I said. Delia might as well know. 'I don't know anything about - ' I looked at the emblem on my polo shirt '- about Pinkert PISS,' I said. 'I don't have any qualifications.'

Delia gazed out at the rainforest, dripping and sagging under the weight of the monsoon. 'Haven't you noticed? Neither does anyone else here,' she said. 'There aren't any maps that I know of, but I can draw you a rough one. There's a whiteboard in the meeting room just inside.'

We stood up and took a few steps and then I heard a shrieking noise that sounded almost human. It sounded even louder now that the rain had lightened up.

'Did you hear that?'

'I'm not hard of hearing, Gar,' Delia said.

We stood still and listened, but there was only the rain pattering the volume up again.

'What do you think? Peacock?'

She took a deep breath and sighed it out loudly. 'Why not?'

I locked the door behind us, as though it could make a difference.

CHAPTER 36

Delia was a good map-maker. She sketched the central U-shaped building we occupied, and positioned several smaller buildings nearby. There was the new conference centre about 150 yards away on the northern side, and there were smaller structures previously used by the monks when they had a going concern with their arts and crafts. They had a pottery shed with a kiln, another shed for wood-turning and carving activities, and a maintenance shed which she said was more like a combination barn and garage. It used to house the one car they'd owned, and there was room for a workbench and tools, and a chicken run. The chickens were long gone. They even had a small sawmill down the hill on the way to the creek Delia had drawn in behind U central.

'The creek winds all the way around here?' I asked Delia. It was like a snake with quite a few baby snakes branching off it.

'It's pretty big, more like a river. People built holiday shacks along the banks before the national park boundary was established. Some of them would still be there.'

'So there might be people down there, too.' People with phones that worked. Suddenly, there was the possibility of another way out, although making our way down to the creek and then following it to some kind of civilisation, or at least an occupied home, would mean we'd be sitting ducks. Which was pretty much our position now.

'What do you think?' Delia asked.

'I'm not sure,' I said. 'It would help if I knew more about the Auroras, Delia. This person isn't here for fun. Whatever they did, or whatever he thinks they did, it must have been fatal for someone.' And it had to do with the diamond studs, or else they were simply a means of keeping score. Two down, four to go.

'I could be blunt and call them all skanks. But that won't help. They're like other stockbrokers I've worked for. They love free markets, de-regulation, no regulation. They love money. They took their lead from Philip Downer.'

'Which was?'

'He's a hard man. He values success; they all wanted success - most people do. Downer doesn't care how he achieves it.'

'Didn't. Didn't care. He's in the cooler.'

'Oh. Yes. Sorry.' Delia returned her gaze to the map.

'It's all right,' I said. 'What about them as individuals. Would one be more likely to be targeted? Maybe this guy doesn't want everyone.' And maybe a mid-sized porcine creature would fly past our window at any moment.

'Butler, well, you know his form. The turd-in-a-tie is a know-it-all prick, and he has very poor office manners. Forty-something, lives on takeaways and Heineken, likes the odd illegal substance. He's overweight as you could see, high cholesterol, two divorces, used to be regarded as some kind of financial wunderkind, kisses up and kicks down. But he loves his dog, Oscar, so that's a saving grace. Anyone that loves a pet can't be all bad.'

'Yes, it certainly is a weighty counterbalance. You seem to know an awful lot.'

'Research for Dean. And there's no need for sarcasm.'

There was no need, but it helped. 'Dave Oliver?'

'Cruising to retirement until the GEM hit.'

'The gem?'

'The Global Economic Meltdown. Global financial crisis. He's got three divorces under his belt, but then he's older than Butler. Bit of a hippie type for a stockbroker. He had long hair until recently - I think Downer told him to shape up and look as though he knew what he was doing. That was after the complaints started. Oh, and he has a tattoo on his upper arm - a stock graph going up and off the scale.'

'Original. What's he like as a person?'

'Barely contained rage. He comes across as quiet and calm, with that oily voice, but he has this vibe - he smiles but the smile never makes it to his eyes. And those eyes? They aren't his.'

'They're not?'

'They're fake - coloured contacts - they always pick Nazi SS blue, or that crazy emerald green. Have you noticed that?'

'Can't say I have, but when you spend as much time at sea as I have in recent years, you tend to miss the trends.'

'He has four kids from the three marriages - private schools, holidays, big-time maintenance payments.'

'That might encourage a bit of unethical behaviour.'

'He's on Xanax and Zoloft - washes them down with Johnnie Walker and Stolie.'

'That could account for the unusual vibe he gives off.' A bunch of drunk sociopaths addicted to calmatives and anti-depressants. Even though they sounded like people you wouldn't want to know, there were a lot of them around. The Auroras didn't have a lock on bad behaviour and multiple divorces, but the lollygagging with money - that was their common ground. And it must be connected with the Antarctic cruise and those diamond studs.

'Did you find out anything about the trip to the Southern Ocean and the Antarctic?' The studs seemed to mean something to our stalker.

'I wasn't working for them then. But - ' Delia stared hard at the map on the whiteboard. She leaned over and drew an iceberg just like the ones on the diamond studs.

'It looks like a profit and loss graph, doesn't it?' I said.

Delia nodded. 'I remember they were discussing the Antarctic cruise at a lunchtime meeting a while ago - the six of them who have the studs. They'd already started the layoffs by then. When the lunch order arrived, I took it in to them. Naturally, I was the invisible woman, and Philip Downer was giving them a pep talk, or that's how it seemed to me. Now, let me get this right. He said something like, 'It's so you never forget you can overcome anything. You can rise above it. You win.' And he was fingering the bloody stud as he spoke.'

'And they all wore them. All the time?'

'Yes, except for Sarah Harding. She seemed to be the holdout. She wouldn't wear it, and Philip wasn't happy about that. In the end, she compromised and wore it on a necklace, but underneath her blouse. She was sick of Philip carrying on. It was as though she'd betrayed their secret club or something.'

Delia and I frowned and looked at each other.

'Then Butler noticed I was there, and that was that. They shut up and ate their lunch, Downer sent me off to find them a getaway for this year. A cheap one.'

'So it was you who came up with this place?'

'Dean, really. He'd been working on it for a while, you know, in anticipation, knowing they do this every year. And there's some family connection with one of them, I don't know who. Dean called it synchronicity. What better place for him to have some innocent fun?' She shook her head, picked up the whiteboard marker and circled one of the buildings she'd drawn. 'I think this might be the best spot for Custer's last stand, Garfield.'

'The Indians won that one, Delia,' I said.

'Well, they kind of deserved to, didn't they?' she said, and pushed the button to print me a copy of her stylish drawing.

CHAPTER 37

We couldn't simply hole up in the conference centre and wait for my message to Henry to bear fruit. If I could find Dean's van, we could make a run for it across the bridge. But if that made us too obvious and kill-worthy, we'd have to go down to the creek and hoof it along the banks until we found someone to take us out of here. I didn't know what to suggest to them.

'Do you think if I'd really earned that certificate in protection and security, we'd be out of here by now?' I asked Delia. Seeing the head, holding it in my hands, had left me with a sense of guilt. I felt responsible for Philip Downer and Melanie Rogers-Hilton, and I'd never met them. There was all the old pain jostling for space; Dad and Mum in the car, lost and burned; and Rita, bobbing in the ocean, and surviving to leave me, too. I was verging on feeling sorry for myself.

'I think we should concentrate on now, Garfield,' she replied. 'We need to get some transport other than our own feet.'

Delia suggested that we try to find a motorbike or pushbike so I could get to the van more quickly. She had a vague memory of a monk-made contraption, a bike attached to a sort of flat-bed tray; it was used to ride along the walking paths and collect fallen timber for the sawmill and the monks' craftworks. And they'd take firewood down to the creek, too, load it onto their little barge and sell it cheap to residents along the banks. They were industrious people.

'You never know, Garfield, the bike might still be there. They might have kept it in good order. The place was still operational until recently, so there's no reason why they wouldn't have kept up the wood-work. It'd be a novelty for the paying guests.'

We hurried down the path to the sawmill, which was on the way to the creek. I'd told Oliver and Leason to lock themselves, Sarah Harding and

119

Dean in until we returned. They had no interest at all in coming with us, and no plans to go out and look for Butler. Delia spoke briefly with Dean, who recalled a bike but couldn't remember its location.

The path to the sawmill was like the one to the hill of hope for mobile phones: muddy, wet, covered in fallen debris, full of curves, but with a gentle downhill slope. It positively encouraged moving slowly, contemplating each and every twist and turn, each and every boulder, rock, pebble, and grain of soil; the fronds and leaves of every palm, fern, shrub and tree. It was a lovely path for fine weather, and killer-free vacations.

'How much further, Delia?' I asked. 'Why is this building so far away from the main centre?' Wouldn't they want some convenience if they were hauling timber?

'Well, it's near the creek, for the firewood transport. And the outbuildings are meditation centres. Each place was meant to be a retreat for working meditation. You don't have to sit to meditate, you can do it anywhere, anytime.'

'Like sex,' I said, before I could shut myself up. 'Sorry, I meant - what did I mean?' Delia, I realised, was an attractive woman, and I - despite my fraudulent presence courtesy of Henry's haste - I was tall, male, and yes, a dab hand in the kitchen.

'It's all right, Garfield, we'll have an orgy once this is over, and relieve everyone's tension.' She gave a little laugh and pointed down the hill. 'See that very tall tree fern, the one near the stand of king ferns? Not much further from there. I remember coming down here once or twice to help them stack the firewood and bag the sawdust.'

'Some holiday,' I said.

'Dean believes in learning twenty-four-seven. He didn't want me to end up with nothing to fall back on if he couldn't leave me a fortune. And now he can't, thanks to the Auroras.'

There was no bitterness in Delia's voice, but I suspected she didn't entirely and absolutely disapprove of our stalker's presence if not his methods.

'Speaking of the Auroras,' I said, 'what about Sarah Harding and Peter Leason? Did your research turn up anything on them that might attract a killer?'

'Let me see. Sarah Harding is a human resources person first and a stockbroker second, but still a stockbroker. An MBA, public sector job in the capital, very briefly and early on, then head-hunted by a major recruitment firm. From there, she met Philip Downer.

'Somewhere in there, she had the relationship that produced her son, Evan - beautiful little boy. That bloke didn't last, though. Downer recruited her when the Auroras were growing and growing and they had staff working in the air-conditioning ducts and out on ledges, they were so busy and profitable.'

For a moment I thought she was going to spit in distaste.

'But she doesn't wear the diamond stud,' I said. 'Not obviously.'

'Even though she still hangs around with the stud wearers. Guilt by association.' She paused. 'And she has poor taste in men.'

I could imagine Delia trying at that moment, like me, to push the thought of Sarah Harding engaging in intimate activities with Graham Butler away into the wilderness.

'What about Leason?' I said. The first man down, temporarily, courtesy of Dean. Well, the first man before Philip Downer's head turned up, and that wasn't temporary. 'Do you think he's on drugs, like Butler suggested?'

'He's a quiet one; and he's all business in the office. Numbers rule. He's a city boy, his wife is rich in her own right, they live in a mansion and take holidays to Bora Bora. Or used to. But he's way out of his comfort zone here.'

'Who isn't?'

Delia nodded. 'I wouldn't be surprised if he's taking Prozac or Zoloft, like half the population.'

I wouldn't have minded being in that half at the moment. My stomach kept reminding me regularly that it was time to panic and become disoriented and confused. More disoriented and confused. We walked on in silence; even the sounds of our footsteps disappeared into the path's bed of leaf litter, and the light mist of rain seemed to hush everything. I took some deep breaths and tried to ground myself in the rainforest. It was, after all, a very beautiful place.

Eventually, the path opened to a clearing and there was the sawmill, a long, rectangular shed with a tin roof and hessian blinds around the sides for walls. Some of the hessian was rotting off its rollers, torn with age and weather, and blackened with mould.

'Impressive,' I said, for something to say, and to challenge the silence. I could have sworn I could smell freshly cut timber.

'Can you smell that?' Delia asked.

She took a few steps forward toward the sawmill's entrance, which was simply a gap in the hessian at the end of the building. I caught up with her and together we walked inside to an empty space where I assumed they'd stack their orders once the milling was done, or else gather for a spot of meditation. The hessian blinds dimmed the light from outside, but you could see the machinery set-up in the middle several metres away and the shelving running down either side where Delia used to help stack the firewood. The shelving on one side was empty, but the other side still held some off-cuts of varying sizes. The scent of cut wood was stronger in here, lovely really, clean, but who'd made it? There was something else, too, beneath the timber smell, starting to compete with it.

'There's something sickly, Garfield. I think an animal's died in here recently.' Delia looked around and then down to the other end of the shed. 'I can see a bike wheel there.' She took off towards the circular saw on the bench in the centre of the shed, but as she came abreast of it, I saw her hesitate and then stop. She tottered sideways and I ran down to her.

'Oh, God.' She fell back against the shelving.

I grabbed her arm and helped her down to sit on the floor, which was covered in a thin film of fresh sawdust. I looked around and saw what else was there. At first, it looked like pink and red and white flower petals had been sprinkled on top of the sawdust. I reached out and swept up a handful of them. The white was hard and the red and pink were brittle and flaky. They weren't petals. I dropped them and wiped my hand on my moleskins.

I stood up and looked at the bench where the circular saw was positioned. The bench was covered in pink and white and red flotsam. Someone had had fun with the saw recently. Lying next to it was the head of an apostle, all cracked plaster, blonde hair and staring blue eyes. It was always amusing to see Jesus and his acolytes represented not as dark-skinned, dark-eyed Middle Eastern residents, but as Anglo-Celtic palefaces. Had this been the practice run before Philip Downer was decapitated? But the saw's blade was relatively clean, and I couldn't see anything more fleshy. He must have decided to work elsewhere.

'It's all right, Delia,' I said, squatting down beside her. She was still breathing hard. 'It's a plaster figure, someone's cut it up on the bench. Probably vandals.' She must have thought it was real. In this light, anything could be misconstrued.

'It's not that.' She struggled to her feet and leaned against the shelving.

'Just relax,' I said. 'I'll check the bike.'

'We have to go, now,' she said, and took off for the end of the shed where she'd seen the bike wheel.

'What's up, Delia?'

She reached the corner where the wheel jutted out from beneath a khaki canvas sheet. I took a few steps to join her and pulled the sheet back to reveal a blue 100cc motorbike. There was no tray attached, but a newly dead carpet snake lay behind the rear wheel, a victim of the rainforest's natural selection program.

'Come on,' she said, grabbing the handlebars and pulling the bike away from the wall, and the snake.

As she held it steady, I checked the fuel tank. It was about half full and the key was in the ignition. Before I could do anything else, Delia threw a leg over the seat, turned the ignition, pumped the accelerator and revved the bike into life. It was rough for half a minute and then smoothed out enough for Delia to put it into gear.

'Garfield, we have to go, now.'

It was a tight fit, but I climbed on behind her and she guided the bike along the side of the saw bench and out into the clearing. She gunned it a few times and we took off along the walking path. It was slow going at first, but faster than our walking pace had been.

'Delia, what is it?' I said, leaning forward. 'What's wrong?'

'It's Dad, there's something wrong, I can feel it,' she said. 'I know it, Garfield.' I put my arms around her waist and leaned into the next bend with her, urging the bike to go faster.

CHAPTER 38

'Delia,' I said, as we reached the Eyrie's main building, 'we have to be careful here.'

When the bike's engine died, there was silence, or at least the relative silence of the wet rainforest: dripping water on top of the shushing of the misty showers, a few birds calling and complaining, a palm frond falling somewhere close.

Delia took no notice of me; she was off the bike and up to the front door in seconds. She proceeded to bang loudly on, and kick the door and yell 'hello, let us in,' as she wiggled the handle.

'Delia,' I said again, joining her at the door. 'We don't know how things are.' What I couldn't say was that they might all be dead inside. Then there was scuffling on the other side and the door opened as Delia banged again. She lurched forward and ran past Sarah Harding up the stairs. I followed her in and Ms Harding brought up the rear.

Upstairs, Delia was trying to open Dean's locked door.

'Delia, let me,' I said, as Ms Harding joined us, and Oliver and Leason appeared at the end of the corridor.

I rattled the door handle and called out to Dean.

'Mr Porter,' I said, 'are you awake? Can you come to the door?'

We all waited to hear mutterings of annoyance and Dean's feet shuffling across the room, but there was no movement. I couldn't hear the bed creak or squeak, and there was no human voice to be heard.

'Maybe he's had a setback,' Ms Harding offered. 'He could be very fatigued - you know, with the pain.' She hesitated. 'Asleep - deeply asleep.'

Dead was what she meant, and it was what I feared, too, after Delia's reaction at the sawmill. I pressed my shoulder against the door and gave it a push to gauge its strength and fit within the doorframe. A few taps revealed that it wasn't solid wood, but they built these old places to last.

The idiot-repelling boots would probably be a better bet than my shoulder.

I motioned for Delia to move aside and took a couple of steps back, then brought my leg up and stabbed my right boot at the keyhole with all the strength I could gather. It took three more kicks and some suppressed cursing before it started to give. Leason came forward and helped with a couple more kicks and then we heard splintering. The lock gave and something metal pinged onto the floor as the door swung inwards.

Delia moved quickly past us and went to the bed where Dean lay. His head was off the pillow and the sheet covering him was tangled around his body as though he'd been tussling with a nightmare.

'He's dead.' Delia stood by the bed. She took a step closer.

'Wait.' I went to the other side of the bed. I felt for the carotid pulse in his neck. There was nothing. 'Dean,' I said, knowing there would be no answer. I leaned down and listened to his chest - no heartbeat. His eyes were closed, so I carefully raised one eyelid and looked for signs of anything alive in there. The pupil was still shiny but there was no movement. His body was warm, and I expected him to wake up, even though I knew he wouldn't.

'Who could have done this?' Sarah Harding stood by the door with the other Auroras. 'Is it the stalker?'

I grabbed a chair, took it around to Delia's side of the bed, and guided her into it. She sat in silence, staring at Dean's face. After a moment, she took his hand in both of hers. I went to the door and ushered the others out into the corridor.

'I don't think anyone did this,' I said. 'I think it's a heart attack, or a stroke, something like that.'

'Natural causes?' Leason seemed surprised. 'That bloke came here to kill us and now he's dead of natural causes and some other killer is out there picking us off? God.'

'No, he didn't come here to kill you,' I said. 'He came here to annoy you and give you some payback for what you did to his investments, and what happened to his brother, Max.'

'What are you talking about?' Oliver asked. There was some belligerence in his voice, and I badly wanted to knock it right out of him.

'Dean's brother, Max, killed himself after they lost all their money. You did the investing for them.'

'People make their own choices about their lives. And no-one knew this financial crisis was coming so hard,' Oliver said, not missing a beat. 'It wasn't predictable.'

'Even though you and your cronies created it,' I said. 'Greedy bastards.'

'Listen here, you've got no business even talking to us, you twat.' Oliver, again. 'You're our servant, PISS boy.'

I reached out, grabbed a handful of his shirt, and marched him backwards very quickly along the corridor. I was taller, and stronger, and Oliver was unfit, shocked out of his tiny stockbroker's mind.

When we got to the staircase, I pushed him sideways and leaned him back over the baluster. Leason and Harding flapped around behind us, but they didn't come closer.

'You're a disgrace,' I said, and stared hard into his eyes, my face millimetres from his. 'And you're not worth an assault charge.' I released my grip and took a few steps back, waiting for Oliver to stand up straight, which he did after a while. His face was red verging on purple, and he looked to be a missed heartbeat this side of a conniption. 'There are no servants here,' I said, breathing deeply, 'we're all prey, and I'm the only one you can rely on to get you out of here.'

As though on cue, Delia walked past our little group and took the stairs two at a time. I forgot about Oliver and chased her down.

'Delia, what are you doing?'

'I'm going to find our stalker,' she said, 'or a way out. Whichever comes first. And if I find him first, well,' she paused, 'he'd better be in good form.'

She made for the front door and as she pulled it open, I grabbed her arm and turned her around.

'Delia, you can't leave here,' I said.

'Yes, Garfield, I can.'

She shook me off, hustled over to the bike and took off. I yelled after her; of course, she ignored me.

CHAPTER 39

OPERATION BLUEWATER POLARIS #004?

Guy Friendly liked the rainforest, not as much as the desert, never as much as the desert, admittedly, but okay, it was growing on him, this place, like an affectionate, quietly insistent creeper, engaging in its own moist, overbearing way. Naturally, it would kill him and all who stealthily stalked within it if it got the chance. Already, he'd had to deal with a flash flood, remove several leeches from his body, dodge a family of red-bellied black snakes, and then, there were the visitors. He knew they'd move from the main building soon enough, and the sheep would be sorted, finally.

He was tidying up after Butler when he heard the distant engine of a motorbike. He darted down to the main path and watched from behind the safety of a giant boulder. The noise took a long time to come closer; there was little else to compete with it here in the quiet; just the rustle of dripping trees and the seeming fixture of the continual showers. If he'd been closer to his equipment stash, he could have rigged a wire across the thoroughfare and had some fun with another potential decapitee. He hadn't really taken to the idea of removing heads, but it seemed to be the most effectively terrifying thing to do. It was business, that's all. In Iraq and Afghanistan, the rebels, the Taliban, al-Queda, used it as a matter of course. They were regarded as monsters and he couldn't, wouldn't disagree, even as he created his own little world of torture and cruelty.

The bike came into view as it rounded the corner and revved faster along this straight stretch; he could see clearly that it was a woman, her long hair flowing behind her. No helmet, how irresponsible. Was it Harding, or the other one, the young dogsbody who seemed to have to run the entire office since the meltdown took off? He'd been into the place several times over recent months as delivery man, and plumber, and electrician. It was amazing how doors opened when you had a uniform, a clipboard or a tool-box. Look at Melanie Rogers-Hilton. And a bonus ladder helped with the electrical disguise. People trusted tradesmen and service industry types; they seemed to personify salt of the earth and, he'd noticed, they were faceless. People saw the uniform, they stared at the upside-down clipboard, waiting to be asked for a signature; they gazed at the toolkit, men and women both, wondering what little gems of interest lay within. There was a kid in every adult longing to dress up and prance around with a hammer in one hand and a shifting spanner in the other.

No-one remembered him from one visit to the next, one uniform to the next, although he'd scored a couple of second glances from the dogsbody. She was a clever one, that Delia; he hoped she'd keep out of his way here and let him do his job. Otherwise. It was Delia, after all, who'd told him in idle conversation as she signed a docket, that the Auroras were coming here for their annual getaway. Her tone as she spoke about them had been heavy with contempt and he'd instantly taken a liking to her for that reason alone, quite apart from her looks. He didn't want any more collateral damage; having to dump Henry's man over the cliff had been more than enough, far more than enough. That single episode had encouraged second, third and fourth thoughts, and he'd had to redouble his commitment, toughen himself and make at least that part of the past stay in its box.

Think positive. If this rider was Harding, he'd take his opportunity. She could join Butler and the two of them would finally be together forever, mix and match heads, and other parts. If it was Delia the dogsbody, well, wait and see. And it wasn't long at all. She came to a stop on the path five metres from where he crouched. She was breathing hard and her hair and the determined little face reminded him, yet again, of Jacinta. She got off the bike and flicked down the stand.

'Murderer,' she yelled, right at him. 'You fucking murderer.'

It was like a physical attack. Murderer? What did she mean? She'd had nothing to do with the cruise, she wasn't even working with them then. She certainly wasn't so fond of them that she'd ride out and accuse the rainforest so forcefully. He watched her carefully as she stood there. She was shaking all over, and now she'd begun to moan, and cry. She was weeping, for god's sake. He felt embarrassed to be watching this full flight of emotion. What had happened to her? She was simply the aide-de-camp in this story. She fell to her knees and leaned back on her heels and continued to cry. He wanted to go to her, comfort her, tell her it would all be all right.

And then she was up. From the knees down, her jeans were darkened by the damp forest floor. She walked up and down the path, still agitated, hands on her hips. She muttered to herself and let out a few yells of - what was it? - frustration? There was no accounting for this behaviour. She hadn't lost anyone close to her - had she? No, he couldn't entertain this fantasy. He willed her to stay on the path, to resist the urge to search for him, or whoever it was she thought she'd named as 'murderer.'

He urged her to move, take herself anywhere but here, escape if she could. He had to get on with it, and who knew when the rest of them might decide to move; then the feast would be on the hoof and he'd be spoiled for choice. That's how he preferred to see it, rather than as a further burden to be wrestled with out in the bush, quarry with half a chance to get themselves away. If they twigged - they probably had already - he'd have to smarten up.

Delia returned to the bike and started it up. She revved the motor viciously and took off in the direction of the bridge. Guy Friendly leaned against the boulder and listened to the engine's noise grow fainter and disappear altogether. He relaxed his shoulders and flexed his hands and fingers. After Delia, certainly after Butler, he wanted to relax, make himself a cup of tea and simply listen to his breath for a while. He wanted space, in his body and his mind, but it couldn't be, not yet.

He wished Delia well even as he knew what she'd find, at the bridge and elsewhere. It was time to organise Butler for his finale. It was a risk, but it would force them to move to where he wanted them to be, if they hadn't already figured it out for themselves. Then he could find himself a dress circle seat and watch the fireworks unfold, discover if shame ever figured in the Auroras' hearts.

CHAPTER 40

'We're moving,' I said, injecting what I thought was an authoritative tone into my voice. 'And we have to stay together.'

'You did a great job of keeping our girl Friday together,' Leason said. 'And when are you going to go out and get Butler?'

'I'm not,' I said. 'Mr Butler is an adult, and he's decided to stay out there and look around. Good luck to him.'

Did I sound convincingly hard? They stared at me, Leason, Oliver, and Harding, but more in puzzlement than anger judging by their faces. I was issuing orders, and I was shocked, so there was a fair chance they'd be wondering, too. In the army, I'd been a 'grunt,' or as civilians like to say, an 'AJ,' an Army Jerk, lowest of the low, no ambition to rise to commissioned officer class, or even a regular combat role. I'd never volunteered to go overseas, even on peacekeeping missions. I'd gone, reluctantly, with my battalion, because I had no choice, not really. Peer pressure, regimental pride, identification as a valued member of the supporting cast to the actual, ballsy, hero fighters like Gianni, the usual convincers. I'd always wanted to emulate Gianni, even after the army, until he died. That put the value of peeling potatoes into perspective.

I joined the forces for stability after Mum and Dad, and it served its purpose. I came out stable - less unstable - and with a skill, and then I wandered and sailed and tried to love the lovely and daunting Rita, until I returned to one of my saviours, Henry, who sent me to this saturated, green circle of Hell. I'd be a Warrant Officer by now, at least, had I shown the slightest inclination towards career advancement. Officer training, or ten years of humping my swag around the world to end up in a rainforest populated by serial killers - which one of these? Hmm.

'You might as well know, I'm having you charged with assault when we get out of here, Fletcher.'

It was Dave Oliver, CEO, keeper of the flame of stockbroking pride.

'Who do you think might want to kill you, Mr Oliver?' I asked him. 'And do you think he'll be more successful if you're alone here, or with the rest of us down the hill?'

'Don't change the subject. I have witnesses.' He eyeballed Leason and Harding, but they looked away, and seemed disinclined to approve his plan with any enthusiasm.

'The subject today is survival, Mr Oliver. It's up to you how you manage that.'

'What about your brother, Dave,' Sarah Harding said. 'You know, with what happened.'

'Coincidence, Sarah.' Oliver was dismissive, but Leason had cottoned on to what Sarah Harding had suggested.

'Your brother?' I asked.

'My brother is a priest, ex-priest. He used to run this place, years ago, and then he bought it when his order disbanded. It was a long time after he left, and he got it cheap, thanks to me.'

'Lost it cheap, too, Dave, don't forget,' said Ms Harding.

We were in the kitchen again, and Ms Harding had decided to make sandwiches, a lot of sandwiches, with whatever was in the fridge. She wouldn't go near the freezer, and she spent quite some time finding another bread board and a new set of knives from the most obscure drawers.

'He kept his house, Sarah, he still has a roof over his head, and he overcapitalised on this place.'

'At your suggestion,' Sarah said, slapping ham on bread with more than average gusto.

'Your brother,' I said, 'could he have -'

'What? Gone psychotic on me and decided on payback? I hardly think so. He's not a priest anymore, but he's far more spiritual these days. He doesn't give a shit about this stuff.'

'But he must have for a while,' I said, 'and recently, or else why bother with reinventing the place. And if not him, there must have been other investors who got burned.' Every investor seemed to have been burned lately. Another reason to have no money in the first place. And did Dean know about the specifics of the connection with Dave Oliver's brother? Delia had mentioned a relationship.

'Of course there were other investors,' said Oliver, 'and I have no doubt some of them made abusive phone calls to me. But my brother is my brother, and besides, you'd be amazed at how quickly people learn to adapt when they have no choice but to downsize. Look at us, we're here, not half a world away, cruising.' He smiled a smug sort of smile that I think was intended for only himself.

'Why does it matter who it is?' Ms Harding asked. 'Isn't it enough that he's killing us?'

'If we can work out why he's doing it, maybe we can reason with him.' Was I that naïve, to imagine we could negotiate? Maybe I was. Maybe a spiritual ex-priest would be an easier choice than - who? The decapitator, the ear-ring collector?

'Where do you propose we go then, Mr Fletcher?' Leason stood at the bench where Sarah Harding wielded her knife through a stack of half a dozen ham, cheese and tomato sandwiches. He took a triangle off the top as her knife reached the bottom of the pile.

'Delia suggested the conference centre. We can - '

'Delia? She's the one who brought us here in the first place, so her father could try and do us in.' Leason was chewing and spitting out words at the same time. It wasn't a good look.

'The conference centre is the best idea. We've been down there and it's safer than this monster of a place.' Sarah Harding began wrapping the sandwiches in plastic wrap. 'Let's go now before it's too late.' She nodded at me, and then busied herself at the pantry gathering a few six-packs of bottled water.

I couldn't help wondering if it was the same roll of wrap the killer used to cover the ear. Would there be fingerprints, or other forensic matter, and did any of it matter at all? It was obvious that the killer had everyone's measure, including his own.

'What about Delia?' Oliver asked. 'She's out there with Butler, and neither of them know anything about the place. They could be in trouble.'

I tossed up whether or not to explain Delia's history with the Apostles' Eyrie, and decided that it didn't matter which way the coin fell, it was better not to share for the moment.

'What about our driver, Dean?' Oliver came close to me and lowered his voice so Leason, now standing at the kitchen's rear door watching the rain, couldn't hear him. 'You do realise there's a possibility he's the killer? And Delia's his accomplice. She could be out there now setting up booby-traps, or hunting Butler down.'

'You've seen too many movies, Mr Oliver,' I said. 'Delia's no killer, she's just lost her father and she's heartbroken. We're going to the conference centre in five minutes, and when Delia and Mr Butler return, we'll hike out. So get yourselves organised and wear sturdy boots if you've got any.'

I went up to my room to grab my bag and I couldn't help thinking about Delia and her apparent duplicity with the Auroras. She'd helped her father stalk them for weeks, during which time she lightly poisoned complainers like Butler with her fish poo coffee and laxative muffins. But could she graduate to killing now that her uncle and her father were dead, victims, in her eyes, of the Auroras greed? Ms Harding thought it was a strong man who'd lowered me over the cliff, but I'd been surprised and drugged and the 'strong man' could have used some leverage with a rope looped around a boulder or tree to help lower me down. Ms Harding, from her account, was far enough away not to see my attacker's face, or to know exactly what he, or she, did with the ropes and pulleys. And I'd never asked Delia whether or not she was an only child. I knew very little about her, other than what she'd chosen to reveal. Perhaps she had an even angrier brother.

We met in the foyer with our food and water, and dressed in hiking gear, or as close to hiking gear as we'd brought with us for a playful weekend 'retreat.' As we started for the door, I heard the motorbike.

'Here's our killer now,' Leason said. 'Like father, like daughter. I wonder if she's brought Butler's head with her?'

Oliver had opened the door and walked out ahead of us. 'What's that?' His voice sounded strange.

I walked out and stood just behind him, following his line of sight. It was hard to tell from where we were, at a distance of 15 yards or so, whether or not it was a mannequin, or a person. Then the arm appeared to move.

'Graham,' Oliver screamed, and took off across the gravel driveway towards the rainforest and the stand of giant tree ferns.

'Wait,' I yelled after him. I had a sudden, sickly feeling deep inside. 'Stop, Oliver, stop.' I started to run, but he was quick for an overweight desk jockey. There was no chance of a crash tackle.

As Delia rode up to the covered walkway, the tree ferns exploded with several very loud bangs and the area directly in front of David Oliver turned from green to pink.

CHAPTER 41

When Graham Butler exploded, Dave Oliver was lifted off his feet and blown back towards me. He acted as a partial shield for me since I was directly behind him, so I had only scratches, and a gravel rash where I'd hit the ground hard on my knee and ripped my moleskins.

The blast knocked Delia from the motorbike, but, like me, she sustained minor injuries, some scratches, and cuts to her elbow when she landed on the concrete walkway. Maybe we all had slight concussion, too, including Leason and Harding, who were standing in the doorway when the bomb went off. That would partially account for our general state of mute shock. Dave Oliver's face and neck looked like some kind of Jackson Pollock painting, bloody red lines, strafings of black gravel-shot and brown sand blast. The effect made him look broken all over. He was a mess, but Graham Butler was the biggest mess of all. The explosion blew him into pink mist. The army bomb squad had nicknames for every kind of event, and pink mist was how they described people who got too close to bomb blasts.

But it seemed to me that this blast wasn't intended to kill anyone other than Butler, or else to highlight the fact that he was already gone and bring that fact forcefully to our attention. Oliver and I both thought we saw his arm move, but it could have been a trick of the light, or the post-mortem spasm of a recently dead body. Otherwise, it seemed too cruel to consider: there he was strung up to the stand of tree ferns like a scarecrow, his clothes in shreds from whatever had been done to him already. And then he had to wait, helpless, and presumably conscious, for us to emerge so that the show could proceed. I assumed that was the killer's intention. It was a public performance and we were the audience. If he'd wanted to terrify us more than we were already, he'd succeeded with bells and whistles.

Immediately after the explosion, my temporary deafness and ringing ears turned the scene into a tableau for a minute or so. Leason and Sarah Harding were the only two bodies left standing, and they stood rooted to the spot in the doorway. Delia, Oliver and I lay on the ground covered in debris: plant matter, dirt, gravel, blood spatter, pieces of Butler; pink mist. I watched as everything fell or floated down and settled silently. The area look as though a small, powerful cyclone had swooped on us, inhaling and shredding almost everything, and then spitting it all back at us with venom and malice.

I ended up facing back towards the main building and saw Delia, on the covered walkway, push herself up to a sitting position. She'd landed a couple of body lengths from the motorbike. She stared at me, or in my general direction, and slowly shook her head. I turned back to the forest where we'd seen Butler moments before. The tree ferns were all but destroyed; the bomb left a clump of stumps, shattered and desiccated trunks and torn up fronds. I tried not to look too closely at the other fallout spread over virtually everything, the pink and red and the slivers of white bone, strips of fabric that used to be Butler's clothing.

Oliver groaned loudly. He covered his ear with one hand and tried to wipe stuff off his face with the other. I stumbled over to him and checked him for potentially fatal shrapnel wounds. Most of it appeared superficial, but no less horrible given the source. I pulled out a handkerchief and wiped the top layer of mess off his face. He didn't look much better.

'What have you done?'

I looked up and saw Leason striding down the covered walkway to where Delia sat stunned on the concrete. He stood over her and repeated his question. Delia simply stared up at him, uncomprehending.

'You did this,' he said, yelled. 'You killed Graham. You set this off, this fucking bomb, you bitch.' He tried to grab Delia by her arm, but suddenly she rose to the occasion and shook him off so hard that he fell back and then down in the muddy soil next to the walkway.

By the time I reached them, Delia was shaking all over and Leason was crying.

'Delia,' I said, 'it's okay.' Why people say things are okay when they clearly aren't is one of life's mysteries. I guess we look for comfort wherever we can find it, even if we have to delude ourselves and appear as idiots.

'The bridge is gone, Garfield' she said, 'and Dad's van - the tyres are slashed.'

She started to buckle and I grabbed her and held her close to me.

'We have to go,' I said, loudly enough for the others to hear. 'Come on, now. Leason, help Oliver. Sarah, bring some water and the sandwiches, forget the rest.' I took one last look around at the scene and thought I saw some larger body parts near the giant strangler fig. Police forensics could take care of it all, if they ever made it to the party. There was no point in investigating further. Butler was dead, we were terrified, and the killer was surely watching us from somewhere in the shrubbery. I half pulled, half dragged Delia along behind the others down the path to the conference centre.

I bolted and locked both entrances after I'd given the place the once over, just in case our stalker was likely to jump out of the coat closet and yell 'surprise.' He had form, after all, with surprises. The others waited politely at the rear entrance in the rain mist, looking like a pack of survivors from a Basra bombing raid.

I secured the windows, closed the blinds, and turned the air-conditioner up, blasting cool air through the meeting room and adjoining kitchen and rest-rooms. It might help shiver and shake us out of our stupor. If our killer wanted to poison us with some kind of chemical or gas, he could easily stand outside and feed it to the air-conditioner's intake vent. But somehow, I thought he'd find that too easy, not as sporting as he liked things to be, or as dramatic. And he seemed to prefer picking off his victims one at a time.

I sat Oliver down on a kitchen chair, got him some handy wipes, and let him groan and rest. What was the use of conversation when we all knew what was happening? Sarah Harding filled the urn and set it on high, and Delia wandered into the meeting room. Leason shadowed me, following me from room to room as I double-checked more carefully for incendiary devices or other instruments of harm, whatever they might be.

There was very little to see. The kitchen cupboards and drawers contained packets of plastic cutlery, most of them unopened, paper plates, boxes of tea and coffee bags, and sugar sticks, cylinders of polystyrene cups, and a few packs of assorted sweet biscuits and savoury crackers: all the hallmarks of disposable conference going. There were jiggers of long-life milk sitting in a cereal bowl, but no ears or other body parts in the small refrigerator, and I was relieved to discover no conventional oven or wood stove, but only a small microwave for nuking lunches and drinks, and it was empty.

'What are we going to do?' Leason asked as I moved out of the kitchen and down the short corridor to the men's and women's toilets.

'What do you mean?' I asked back. I had no time for more accusations or confrontations. I pushed open the women's toilet door with my boot. Leason stared in from around my shoulder. A harmless and clean white toilet, and a narrow sink with soap and paper towel dispensers on either side of it.

'Where are we going?'

'Where would you like to go, Leason?' I asked him. 'I'd really appreciate your thoughts on this one.' I was more and more suspicious that this stalker had more at stake than money. Greed and loss could provoke a lot of reactions, but this was too much, wasn't it? Three people dead, and the rest on borrowed time. Maybe I was too naive.

'What do you mean, my thoughts? You're the security man.' Leason sounded frustrated but the fear was lurking just beneath the anger. 'Get us out of here.'

'I think we need to sort a few things out first.' I walked into the meeting room to see Delia sitting at the oval conference table. 'We'll have a meeting. Here, in the meeting room.'

Leason looked around and frowned. 'Where's our stuff?' He stared at the big table and around the room again.

'What stuff?' I asked.

'The stuff we were working on this morning.' He moved to the other side of the room and I looked under the table. There weren't any hidden corners in here.

'Jesus,' Leason said, and I saw him lean down. 'Our stuff's in the rubbish bin.'

I went to join him and sure enough, there were manilla folders and papers shoved into the wastepaper bin. 'Were they important?' I asked.

Leason glared at me as though I'd insulted his sainted mother, so I decided to ignore him and focus on what was on the table now. There were six white file folders placed in front of six chairs. Presumably, they represented each of the Auroras, including the dead ones.

The chairs faced the large TV screen attached to the wall. Beneath it, on a small grey table, sat a DVD player. Next to the DVD player was a boombox. In front of both machines were white cards. The boom-box card had the number 1 written on it and the words, 'Turn me on first,' in black marker. The DVD card sported the number 2 and this message, 'Read your folders, then play me.'

The author obviously saw us as process-driven people, agreeable to following orders. Why not? This guy held all the cards at the moment, and the envelopes, so who were we to upset his natural order? The thought occurred to me that I'd upset his natural order by not rolling off the cliff, unless that was what he wanted, someone like me to herd these kittens around his killing field.

As we stood there, Sarah Harding helped Dave Oliver into the room. She appeared to be in shock, and had so far said nothing about Graham Butler or anything else. I wondered how much of his disappearance she'd witnessed, and I was grateful that she'd been far enough away to at least avoid contact with the fleshy fallout.

There wasn't much I could do for any of them at the moment, other than follow instructions. I turned on the boom-box; after a few seconds, twangy guitar music started up. I would have recognised the song anywhere, a hit we soldiers used to sing at the tops of our voices to comfort ourselves and each other. But I didn't feel comforted by it today.

CHAPTER 42

The song's title said it all: 'Unwell,' but I, like my army buddies, preferred everyone's favourite lines about not being crazy but merely a little unwell, emphasised in the next breath and at howling volume with the insistence on no craziness, not at all, just a simple, tiny, little bit of impairment. Everyone knew you had to be extremely unwell and entirely impaired to be where we were, doing what we were doing, even when we didn't truly realise it. Singing a song, as mindlessly as possible, made it more acceptable, our way of life, killing, being killed, or, in my case, supporting killers with good food, victuals for the victorious in battle, and the limping.

This time, 'Unwell' was sung by our stalker. He sang quietly, and he was a reasonable guitarist. And then he stopped at the end of the first chorus of unwell and impaired.

'Just kidding, folks,' he said. 'I'm not unwell, or impaired. Not so you'd notice.' And then he paused. 'But you have noticed, haven't you? There's a little something going on. For those of you who are behind on the details, you might want to consult the remaining heads of Polaris Securities and Investments. Those that have heads.' He laughed. 'I'd suggest you do that before you watch the DVD, because it will come as a shock, I assure you. It shocked me.' Then, the voice was replaced by a different style of music. It took a while to realise because it was so quiet and slow, but then it began to build. It was Ravel's 'Bolero.' A psychopath's sense of humor.

'This is creepy.' Sarah Harding broke the spell; she wrapped her arms around herself and shivered. 'Who is this man? I don't know what he wants us to say.'

'He believes you know what it is,' Delia said. 'Something to do with those studs you all wear.'

'I don't wear the stud,' said Sarah Harding. 'I don't wear it.' She put her hand to her neck. 'It's a necklace, anyway. Mine is.'

'So, what happened on your cruise?' Delia asked. Ah, the direct, provocative approach.

'Can you turn that thing off, Mr Fletcher. Please.' Ms Harding wriggled around in her seat, still cold.

I went to the boom-box and flicked it off. The singer had recorded his words and the songs on a tape. I removed the tape from the machine and held it by one corner. There was nothing on the label, no title, like, 'Hello, I'm Jonesy, and I'll be your killer today,' or 'Nah-na-ni-na-nah.' An old-fashioned cassette tape, not a CD. I placed it next to the boom-box, then faced the room like a facilitator at a workshop. All I lacked was a laser pointer, and knowledge.

'As Delia asked, Ms Harding, what happened on your cruise? Whom did you tick off?' This wasn't about money, this was far more personal, and I'd known that much, at least, for a little while.

'We didn't tick off anyone,' Dave Oliver said, and then groaned and clutched at his ribs. 'There was an incident.'

'Dave.' Leason stared at Oliver as though he'd turned into another species. 'It wasn't our fault.'

'Whose fault was it, Pete?' Oliver held Leason's gaze.

'Nobody's,' Leason said at last. 'The incident was an accident, and she was as much to blame as anyone.'

'She?' At first I thought he meant Sarah Harding, but there was no reaction from the chief of human resources.

Oliver coughed and coughed. I grabbed him a bottle of water, and he drank half of it before he calmed down.

'So if we watch this conveniently loaded and ready DVD, that's what we'll see, an accident?' I went back to the table where the DVD sat, waiting for its moment in the rain. 'An accident provoked this carnage.' Our man was either easily roused to violence, or the Auroras - what did he call them, Polaris Securities and Investments? - were hiding something. My bet was on the latter, with bonus psychopathy thrown in for extra spiciness.

'Play the DVD, Garfield,' said Delia.

She sat down at the table and glanced at the five white folders. 'Wait, the folders. The DVD card says to read the folders.'

She opened the one in front of her and picked up the one sheet of paper inside. At the same time, Sarah Harding opened hers. From where I stood, they looked the same. Oliver and Leason grabbed at their folders and opened them.

'God, what a prick,' said Leason, crunching his sheet in his fist.

Oliver turned his sheet face down and left it on the table. Sarah Harding held onto hers and it started shaking and shaking more as her panic rose. Delia simply placed her sheet back in its folder.

I leaned over and picked up the last folder and, as I did, I dislodged the sheet of paper inside. The blasting current from the air-conditioner next to where I stood picked it up and helped it float slowly down to the carpeted floor. It looked like a giant, rectangular snowflake and it landed face up. The line of text at the top of the page said, 'The rest of your life,' and the rest of the sheet was blank.

'He has a sense of humour,' I said. 'Black humour, yes, but that could be a good thing; we might be able to reason with him.'

'A comedian psychopath,' said Oliver, and gave another cough. 'Sure, he'll be reasonable, of course he will. He thinks we killed someone.' He looked over at Sarah Harding. 'He thinks you killed someone.'

'Me?' Sarah Harding pushed herself back into her chair. 'Why me?'

'You're a woman, Sarah, you should have been the compassionate one. The one who remembered.'

'Dave,' said Leason, 'that's enough. It was everyone, including you.'

'And now,' Dave continued, punctuating every couple of words with a cough, 'we're going to watch whatever this piece of garbage is,' he pointed to the TV screen, 'and then he'll swoop in on us here in our 'safe house' and do us in. God.' He pushed himself back and then leaned forward again. No position was comfortable.

Leason got up and came around to Sarah Harding. 'Sarah, can I see you in the kitchen, please?' But his polite request was accompanied by a firm hand on her shoulder, which slid down to her elbow and pulled her up. Ms Harding looked startled, but she seemed to understand something in his tone, something that Delia and I didn't detect. It was some kind of stockbroker dog whistle.

Meanwhile, Oliver could stand sitting no longer, and asked me to help him onto the floor, which was when I saw the box, the chef's box of mystery, wedged in between the two long, solid columns of timber running for two-thirds of its length and forming the legs of the conference table.

'Shit,' said Oliver, 'it's a bomb.' He reached out towards the box and then he fainted.

CHAPTER 43

Dave Oliver was on his side, groaning quietly. Actually, it was more of a whimper, and I felt like joining him there on the soft carpet, waiting for somebody's, anybody's mother to come and save us. Instead, I dragged out the chef's box, still wrapped in hessian. We might as well get it over with before we watched the DVD, even though it wasn't included in our stalker's numbered instructions. Perhaps it was his private joke, something for him to enjoy beneath the table as we watched above.

'Do you think - could it be a bomb, Gar?' Delia asked. She was crouched on the other side of the table, staring at the box.

'No, I don't,' I said. 'It isn't. No.' Convincing.

'Maybe we should just leave. We could go to the creek and find someone.'

'Delia, we're in the middle of a monsoonal dumping in a rainforest off the beaten track. Anyone with any sense will be indoors waiting it out.' Like us. Waiting for the psychopath with our cocoa. Speaking of which.

'Mr Leason, Ms Harding, would you come in here, please.' I waited, and waited.

Delia got up and went out to the kitchen. 'The back door is open, Gar,' she called. 'They're gone.'

I heard the door slam. Delia shot the barrel bolt and returned to the conference room. 'Where do you think they are?'

'I don't think they want to see the DVD.' Which was no answer. 'Maybe they've gone back to the main building.'

'Let's watch it, then,' she said. 'It's no skin off our nose, and these bastards got us into this in the first place.'

I decided not to remind Delia about her father's plans, and her own participation in them. Instead, I pulled the chef's box out. It felt different for some reason, as though something was moving inside. It couldn't be anything living, the box was too well sealed. I took to the hessian - which, I noticed, had been rewrapped - with my apple-peeling pocket knife. Just enough to start a thread a-pulling. There were no locks, but four clip-style buckles, one at either end and two along the side.

'Are you ready?' I asked Delia, standing beside me. She nodded. I glanced back at Oliver, but he was still enjoying or enduring a siesta. I flicked the last buckle and slowly pulled up the lid, surreptitiously checking, despite my reassurances to Delia, for tell-tale signs of rigging and explosive devices, not that it would do me much good now. There were none.

'What?' Delia said, staring into the box. 'What's this?'

I remembered what it had felt like when we first found it on the road. Heavy, of course, but not sloshing, and there had been sections that felt colder to the touch than other parts. We'd probably carried Downer's head with us inside this box. The killer probably thought we'd open it, and when we didn't, he did it himself and put on the roast. There was no need to add to everyone's discomfort with that theory.

'It used to be frozen,' I said, and dipped my hand into it. The water was still cold - the time in the cooler would have helped - and there were still a few small, transparent pieces of ice floating around. Sitting on the bottom at one end was a diamond iceberg stud. I reached in and pulled it out. A tiny piece of flesh was stuck to the back of it; our stalker hadn't bothered with the nicety of removing the clasp before he removed the stud from the ear.

'Butler's?' Delia suggested.

We stood up and I put the earring on the table.

'Only one thing left to do,' I said. 'Do you want to do the honours?'

'Shouldn't we wait for Leason and Harding? And what about him?' She threw a glance at Oliver curled up on the floor, looking like an overgrown, battered baby.

'Bugger them,' I said. 'We need to know how motivated our man is.' His motivation was his strength and his commitment. So far, his strength was as the strength of ten, though without Sir Lancelot's purity, at least from our perspective.

'Are we worried about bombs here?' She grabbed the remote and sat beside me. 'Could this be a detonator, Gar?' We both stared at the little black stick in her hand.

'He wouldn't go to this much trouble and then blow us up.' I was fairly certain he wouldn't.

Delia hesitated briefly and then pressed 'Play.'

CHAPTER 44

OPERATION BLUEWATER POLARIS #005, 006.

Why hadn't he anticipated this? It was entirely on the cards, and yet, he'd been certain they'd watch. Too certain. Lack of flexibility in the field had defeated better men than he'd ever been or would be. He'd seen their bodies: burned, bullet-riddled, broken. He'd even killed some of them, but that didn't mean he was the victor, it simply meant he'd managed the situation better on the day, at the precise moment when it mattered.

So, the Chief Operating Officer, and the Chief Human Resources Officer, together for the last time, moving fairly quickly along the walking path to the waterfall. He wondered whether or not they'd ever been friends, Leason and Harding, or if the exigencies of their offices precluded such privileges. And friendship, make no mistake, was a privilege afforded to so few. He'd had friends, but after Jacinta, the best friend of all, none of them seemed to exist anymore; he'd rendered everyone and everything invisible, mute, irrelevant. Except for Jacinta, who'd been made invisible, mute, irrelevant, by these two and their cronies.

Flexibility. He felt the anger rising, the pumping in his chest, the heat in his hands, the pricking behind his eyes, his throat congested, his desire to scream a scream of rage for a very long time. Redirect. He left the hide he'd set up not far from the conference centre and followed them. He bet himself that he could crash around like a demented camel and they wouldn't notice, such was their fear, and determination to escape, even going the wrong way. They were talking loudly as they went, stealthy operators.

'I can't believe it,' Harding said. 'I just can't believe it.'

And what had they brought with them? Weapons, even rudimentary ones, a butter knife?

'So you keep telling me, Sarah. And yet, here we are.' Leason pulled at his T-shirt, soaking wet.

No, no weapons. Bottles of water, when they were surrounded by it; streams, creeks, rivers, waterfalls of it. He'd concede that bottles were convenient, but they weren't weapons.

'How anyone could be so stupid to think nothing would come of it. How we could think - you - you might have been suspicious, you're the paranoid type.'

Was there an eye dropper's worth of contempt in the voice of Ms Human Resources?

'It's been over a year, Sarah, over a fucking year, and no-one, no-one came forward - not at the inquest, not even after the bloody media reports.'

'Her husband was a wimp.' Harding spat the words at the path in front of them, apparently disgusted that Jacinta's partner hadn't the strength of purpose to accuse, or seek revenge. 'He didn't even blame us.' There - she wanted to be punished, she did. 'He forgave everyone - what kind of person does that?'

A broken person, a man more broken than Guy Friendly knew himself to be. That's the kind of person who forgives, Sarah Harding.

'Someone has,' said Leason.

'Has what?'

'Decided to blame us.'

'I still think - there's a possibility - Pete, it could just as likely be some big Philip Downer gag - some kind of organised candid camera deal to make money, or something. You know how desperate he is, and you don't really think that security guy, Fletcher, knows anything, do you?'

But her words, Friendly observed, didn't carry the volume they'd had previously. You don't really believe that, do you, MBA girl?

'Sarah, this may not be real enough for you, but I could do with a little less real. Philip's dead, it's his head, not a rubber dummy. Melanie's dead for sure, that was her stud that came out of Philip's mouth. We know exactly how many of them were made. Butler's in pieces all over the place. You think all that's a joke?'

Harding didn't speak, but shook her head and picked up her pace, walking ahead of Leason. Then she stopped abruptly and turned to face him. He had no choice but to stop.

'We couldn't have saved her, you know, Sarah.' Leason stood waiting for agreement, but it didn't come.

'Not once it was too late, Pete, of course not.' Harding paused.

'Of course, as HR person on the trip, you could have looked out for her.'

'What?'

'Never mind, it's all over now.' Leason backpedalled. 'We had to save ourselves. There was no point in telling them what happened. What would that have achieved for anyone, especially us?'

'It wouldn't have achieved anything,' Harding said, 'other than justice, whatever that is. Obviously, someone's decided to take things into his own hands, now that he's found out what happened.'

Clever Ms Harding, Guy Friendly thought, the truth will set you free, one way or another.

'He might think he has, but how did he find out? Who told him, and did they mention that she had some responsibility too. A lot. She did, don't deny it, Sarah. She could have planned better. She was the one who wanted to do it. She was careless, and she got what she deserved.'

Harding remained silent this time. Just as well, or Friendly might have simply Glocked them with the 9mm then and there. He took a very deep breath, held it for several seconds, and then let it go in a rush.

He'd bring them down the easy way, well, one of them, maybe both. There had to be a bit of sport now, especially after that revelation. He followed them until they reached the fork in the path. They weren't to know the bifurcation was simply to provide tourists with alternative, ferny routes to the same destination. But it was his chance for more accuracy while they stood there like dodo birds about to discover that their flightlessness, and imminent extinction, were real.

'Which way now?' Harding asked her Chief Operating Officer, but the COO was clueless. He moved his head this way and that, gazing along each sodden alternative, indecisive.

Indecision, another attitude that'll get you defragged in the field, young Jedi.

He drew the gun, removed the safety, cocked it, and edged closer. The mist had turned into a drizzle again. It didn't really matter where he hit the target, as long as it stuck for a few seconds. He held the gun in both hands and leaned against a tree fern. He squeezed off a round, smooth and simple, and watched as the target simultaneously screamed, grabbed for the entry wound, and fell over.

Show time.

CHAPTER 45

Fade to white. There was silence in the room. Even Oliver was quiet, lying there on the floor. He'd woken up, I noticed, but had remained where he was, and now he stared at the ceiling tiles, apparently unable to face whatever it was he'd done, or hadn't done.

We waited for something to appear on the white screen. Eventually, there was noise, along with the whiteout. It was low at first, and accompanied by a line of text across the centre of the screen that said, 'You must remember this.' The noise grew in volume and became a roaring wind, howling, a bit scary to tell you the truth, even though I was sitting in the middle of a humid rainforest on solid ground. Never mind the psychopath outside.

That noise was the noise of the Antarctic; I'd only experienced it once, right before I'd taken to the more pacific, temperate waters of the eastern seaboard. But that one time, on a trawler down in the Great Southern Ocean and further south, that was enough for me. I'm a lad of the tropics; I like my board shorts and bare feet; I like to eat outdoors as much as possible, I love to listen to music on jasmine-scented verandahs, and smoke a little weed as the sun sets with a sea breeze kicking in on a high eighties day. I don't like the cold, and this wind was cold, this white was freezing.

'A blizzard?' Delia said.

I shrugged. 'I guess so. Something to do with the iceberg studs - there's no doubt now.'

A voiceover narration began as the whiteout slowly lifted and the volume of the blizzard moderated. The voice sounded like the unwell, impaired singer we'd heard on the audio tape, but there was a hint of distortion, too. It wasn't his real voice.

'On October 4, 2007,' the voice began, 'the Liberian registered ship, Magellan, dropped anchor outside Stockford Bay, a little-known, beautiful

147

Antarctic destination. Stockford Bay is exclusive because it's, well, exclusive. It was made that way by rich people. Only those with connections and fat bank accounts, or very long, unaccounted-for lines of credit, go there. The Magellan was chartered by Bluewater Polaris Securities and Investments, but we'll use the shorter, more familiar, Polaris, if it's all the same to you.'

The whiteout dissolved to an ice-covered landscape filmed from offshore. The water was a deep, deep blue and very still. The snowy, icy land was blindingly white, the day was perfect and sunny, and you could see penguins and seals onshore. Birds flew and swooped around as if on cue. There were inlets and fjords here and there where small boats could probably land; great, jutting ice ridges, plenty of places for excursions into massive overhanging ice canopies, if you weren't afraid of sudden collapses, or shearing. It was a wonderful advertisement for Stockford Bay.

'On October 5, the Polaris group and a researcher/photographer, disembarked from Magellan and took a cabin cruiser into the shallows of the bay, for recreational activities. The trip was organised by the Polaris group's founder and Chairman, Philip Downer. Philip liked adventure holidays, and he was prepared to pay out a lot of other people's money to enjoy them every year.'

A picture of Downer appeared on the screen. It was part of a newspaper article with the slug, 'Tragedy hits Polaris Cruisers,' but the story's print was too small to read. There was another photo at the bottom of the article, a group shot, presumably of the Polaris people.

'Mr Downer and his cohort, Melanie Rogers-Hilton, Peter Leason, David Oliver, Graham Butler, and Sarah Harding, with their photographer/researcher, took a rubber ducky to shore and frolicked for some time. They ate, they drank, they ate some more, six of them drank a lot more.'

As each name was announced, a picture of the person, grinning from ear to ear, appeared on screen and remained there for several seconds. They were in cold weather gear: fleecy coats, gloves, thick beanies and hats. The men had grown beards. They must have been taken by the official photographer/researcher, but at the end of the six Polaris pictures, that was it, there wasn't a shot of the photographer. Maybe he was camera shy; a lot of snappers are only happy on the other side of the lens. I can understand that; I'm usually only happy on the other side of the chopping board when I'm in a kitchen: preparing, cooking, plating up.

'Late in the afternoon, the Polaris group began to feel the cold, despite their alcoholic insulation. They packed up and rubber duckied their impaired way back to deeper water, and the cabin cruiser. They decided to wait a while before returning to the mother ship, the Magellan. They were very tired after their long day of adventurous tripping in and out of the bay's many attractions, and the weather was closing in. But they didn't want to be seen as irresponsible high flyers; a measure of sobriety was called for.'

For dramatic effect, the lovely scene of Stockford Bay, which had returned to the screen after the Polaris faces, began to fade to white again, and again, the text, 'You must remember this,' appeared, this time accompanied by a guitar playing the tune from Casablanca. The music continued for a minute, during which time Delia turned to me and asked, 'Why is he doing this? Any clues?'

'No idea. Maybe it really is connected with the stockmarket. Maybe the cruise company went broke, and Polaris had something to do with it. Maybe they didn't pay for the trip. But that article with Downer's photo said there was a tragedy.'

'Something like Uncle Max, and Dad.' Delia reached for her water bottle and Dave Oliver pushed himself up to lean against the wall.

'I'm going to throw up,' he said.

I moved faster than I had all day, grabbed Oliver by his upper arms and lifted him despite his squeaks of pain. I hustled him down the hall and shoved him into the toilet, slamming the door for extra emphasis. Delia came along behind me with a bottle of water, opened the door and threw it in like a grenade. She slammed the door harder.

'I put the DVD on pause,' she said.

We hurried along the corridor to the sound of Oliver heaving up something that must have resembled shame, or self-loathing. I didn't want to know what that looked like.

CHAPTER 46

OPERATION BLUEWATER POLARIS #005, 006.

'Trust me,' said Guy Friendly, tightening the rope.

It had been easy enough, after the first shot, to subdue Leason, who stood over Harding, his mouth open, eyes bulging at the small tranquilliser dart lodged in her back. Friendly walked up to him and said hello. Leason almost fainted, and then decided to make a run for it. A gentleman to the end, ready to light out and leave her to her fate. At least he was true to form. Stupidly avaricious stockbroker, ridiculous adventurer, and now, hopeless runner. He'd wanted to use Leason as a pack horse to transport Harding; he still could.

'Stop, now,' he'd called after the fleeing Leason. Nothing. And then Leason tripped and fell. Friendly ran to catch up with him before he could get up. 'Not having much luck, are you, pal.' He hauled Leason to his feet and shook him a bit. It felt good. He shook him some more, and Leason began to resist, so he slapped his face and said, 'I'm in charge here.' Leason became still but his breathing was ragged and fast.

Friendly removed the dart from Harding's back, and had Leason pick her up and carry her over his shoulder to the clearing near the waterfall where he got the two of them organised.

'I said you could trust me,' Friendly told Leason, as Harding began to awaken. He splashed some water on her face to hurry things along. It was getting late and he didn't want to be at this after dark.

The two of them were tied to strangler figs growing right on the edge of the cliff. Leason and Harding were positioned side on to each other, one tree a piece.

'What are you doing?' Leason strained against the ropes and found he could move forward, but the moment he stopped straining, something pulled him back sharply and winded him against the fig's trunk.

'I wouldn't do that too often if I were you,' Friendly said. 'The rebound makes them tighten some more. A little trick from the Middle East. It's all in the way you tie them off, buddy.' Leason wasn't to know he'd jerry-rigged counter-weighting rocks behind the tree and over the ledge, so that what felt like tightening ropes was simply the dead weight of the attached rocks pulling him back. Gravity, what a hoot; and the power of psychological suggestion, mmm-hmm, tasty stuff.

Of course, if Leason went too far too fast, or in the wrong direction, the section of rope looped around his neck could snap a few vertebrae and end it fairly quickly, or leave him a quadriplegic, maybe a tetra-. Friendly had had a few friends who were quads and tets, the result of war injuries, bombs and the like. Some of them, over the years, had asked him to help them out of their troubles, and he'd obliged. It was the least he could do, he'd always believed, given his strapping good health, his amazing good luck, and his desire to end suffering. He'd given them all decent burials, necessarily in deserted places, usually desert places off the beaten track, no family present, obviously, but they'd been loved, at the end. He'd loved them, so much that he was willing to take their pain upon himself and send them to the exit with smiles on their ravaged faces. There weren't any smiles today.

Harding, who'd finally woken up, looked horrified. She was similarly restrained.

'Of course, you two don't have to put up with the cold, but I've done my best to replicate Jacinta's position in other ways.' He hadn't, not really, but the restraints were close enough. Jacinta's choices had been so limited, so circumscribed, so avoidable had one or both of these creatures bothered to think the right thought, just a simple memory, at the right moment. She'd been fit and healthy, but they'd left her to paralysis and no way out.

'There's a way out of this, if you'd care to think about it for a moment or two. Or an eternity.' Friendly laughed out loud as he placed the filleting knife between the two trees. 'There it is.' He stood back and watched them stare at the big knife. 'All you have to do is secure the knife and you can cut yourself loose. It's sharp, it's one of mine. And see, I've even left your hands free, for grasping. You know all about how to grasp.'

The two captives flexed their hands instinctively. They were free, all right, but their arms were roped to their sides, preventing more than minimal movement, and then only from the wrists down. Any lunge for the knife would have to be accurate, and the return slamming against the figs would eventually take its toll. And there was the additional neck-snapping bonus. It was the best he could do with minimal notice. He hadn't wanted to be anything but spontaneous really, out here with nature, especially after all the months of planning, and especially after Downer and Rogers-Hilton; they'd been an effort, and they'd potentially exposed him to suburban sticky-beaks. Out here, the only beaks belonged to the birds, wily buggers, and they didn't give a pinfeather.

'We can't get out of here,' Leason said, almost crying, 'we can't. We can't, Sarah. And we've seen his face.'

'It's a shame you didn't put that kind of feeling into your Antarctic expedition,' Friendly said. 'You might have saved someone.'

'Who, who the fuck are you?' Harding screamed, as best she could after the mild anaesthetic; it would have left her mouth and throat dry. Not a bad scream, in the circumstances, but nowhere near as heartfelt as Delia's earlier effort on the track. What was that about?

'You know me, Sarah.' Friendly walked slowly over to Sarah Harding and stood in front of her. 'Think.'

'I don't - I can't remember.'

'Sure you can.' He held her chin with his right hand and made her hold his gaze. 'Think again, just a little bit more.' He turned his head and gave her each profile. 'Imagine me without the beard.'

'Delivery guy?' She gasped, and then coughed. He let her go and moved back.

'I gave you the idea for Henry Pinkert's gang of too-few-to-mention.' He watched as the memory returned to her.

A few weeks before this adventure getaway was due to commence, Friendly had struck up conversations with Sarah Harding and Delia during his visits to the Auroras' offices with his courier deliveries. It had been a simple matter to suggest Pinkert's firm when the question of compromised security had arisen.

The Auroras were terrified of their clients, so much so that they travelled everywhere together. He'd watched them taking their lunches with each other, conferencing only in their own offices, coming and going at odd times with the apparent intention of confusing would-be stalkers looking for routines. There was building security, but they'd needed protection for their little business holiday, and Guy, being the friendly fellow he was, had casually thrown out the bait during one of his delivery runs. He knew that, like nine out of ten people, they'd be too lazy to look any further afield. The only problem was that Henry had managed to obtain the services of someone halfway decent at the last minute, someone he didn't want to hurt.

'So,' Friendly said, gazing first at Harding and then Leason, 'go to it, campers. There's no time like the present.'

'Wait a minute,' said Leason, gathering what was left of his chutzpah, 'that doesn't mean anything. Delivery guy? What are you doing this for?'

'It's hard to believe that you have a master's degree - what's it in again, fleecing and deceiving, an honours thesis in manipulation and theft?'

'You're a fucking smart arse now, but the police will be here soon,' said

Leason, and he began to wriggle around, trying to loosen the unloosenable ropes. 'Your feet won't touch the ground they'll have you behind bars so fast.'

'Balls, who'd have thought?' Guy Friendly walked up close to Leason and stared at him. Leason stared back, but that rasping breath, the beginning of the shakes, they gave him away. 'Jacinta Hurley, Mr Leason, like I said.' He reached up and ripped the diamond iceberg stud from Leason's earlobe. Leason screamed in pain and Guy Friendly winced at the piercing sound. Leason trembled and tried to move this way and that as blood ran and dripped from his torn ear. He began to hyperventilate.

He turned to face Sarah Harding, who'd been trying to move sideways towards the knife. 'Jacinta Hurley, Ms Harding. She was the love of my life. You killed her.' He walked over to Sarah Harding and reached inside the top of her T-shirt, pulling out the gold chain from which her diamond iceberg stud dangled. 'Hmm. Well, I guess you aren't as ostentatious about it.' He wrenched at the chain and it snapped, leaving a red line against the left side of Harding's neck. A few beads of blood appeared on top of the mark. 'You're a delicate flower, Ms Harding, aren't you,' said Friendly, watching the red droplets form.

He stepped back and stood facing the two of them. 'It's a simple equation, your six pathetic lives for her one precious life. Personally, I'd put the ratio a lot higher, but you know, you can't always fudge the figures. Well, yes you can, for a while, just the way you fudged Jacinta's death and got away with it, for a while. Questions? No? I didn't think so.'

'You can't do this,' Leason said, 'you can't just leave us here. We'll die. No one knows we're here. No one knows, you maniac. You can't bring Jacinta back.' Leason began to cry.

Friendly pulled a cloth from his pocket and walked up to Leason, holding his nose until he had no choice but to open his mouth. He stuffed the cloth in as far as it would go without choking him and then pulled a roll of tape from his other pocket and added some strips across Leason's mouth. Insurance.

'Ms Harding?' he said, turning to the Auroras second most senior woman. She must have had to step on a lot of heads to get here. Some reward for effort. 'Anything? Remorse? Regret?'

'I have a son,' she said, breaking down at last.

'I'm sorry,' Friendly said, 'I know what it's like to lose a parent.' He waited a beat, two. 'Jacinta might have had a son, or a daughter. Did you know that?'

But Sarah Harding, he could tell, was too far gone into her own grief to imagine anyone else's. He decided on only tape for her; she continued to sob, her nose running, her eyes streaming. He did feel some sympathy for her, or rather, for her offspring, for the loss, and the gain.

Friendly walked around each tree and checked the ropes; he leaned over the ledge and made sure the rocks he'd levered down were still well bound and free of obstacles. They looked like a couple of clock pendulums, rough ones, but effective. He leaned close to Leason and listened to his ragged breathing, smiled into his terrorised face. He didn't menace Harding as much this time; she was doing a wonderful job of that to herself. If the brokers couldn't yell, and they couldn't move, then it was up to Nature, perhaps. He hadn't quite decided, and it wasn't so much flexibility as feeling out of sorts, but he'd come this far, and there were still decisions to be made about the others, the 'innocent' others.

'That filleting knife,' Friendly told them, relaxing against a boulder and surveying his work, 'it's my favourite, you know, my very favourite.' He smiled, and watched doubt enter their eyes.

CHAPTER 47

'Do we wait?' Delia stood at the meeting room door looking down the corridor.

'Bugger him,' I said, 'let's get through this. Okay? Are you okay?'

'Sure,' Delia said, though she clearly wasn't, and returned to her seat.

I grabbed the remote and pressed 'Play,' then rewound it a bit in case we'd missed anything. They'd returned to the cabin cruiser and the weather was closing in. They were urged to remember this.

'The next morning,' said the narrator, the Casablanca music receding to the background, 'rather later than usual, the Polaris adventurers emerged from beneath their various rocks on the Magellan.'

The screen changed from whiteout to a white ship slowly cruising through deep blue water. It looked as though it could have been lifted from an ad. or an internet web site.

'They'd returned to the mother ship late the previous evening, after a few hours of improving sobriety, and weather - it didn't worsen, after all. They were hung-over, but filled with the joy of living for another day in one of the Earth's most beautiful landscapes.'

I thought I noticed a slight change in the narrator's tone, a sort of hardening from detached news broadcast style to someone far more involved.

'Imagine their surprise, and dismay, when the alarm was raised by a crew member, who'd found a body - a body - on a rubber ducky in the aft section of the ship. Was it a Polaris colleague? Was it a Magellan crew member? Was it a stowaway?'

'I'm betting it's none of the above,' said Delia, slouching down in her seat, waiting for the reveal as the ship on the screen sailed on oblivious.

'The Magellan's captain ordered the ship's doctor to the aft deck to examine the body. Alas, there was no hope. This poor wretch had apparently spent the night in the ducky with a bottle of vodka. The ducky was at least partially exposed to the harsh weather because of its location at the rear of the ship from where the smaller boats were launched each day for groups of explorers like the Polaris gang. And surprise, surprise, the rubber ducky was their rubber ducky, the very one they'd used the day before, the very one captained by Polaris CEO, Philip Downer. The doctor pronounced the body deceased, with a provisional cause of death due to exposure by misadventure.'

Then a still photograph took the place of the cruise ship. It was a head and shoulders shot of a woman dressed in cold weather gear. You could only see her face encircled by the collar of her jacket, and her fur hat. Her smile made it all the way to her eyes. She was pretty by any standard, dark eyes, dark hair, what you could see of it, mid-thirties perhaps.

'Do you recognise that face, Delia?' I asked.

'Never seen her before.'

'The body was removed to the sick bay, where it remained for the rest of the cruise. Yes, they finished the cruise. The body wasn't going anywhere, not now. In due course, the coroner investigated, the media reported the story, the deceased's family buried their loved one, dead due to her own silliness, apparently. Everyone went back to their lives.'

Again, the earlier photographs of the Polaris six appeared on the screen, one by one, and for several seconds each. The Casablanca music increased in volume. As I watched, the sense of recognition I'd felt when I first met the Auroras, returned.

'There's something familiar about this,' I told Delia.

'But of course,' said the narrator, his voice calm but insistent, 'you, the remaining members of the Polaris adventure getaway gang, you know what really happened. And you know why you're all going to die. I'm Guy Friendly, and I've been your host.'

The photograph of the woman reappeared, smiling at us. 'You Must Remember This,' was abruptly replaced by something I hadn't heard since I was a kid at the Nonna's place: Benny Goodman's Sing Sing Sing. It was one of his most famous songs, with a driving drumbeat and a jazzy melody. At first, I thought it was a strange choice because it was so full of life and possibility, and joy, which was why Nonna Lucia had loved it. And then I thought that our man in the rainforest, Guy Friendly, could barely stand to be alive when this woman was dead.

'It must be her husband,' Delia whispered.

There was a noise behind me, and I turned to see Dave Oliver leaning against the doorframe. He was as pale as the white wall beside him.

'Jesus,' he said, staring at the woman on the screen.

'Do you know her?' I asked.

He gazed at me as though I'd spoken gibberish. 'Who is she, Dave?' I stood up and went over to him, took his arm and brought him to sit at the table.

'That's Jacinta.' His voice was quiet and frightened. He reached up to his ear and felt the diamond stud. 'Christ.'

He fumbled with the stud, but finally removed it. His hands were shaking so hard that when he went to put it on the table, he dropped it and it bounced across the surface and fell onto the carpet near Delia. She leaned down and picked it up, sliding it back across the table to Oliver. He looked down at it as though it was a snake, or a bomb. Then he returned his attention to the screen, and stared at Jacinta.

'Jacinta who?' I asked. As though it would help us to understand.

'We killed her,' he said, and began to cry quietly as the screen faded to white again and the music drifted away to silence.

CHAPTER 48

'Aurora used to be Bluewater Polaris Securities and Investments,' I said.

Delia nodded. 'They changed it after - well, it would have been not long after the Antarctic trip.'

'It coincided with some investment outcomes that - they were not what we'd hoped for,' said Dave Oliver. 'Philip decided we'd be better off with a new listing, so he backgrounded Polaris and we punched up Aurora - same difference, really, it was already part of the documentation, just not emphasised as much as Polaris. Some fiddling around with the paperwork.'

'And you all have this memento of the Antarctic cruise, like some cult, only a woman died. Guy Friendly's woman.' I picked up his diamond stud. 'You said you killed her, so it can't be a mark of respect, can it?' I twirled the stud between my fingers.

Oliver looked uncomfortable, and I was glad. He was the only one left who could give us some clarity, and some idea of what our rainforest stalker had at stake. It wasn't too hard to work out now, though, even without the details.

'It's meant to be a symbol of silence,' said Oliver. 'A vow of silence.'

'Something went wrong, and you covered it up, the six of you.' I reached across the table and grabbed the other diamond stud, the one from the mud crab box.

'Whose is that?' Oliver asked.

'My guess would be Graham Butler's - Mr Friendly removed it before - ' I raised my eyebrows, hoping he'd realise.

'I don't know how this bloke - how did he find out? Someone must have talked.' Oliver shook his head in disbelief - at what, that a duplicitous stockbroker might tell a lie, or that he or she might tell the truth?

'So, what happened, Mr Oliver?' I turned to face him and swung his chair around to face mine. Our knees were almost touching. 'You're probably the last man standing.' I placed the studs on the table beside us.

Oliver looked completely stricken by that possibility.

'No - Sarah and Peter, they'll be back,' he said. 'They have to be back. We have to go and rescue them - you have to help them. Me - you have to protect me.' He tried to get up, but I pushed him back, more gently than I would have preferred.

'Just tell us what you know. You're safe.' At this precise moment in time, that was true. What might happen in the next thirty seconds was in the lap of the stalker. All I knew was that I wanted to get us out of the Apostles' Eyrie in one piece rather than many.

Oliver stared up at the now blank screen, took a deep breath as he'd no doubt been taught at his executive stress reduction seminar, held it for a few seconds, and let it out. I found myself doing the same, mirroring his movements. Delia simply stared at us as a mother might contemplate a pair of somewhat demented children: she was worried but not certain exactly why.

'Jacinta was our photographer, sort of. We met her on the Magellan at one of those dinners they have where everyone wears their best. She was doing a story for some nature magazine, something like that. Philip decided we'd have a record of our trip professionally done, by her. He said we'd post it to the Polaris website for our clients to enjoy. It was a pretty informal arrangement, a cash deal, and it gave her more time for free - she didn't have to hire a boat herself. So she turned up that morning, we took the cabin cruiser out - '

'Wait,' I said. 'Didn't some crew members go with you - wouldn't there be a head count happening?'

'Philip has, had, a boat licence, but there was supposed to be at least one crew member with us. Some regulation or other. Philip got around it - he made sure the captain was looked after, you know, an extra bonus. He wanted it to be just us, the fabulous, pristine six of us on our wonderful icecapade.' Oliver sounded disgusted with himself. Fair enough.

'Plus your invisible photographer.'

'Yes. Jacinta - Jacinta Hurley.'

I looked over at Delia. She shrugged; the name meant nothing to me, either.

'Well, the deal was, she'd come with us for some of the landings, and then we'd drop her off at this particular spot so she could get some real work done for her assignment. Arty stuff, animals, whatever.' He stopped again, and wriggled around.

'Go on,' I said. 'We've got all the time in the world.' Or however much Guy Friendly had allocated. 'Guy Friendly,' I said, surprised. 'He's from Sesame Street. Our man really does have a sense of humour.'

'Our man isn't human,' said Oliver, anger in his voice.

'Our man,' said Delia, her anger rising, 'is very human. He wants his revenge. He wants his partner back.' Just like Delia wanted her father and uncle back.

And our man was no puppet, but I guess he saw us as exactly that. He liked to play, or else that was how he got himself through the tasks he'd set for himself. He reminded me of some of the fellows I served with, especially when they were in combat zones. Total focus, no turning back, absolute dedication to the job. Obsessive, some would say.

'So you got your shots, and Ms Hurley got her free drop-off, and then what?' I asked.

'Yes, we had a few hours with Jacinta, then we dropped her off and we continued with our exploring - we stopped at a few different places. Philip took more photos, we had lunch. It was a big day.'

'By which you mean, you had a lot to drink. Wasn't there a designated driver?' How stupid were these people?

'We didn't need one, Fletcher, we were in the middle of nowhere, no other traffic, we were on holidays, enjoying ourselves.'

'You're incredible,' I said. 'You have this culture of entitlement, like you're kings and queens, even when you've killed someone.' I stared at Oliver and I wanted to smack him. I don't know what I was looking for, some hint of recognition, of understanding. Remorse seemed to be too much to expect.

'It was wrong, okay? We were wrong,' he said. 'I know that.'

'How did Jacinta Hurley end up dead in the dinghy?' Delia sat quietly opposite us. As usual, she homed in like a ground-to-air missile.

'We put her there.' Oliver was fighting with himself, I could see it in his eyes, and the way he kept fidgeting with his wedding ring. Was he still married, or had that bitten the dust, too? I couldn't remember.

'Yes?' It was like peeling a boiled egg: you think you've tapped it in the right spot, you have it ready to glide off in one or two pulls, and then it shatters into tiny pieces that glue themselves to the membrane and your fingers, sharp and unyielding.

'We forgot about her,' he said, and slowly backed away from me, pushing his chair with furtive movements of his feet.

I looked at my hands, resting in my lap. I'd deliberately assumed a meditation position after his comment about the Auroras enjoying themselves. I thought my apparent calmness might calm him down enough to be open with us. I thought it might calm me down enough to refrain from damaging him. But all I could think of was Rita, helpless in the vast ocean, waiting and hoping to be found, and at the very least knowing that we were looking, knowing she was loved and cared for, and remembered, for God's sake.

'How,' I said quietly, 'how can you forget a person?' I leaned forward and Oliver pushed further back.

'We - we were under the weather,' he said, cringing as he recognised the lameness in his response. 'And, things weren't going well at work, either. We were all stressed to the max, you know.'

'Who remembered?' Delia asked. 'Which one of you woke up?'

'No-one really,' Oliver said. 'Sarah wanted to know about the photos, and when we could get them on the website. And then, we realised Jacinta wasn't with us to ask.'

'So you went back to get her?'

Oliver hesitated. 'Pretty much.'

'What does that mean?'

'It means we had a discussion about what would be the best thing to do.'

'To save your arses,' I said flatly. Who'd have thought they'd be so cutthroat? Who'd have thought they wouldn't be?

'It wasn't like that,' Oliver said. 'When we realised, it was terrible. It was freezing outside and we thought a storm was coming. But we went back anyway, even though we were at risk.'

'At risk,' I said. 'Come on, then, give us the risk scenario.'

'We - that is, Philip and I went back to where we'd dropped Jacinta off. At first we couldn't see anything - too much ice, and it wasn't as bright and clear anymore, and the weather - it was threatening. The temperature had dropped incredibly fast. Then we saw a red flash - it was her backpack, in the snow. When we got to the pack, Jacinta was right beside it - she'd frozen to death. No cover anywhere.' Oliver seemed to have become one with his chair; he'd sunk into it, like a battered cushion worn almost flat.

'So you took her back with you, and what? No-one on the Magellan noticed she was dead? Were the crew all drunk, too? And the passengers? She can't have looked too well.'

'We said she was drunk, we carried her in and took her to her cabin. She just looked like she was sleeping. Later on, when people had gone to bed, Graham and Philip took her back to the rubber ducky.'

'And the final indignity was the bottle of booze that you left with her.' Delia stood up and began to pace around the room.

'That wasn't my idea,' said brave Oliver. 'That was Graham. He's a drunk.'

'And you all sang from the same page at the inquest.'

Oliver nodded.

'It was Philip's idea to get the studs,' he said. 'He thought it would always remind us to keep our mouths shut.'

And it would remind them that they'd beaten the odds; they'd won.

'And you've always been quiet, you've managed - until now.' Guy Friendly had already collected three studs, and Oliver had given his up voluntarily. I wondered whether or not he had the other two yet.

'We'll go now,' I said to Delia. I turned to Oliver. 'Get up, or I'll leave you here, and forget you ever existed.'

Delia looked over at me, but she didn't say anything. She gathered some bottles of water, and I ushered Oliver through the door first. Delia pulled me aside as he made his way to the back door.

'Garfield, do you have a plan?' she asked in a whisper.

'Not exactly,' I said. 'This Guy, he knows what he's doing. He'll want to finish the job. So we need to get away if we can, save this bloke - why, I don't know - and ourselves. I'm hoping Henry's got my message by now.'

'That's it?'

'Got anything?' I asked her. I was very open to suggestions.

'Here.' She handed me a bottle of water. 'We're going to confront him, Guy Friendly. He's obviously smart, and dedicated. I can work with that. And we didn't kill his Jacinta.'

She was out the door and handing water to Dave Oliver before I could explain that laxative muffins and fish poo coffee may not work their magic this time.

CHAPTER 49

OPERATION BLUEWATER POLARIS #005, 006.

Watching them was becoming tedious. He'd thought there would be some consolation in seeing them thrash like a couple of fish on a deck waiting for the gaff. But no, his natural instinct to end the suffering began to assert itself almost from the beginning. There was Leason with his antics, struggling forward and sideways, lunging for the knife, never quite making it, and staggering backwards as the counterweight of the heavy boulder responded to gravity and Leason's failing strength. Back he'd go, slamming into the fig's smooth trunk, winded. This was nowhere near as satisfying as Philip Downer had been. The first cut really was the deepest.

Harding tried once or twice, but her lower body weight meant she was exhausted fairly quickly. He should have used a lighter counterweight. In between attempts, she rested against the fig, staring at him, never taking her eyes from him. What did she think, that she'd fake out Guy Friendly? Leason had more chance with his stifled grunts and moaning murmurs, and now that he'd decided to forget about the knife for a while, those noises coming from the back of his throat and forced through his nose, were really annoying. What the hell did he want, apart from a rewind to Friday?

Friendly pushed himself off the flat rock he'd been resting on and went to Leason, who stopped the noises instantly.

'What is it? What do you want?' Friendly asked him, ripping the tape away from his mouth, roughly pulling out the cloth, now caked in saliva and blood.

Leason coughed and half-choked and coughed some more.

'Water,' he croaked, 'water - you fucking coward.' And then he tried to cringe away, which was impossible since he'd cringed as far as he could against the fig.

Friendly stared at him. Coward? What? Perhaps Leason wanted it to end, and thought that provocation might bring sweet relief. He could be right.

'Why can't you fight like a man?' Leason huffed and coughed the words out.

Friendly stood close to Leason. 'Pardon?' he said.

'You heard me, you're a coward, stringing us up like this. Why don't you fight me like a man.'

Where was this bravado coming from? The death throes of a murdering stockbroker were strange indeed.

'God knows how you killed Melanie and Philip,' Leason said, his eyes bulging.

'I killed them in my own good time,' Friendly replied. 'Ms Rogers-Hilton barely felt a thing. I can't say the same for Mr Downer. But then, he was the driving force, his was the final say-so. And you all agreed, so readily.' Friendly stared into Leason's eyes, watching for shame, searching for a hint of contradiction of Friendly's version of how it had happened. There was none.

'Give me a fighting chance, then, be a man for once.' Leason tried to poke out his chest, but he had no luck against the binding ropes.

'You tried to run away before, Mr Leason, remember? You didn't want to fight me.'

'I've changed my mind,' Leason said, angrier now. 'Give me a go, you prick. I'll have you.'

Suddenly, Guy Friendly couldn't help himself. He laughed, and laughed. He laughed so hard, he had to sit down. He gazed up at Leason and then over at Harding, looking disdainful against her fig, still staring him down.

'All right,' he said, giggling stupidly. 'Just give me a minute.' Friendly felt the wonderful feeling of release as his laughter slowly subsided and gave way to a reassuring ache in his sides and the unmistakable heaviness in his limbs and lower body that signalled relaxation. And he was alive, he was alive. He breathed deeply. Jacinta used to tell him you could heal anything with the right balance of laughter and good times and dedication. He could combine all three right here, although he knew, of course, that Jacinta may not see the elements or the result in quite the same therapeutic light. But this was his only recourse, his only response, now that she was gone, a demonstration of his own truth, restoring the balance destroyed by Jacinta's death, her murder, her invisibility. She'd been his guiding white light, his salvation. Who would be his salvation now? Who or what could possibly save him from his own truth?

Friendly got to his feet and stretched away as much of the heaviness as he could, shook off re-imagined Jacinta's disapproval. First he went to Sarah Harding and removed the tape from her mouth.

'You can be his cheer squad.' He smiled at her. She said nothing.

'Are you ready, Mr Leason?'

Leason watched him approach, heard him as he went behind the fig and unhooked the boulder, followed his every move as Friendly released him from the elaborate roping arrangement that ran from his neck to his knees.

The instant he was free, Leason tried to rush Friendly, but he hadn't counted on how weakened he would be as a result of the restraints and his fight against them. The two men grappled with each other, but Leason's legs were rubbery; Friendly threw him off with little effort. He fell heavily onto his side. He'd landed near the filleting knife and quickly reached for it. Friendly stood a couple of metres away, unarmed but ready.

'Come on, my enemy, teach me a lesson,' Friendly said, standing casually, hands on his hips.

Leason changed the knife from one hand to the other and back again. He was either ambidextrous, anxious, or completely stupid. Friendly decided to go with the latter. He tried to relax into his new role as fair-go-psychopath Guy. He predicted that Leason would lunge again, but at first the stockbroker simply stood swaying and glancing down at the knife every couple of seconds. Was he waiting for a bell to signal the first round?

'You can start any time,' Friendly said, a little surprised that Leason hadn't lit out into the scrub straight away.

'Bastard,' Leason said, and moved forward a metre, jabbing the knife ahead of him. Then he lunged, and when he did, Guy Friendly took a step to the side and back; his heel caught on a bulging fig root and he lost his balance momentarily. Leason kept coming and Friendly went down with Leason arriving on top of him. Friendly heard Harding scream, and then yell, 'Kill him, Peter - you fuck.' A murdering stockbroker and a lady with a mouth. Double bonus. But who was the fuck, Guy Friendly, or Leason the lunger? A fifty-fifty split seemed about right, in the circumstances.

Friendly didn't feel it at first, but as he grappled with Leason, he knew something was wrong. Two somethings. There was warmth all over his right forearm, and it wasn't the humidity. Leason had managed a slash with the knife. Friendly only had himself to blame, but the other something was what really worried him. He felt breathless all of a sudden; there had been a localised, specific pushing feeling when Leason fell on top of him, and now there was pain in that same spot on his left side. Some kind of puncture wound? To relieve the pain, he rolled with Leason, who didn't have a plan, that much was obvious. Once he'd managed to force him over and get on top of him, he punched at Leason's face, landing a blow near his right ear. Leason gasped and struggled more. He didn't seem to know what else to do with the knife, which waggled around in his hand, a randomly dangerous implement, making ineffectual stabbing motions into the air. Friendly punched again and again at Leason, landing blows on his jaw and, eventually, his already broken and bruised nose. Leason cried out in pain, but continued to struggle and writhe.

The breathless feeling was sapping Friendly's strength by degrees. He could breathe but it was an effort. He had to end this now. He pushed himself up and back from wrestling with Leason, up onto his knees, and straddled Leason's waist. He caught Leason's right wrist firmly, gripping it harder and harder, twisting the wrist at an odd angle so that Leason cried out.

It happened, eventually: Leason dropped the knife and Guy Friendly grabbed it, and then it was speedy, like lightning. Friendly leaned forward towards Leason and drew the knife blade across his throat. Leason stared in surprise, not at Friendly, but past his shoulder. Then, Friendly heard them, too: voices, people approaching the clearing where Peter Leason's final moments were happening.

'Sarah Harding,' yelled a familiar voice.

Sarah Harding cried, screamed, and struggled against her ropes.

Dark arterial blood spurted from Leason's right carotid vein. He'd be done for in no time.

'Sarah Harding,' called a woman's voice. 'Peter Leason.'

Peter Leason kept staring, even more surprised by hearing his name called. Did he think it was one of god's minions, come to take him home?

'Over there, Garfield, look.' It was the voice of the woman who'd screamed 'Murderer' at Friendly when he was only metres away from her on the road out. Delia. She'd seen them. Time to go.

Friendly stood up and instantly saw stars and blackness as the pain in his side spiked to a new level of intensity. He staggered and fell, landing on top of Leason, whose carotid was pumping blood like a fountain. On the ground, Friendly began to gasp for air, drawing in pain-filled gulps. It had to be a collapsed lung, a pneumothorax. He could survive that. He looked up towards the voices as his vision cleared and saw three blurry figures near Sarah Harding. He couldn't survive them. He pushed himself up, brandished the knife and said, 'Who's next?'

CHAPTER 50

I saw him lying on top of Peter Leason, and I watched Leason's life pumping from his neck onto the forest floor. His face grew paler and paler, but there was nothing I could do. I turned to Dave Oliver and Delia as our stalker slowly got to his feet.

'Get yourselves and Sarah Harding out of here,' I said, 'fast,' and handed Delia my apple-peeling pocket-knife. But Delia, apparently a woman for all seasons, produced her own knife, a long, tapering thing that could have been my Uncle Mick, the butcher's favourite boning knife. I raised my eyebrows.

'The conference centre kitchen,' she said.

She began slicing through the ropes that bound Sarah Harding, staring in horror at Peter Leason, whose eyes were closed now. Dave Oliver didn't know what to do, so he stood, legs apart, half-ready to bolt into the jungle, half-ready to defend what was left of his honor, if such a thing had ever existed for him.

'Go down to the creek,' I told him, 'follow it and you'll find someone to help us.'

'Which way?'

'What?'

'Which way? The creek. Which way do we go?' Oliver was on the verge of a panic attack. He couldn't take his eyes off Guy Friendly, who, no doubt in Oliver's mind, was about to eviscerate, decapitate, and blow all of us up. But I knew for certain that he wouldn't.

'Follow the current,' I said, sounding more confident than I felt.

'Follow the current,' Guy Friendly repeated, smiling at our bedraggled little group. He swayed a bit, but otherwise he seemed to be in charge. That was okay, for the moment.

'Go, now,' I said, as Delia cut away the remaining restraints and Sarah

Harding fell into her arms. Delia pushed her back, and handed her over to Dave Oliver. The two of them held each other like the last life preservers on the Titanic.

'Garfield,' Delia said, 'come with us, while he's winded, or whatever he is.' She risked a glance at Guy, who continued to stand quietly a few metres away, watching us without expression, Leason's blood pooling at his feet.

'Go, Delia,' I said, 'I'll take care of this.'

Delia hesitated, 'Garfield?'

'It's all right, Delia,' I said, 'this is my job. I'm responsible for protecting you. All of you.' Already, Harding and Oliver, arms around each other's waists, were hobbling down the path as fast as their impaired bodies would take them. They knew my place in their scheme of things. 'Go on, I'll be okay.'

She took a look at Guy Friendly and Leason, and gave me a quick hug. 'Don't turn your back on him.' She followed the other two back into the gloom of the rainforest canopy.

With any luck, they'd be picked up before dark. With less luck, Guy Friendly would turn out to be a different man entirely from the one I knew, now that I'd seen him face to face.

I walked over to where Leason lay and knelt down beside him. Guy stood on Leason's other side. I felt for a pulse in his wrist and his neck, but there was nothing. I pushed up his left eyelid and his eye stared back at me, unmoving. I sat back and looked up at his killer.

'Guy Friendly,' I said. 'Cute.'

Guy moved back a metre or so, out of the way of Leason's lost blood, and slowly let himself down to a sitting position. He felt around his left side, prodding with his fingers.

'Pneumothorax, I think,' he said. He took a deep breath and suppressed a gasp of pain. From a pocket on the lower leg of his khaki trousers, he pulled a cotton bandage roll. 'Do the honours?' He held it out to me, and I took it. 'For the arm. First things first.' He pushed up his sleeve, which was all but dripping with blood. 'Leason - a lucky hit, God rest his shifty soul.' He shook his head.

I unrolled the bandage and began a slow, careful wrap of his right forearm.

'Lucky for you it isn't deep,' I said. Poor Leason hadn't had a clue about attack, or defence.

'Aren't you going to ask?' Guy said.

I stopped wrapping. 'I'd have to say, all things considered, that reports of your death have been somewhat exaggerated, Gianni.'

Guy Friendly laughed at that, and caused himself considerable discomfort. He sighed and waited for his breathing to return to its shallower, more tolerable mode.

'Got a clip?' I'd reached the end of the bandage. Guy delved into his pocket once again and came up with a clip, which I hooked firmly in place. 'You need a hospital.'

'Dead men don't need hospitals, Gar.' He began unbuttoning his shirt and I helped him off with it.

'Do you prefer Guy or Gianni, now?' I checked the puncture wound in his left side. It was bleeding, but there wasn't much to show for it. 'I need something to pack this with before I can tape it.' God alone knew what was in there, but I could only make running repairs. On the plus side, he looked as fit as a fiddle, physically.

'Gianni will do, between us.' He produced a roll of black gaffer tape and tore a sleeve, the less bloodied one, from his shirt and folded it into a neat rectangle. He held it against the wound while I taped it firmly around his torso with several loops of the gaffer tape. Once that was done, we both sat back and checked each other out.

'Garfield Fletcher, protective security expert.' He was going to laugh, but checked himself.

'Gianni Magiolo, dead man walking. How did you do that?'

'Die in Iraq? It's an easy place to die, Gar. And I left a bonus piece of myself behind, for DNA purposes.' He held up his left hand and wiggled his forefinger. The top joint was missing. 'All that was left in the pink mist.' He smiled at me, and I didn't know what to do. I smiled back and the image of our own recent pink mist, courtesy of Graham Butler, returned.

'I'm not going to kill you,' he said.

'I know that,' I replied, remembering the trouble he must have taken to lower me over the side of the cliff and onto the ledge. He knew I'd manage to escape, eventually, but he probably hadn't reckoned on help from Ms Harding.

'You don't look too convinced.' He proceeded to rip the other, bloodied sleeve from his shirt before putting it back on.

'Did you ever consider that shock could be an issue here?' I felt numb, and I was getting number, and dumber it seemed. My best childhood friend, my former Army buddy, dead for quite a while, or so I'd thought, was actually a serial killer, a psychopath, a revenge murderer, all of the above?

'I'm sorry about that, but you're the last person I expected to see here. I thought you were still at sea, cooking up cyclones. That's what I get for touting Henry's company to these scallywags at Aurora.'

Scallywags. He really did hate them. Gianni used such terms of endearment when he loathed and detested someone with an intensity that required repression for security purposes. You never let the enemy know what you're really thinking.

'You're the last person I expected to see anywhere,' I said, and suddenly, out of the blue, I felt like crying. When I'd heard the news of Gianni's death in Iraq, courtesy of a roadside explosion, I walked around for a week in a daze. I hadn't seen him in years, not since we'd both left the army for other careers, although we'd kept in irregular touch by email, but I couldn't believe I'd outlived him. And I was right; I hadn't. I rubbed at my eyes.

'Little Gar, always the softie,' said Gianni, leaning over to pat my leg.

'I'm sorry about your Jacinta,' I said. 'This is all about her, isn't it?'

He stared down at his boots. 'Yes.'

'How did you find out, about what really happened?'

'You know?'

'We got Dave Oliver to tell us, after your DVD presentation. He thinks one of them, one of the diamond stud gang, must have spilled their guts.'

'No, spilled guts in other ways, as you're aware,' he said. 'No, Jacinta told me.'

'Jacinta?' How could that be? 'What did you do, have a séance or something?' It wasn't beyond the realms of logic, and Gianni had always been a man with an open mind. I knew a lot of people who'd heard from loved ones via psychics who couldn't possibly have acquired the knowledge they displayed by the usual terrestrial methods of investigation and research. There really are stranger things in heaven and earth.

'A story for another day, Gar,' he said, making an effort to stand up. I moved to help him, and as I got closer, he leaned down and pulled something else from another pocket of his cargo pants. Then I felt an intense stinging in my eyes as something sprayed onto my face.

'Gianni,' I yelled, 'what are you doing?' I tried to wrestle with him, but my eyes were on fire and watering like taps.

'It's only capsicum spray, Gar, harmless.'

Gianni was strong, even with a slashed arm and a collapsed lung. I grappled and mauled, but eventually I went down, lying on the ground in panic and agony. He hadn't punched or kicked or scratched me, but the burning capsicum wouldn't let up.

'Gianni, don't go, we have to sort this,' I screamed. 'Gianni.' Was he still here with me? I didn't have a clue. My entire body was occupied with the excruciating pain in my eyes. It seemed to radiate through my body the way bee stings and ant bites and jellyfish tentacles invade your nervous system and bring you to a shocked standstill. It was hard and sharp and paralysing.

'Take this,' he said, and pressed something into my hand. 'I died in Iraq, Gar, remember.'

It was a bottle, presumably water. I struggled to open it and poured it onto my face, forcing each reluctant eye open and liberally dousing them both. It seemed to take forever for the intensity of the pain to begin subsiding. I realised I was sitting next to dead Peter Leason when I accidentally, blindly leaned against his inert body. At least he was soft, and harmless now, unlike the capsicum spray.

I should have known that Gianni wouldn't stop, not for me or anyone else. And I also knew he couldn't bring himself to really hurt me, and that he was relying on me to protect his identity. The Auroras didn't know who he was, and neither would the police. He was a dead man walking and he wanted me to keep it that way.

CHAPTER 51

A line came to me as I blundered half-blind down the path to the creek. Rita and I used to throw it back and forth at each other when we were kidding around. It was from a movie she'd seen years ago. One of the characters tells her friends the upcoming storyline of a soap opera she stars in: she's been abducted by aliens, and one of her lines is: 'I didn't ask for the anal probe.' The actress has to decide which word to emphasise when she delivers the line, so her friends help by trying out each one in turn. '*I* didn't ask for the anal probe;' 'I *didn't* ask for the anal probe.' At the moment I tripped on yet another tree root, I saw every single word in bold italicised type and I cursed Henry to the top of the canopy. He'd let me get screwed with my pants on and he didn't have a clue he'd been set up. I couldn't even blame him. However.

'Fuck you, Henry,' I yelled, or rather croaked. The capsicum spray had done something nasty to my throat, too.

Guy Friendly - and I had to stay with the alias, for the time being - was either long gone, or hunting my gang of three, and I couldn't have him pegging Delia as anything but an innocent, at least as far as being some kind of several-times-removed accessory to Jacinta's death was concerned. I have to admit I didn't care a great deal about the other two, even Sarah Harding with responsibility for a young son. Dave Oliver had confirmed their monumental negligence in leaving Jacinta behind on the ice, and their unforgivable decision to cover it up, and furthermore, to make it look as though Jacinta had been the stupid and drunken architect of her own demise.

Philip Downer had decided that the diamond iceberg studs would remind the Polaris crowd, now the Auroras, to keep their mouths shut forever or face the courts on charges like involuntary manslaughter, or negligence causing death. But these studs could also be interpreted as a symbol of triumph, a badge of dishonour embraced because they'd fooled everyone, including Jacinta. Somehow, Gianni - Guy - had found out, and decided the law would most likely be an ass in the face of a high-priced legal defence team, and would either acquit them or slap their wrists with suspended sentences. Even gaol time would seem inadequate redress for a grief-stricken lover. And how much, after all, could a prosecutor prove, if all of them denied everything incriminating? They were stockbrokers, masters of the universe, tough as nails, impervious to the wails and groans of deceived, broke and homeless clients, and eager for their bonuses regardless of merit. Eager to move on, and up, and out of the miasma of suffering they'd created, deserving, like aristocrats, of new starts, better opportunities, regal treatment not extended to the masses.

Money alone, or rather, its loss, had been enough to turn on a pressure hose of abusive and threatening phone calls and letters from dudded investors. But death, how did that measure up? The death of a loved one, perhaps the only one, the soulmate? Jacinta. And I knew that Gianni - Guy - was an efficient killer, long before this weekend, but only, as far as I'd known, when he was in uniform.

It was one thing for poor Dean Porter to hatch a plan to seriously disturb and disrupt these fools on their adventure getaway, to somehow scratch back some of his own and his dead brother's dignity.

And Delia, poor Delia, with her laxative muffins and fish poo water, she was an innocent abroad trying to love her father back to health and life. Delia. Delia with her long, sharp, boning knife, Delia and her subversive dedication to infiltrating the Auroras' offices and encouraging them to getaway to the Apostles' Eyrie. Delia, whose father and uncle were both dead as a result of the Auroras' greed, ineptitude, incompetence, and callous ignorance. Delia.

I hurried along the path, calling out Delia's name, and then Sarah Harding's and Dave Oliver's. There was no answer. My eyes were still watering, and the rainforest looked even blurrier than it already was with the rainfall. I heard the creek flowing before I saw it, and I followed what I thought, through the blur, were muddy footprints, along the bank for some time. I was impatient to see some sign of life, of three lives, to be more precise, standing upright and breathing. I looked up from the mud bank to divine a way past an outcropping of slippery, moss-coated boulders, and saw two figures standing about ten metres away.

'Delia,' I called, and one of the figures turned its head towards my voice.

I scrambled over the boulders, slipping this way and that, using sheer momentum to get myself to the other side. I ploughed along towards them, blinking and blinking, trying to clear my vision. As I got closer, I could see that there was a third figure slumped on the ground right in front of Delia: Oliver. She held the boning knife in her hand and Sarah Harding was standing back and off to one side. Delia raised the knife and was about to bring it down.

'Delia, no,' I yelled, and lunged at her as I crossed the last metres of muddy debris. I knocked her off her feet and heard her surprised yelp of pain, but she didn't struggle with me, so I sat up and pushed myself away from her. She'd dropped the knife; I picked it up and held it firmly. 'This isn't the way, Delia,' I said, and stared down at Oliver, who was staring back at me in what looked like terror.

'It's all right,' I said, 'you're safe.' He looked unconvinced.

'Safe from what, Garfield?' Delia asked. She'd picked herself up and was scraping at some twigs and clods of mud on her clothes.

'Delia,' I said, and I had to rub my eyes again. 'You're still blurry.'

'Did you think I - no, you couldn't have, could you?' Delia stood gazing at me, and then she gave a laugh that sounded more bitter than twisted. 'There are easier ways than this, Garfield.'

'Delia was going to cut down those palm fronds so we could avoid sitting on mud, Mr Fletcher.' Sarah Harding pointed at the Golden Cane palm fronds above Dave Oliver. 'They're damp, but at least they're not muddy.'

I looked up at the palm tree and then at Oliver, who'd already decided on a rest, despite the muddy ground.

'I've had enough,' he said in response to my unspoken question.

'No, you haven't,' I told him. 'We need to keep moving. Get up.' Movement might help to cover my embarrassment as well.

'Garfield, a word with you,' said Delia, moving a little way along the bank. I handed Sarah Harding the knife and followed Delia. Oliver ignored my instructions and remained seated. Sarah Harding began hacking at the fronds.

'You didn't think I was going to kill them, did you?' Delia sounded shocked.

'You lost your uncle, Delia, and your father. They lost their retirement savings, their future.'

'They don't have a future any more, Gar, not in this dimension.'

'What about your future? You've lost everything.'

'I'm alive, Garfield, and we can get out of here.' She turned to the creek, which was running fast but there was no danger of flooding. 'What happened with the stalker?'

'He got away,' I said. 'He had capsicum spray. I can't see very well, but it's getting better. We really need to move.'

'He looked strange.'

'He's a killer. Of course he's strange.'

'Not like that.'

'Like what, then?' Had she realised that he knew me? She was an astute observer, there was no doubt about that.

'I can't put my finger on it, but it's something familiar,' she said. 'They really do need to rest, Garfield, for five minutes?'

We both turned our attention to the Auroras, my charges for better or worse, much worse. Four gone - two of them killed on my watch - and two left. I wondered if that would be a good enough strike rate for Guy Friendly, or if Jacinta's life, and his life together with her, warranted absolute retribution. And even if it wasn't good enough for Guy, being Mr Sixty-Six percent, maybe, just maybe, it would be good enough for Gianni Magiolo, my best old friend, Nonna Lucia's sunshine boy.

CHAPTER 52

'We can't travel like this at night,' said Oliver. 'We'll kill ourselves, never mind the fucking psychopath.'

'The psychopath,' Delia said, 'will love the fact that it's dark. He's obviously trained to be a guerrilla, so night manoeuvres probably excite him more than anything else. He probably has those goggles for night vision and an infra-red sight on his rifle.'

Way to go with the reassurance, Delia. I guess it was her way of getting Oliver to move, because as long as he held out, it seemed Sarah Harding - adrift, in shock, and getting shockier since Butler's explosion, and then Leason bleeding out - wasn't prepared to move, either.

'He - he said he was the delivery man.' Sarah Harding spoke quietly, well below her usual confident volume.

'Pardon?' I said.

'The man - Guy Friendly - he was the delivery man. A delivery man to our offices. Do you remember him, Delia?'

Delia hesitated before she spoke and then her eyes widened in recognition. 'He had no beard then,' she said. 'How could I have missed that. That's him. His name was Jack, and he worked for Green Dream Couriers.'

'He left the business cards for Pinkert's,' said Sarah Harding, 'that's why we hired you, Mr Fletcher.'

I watched Ms Harding's face as she mulled over what that could mean, what it might say about any connection I may have with Guy Friendly. What I was certain of was that Green Dream Couriers would have no idea who Jack really was, or where he came from.

'He said,' Sarah Harding began, and then she stopped and appeared to be on the verge of tears. 'He said,' she tried again, 'that Jacinta was pregnant. I'm sure that's what he meant, that she was pregnant when she died.' She stared down at her sneakers, filthy with mud, flecks of blood, and forest floor debris. 'Pregnant.'

'Mother and child,' said Delia, so softly I could just make out the words.

'How could we have known,' Oliver said, grunting himself into a new position on the palm fronds. 'We didn't know. We can't be responsible for that.'

Leopards really don't change their spots, and Oliver was no exception, although I'd normally hesitate before comparing him with a magnificent animal like the leopard.

'Shut up, Dave,' Sarah Harding said. A biting tone had entered her voice. She stood up. 'Let's go.' Remembering what Guy had told her seemed to give her new energy.

'It's too dangerous.' Oliver protested, but when the three of us began to walk away from him, he struggled upright and shuffled along behind.

We took it carefully. It was completely dark, but the rain had stopped, some of the clouds had broken up, and there was just enough moonlight to see a couple of yards ahead of us. We had the creek's noise to our right, keeping us more stable and moving in an only slightly meandering line. I could only hope that there was something up ahead for us to appreciate.

'Do you think he's following us?' Delia asked me. We'd taken the lead after a while, and could hear the other two behind us, muttering indistinctly and arguing.

'If he was, he could have done us in a dozen times over by now.'

'Maybe he's a sadist, and he's just letting us think we're going to escape.'

'He's no sadist, believe me,' I said, before I could stop myself.

'How would you know, Garfield, you met him for all of five minutes.' Delia watched me carefully in the low light.

'Well, he left me with a bottle of water to irrigate my eyes after the capsicum spray. A sadist wouldn't do that.' There was absolutely no point in playing out a true confessions scene with Delia, even though I had no idea what to do with the knowledge I possessed.

'No, I suppose not,' she said. 'Then maybe he's one of those psychopaths that, you know, have very specific targets. Women with red hair, drop ear-rings and a history of horse riding.'

'I think you're right,' I said. In Guy's case, the six people who killed his one true love and their child, and hid their guilty secret, apparently free of remorse or any desire to ever do the right thing. I wondered if any of them would have weakened on their deathbeds and confessed before the certain and boiling oils of hell consumed them. Probably not. At any rate, four of them no longer had to worry, about anything.

'I don't blame him.' Delia lowered her voice. 'I don't blame Dad, either. And I have no regrets, except that this bloody stalker literally scared the life out of my father. For that, I'd cheerfully shoot him, right now.'

177

But her tone lacked the requisite commitment, and belied her words. Delia was a small-time avenger. She'd want him beaten up, and thoroughly, but she was no homicidal Guy Friendly. And eventually, she'd find some way of rationalising that the man was simply doing what he had to do, and Dean Porter got in the way. An accident of fate.

'Up ahead,' said Oliver, 'see? There's a light. My brother's house, and he's there. He's got to be there.' Oliver tried to shuffle faster, but his fractured ribs kept him at a snail's pace.

'Your brother,' I said, shocked. I stood in front of him and he came to a stop. 'You've had a brother nearby all along and you didn't tell us?' What was this bozo thinking? That he'd be the last man standing and manage to get to safety while the rest of us perished?

'He isn't always here, this is the house I saved for him, when he lost the Eyrie.'

'This house?' Sarah Harding was as much in the dark as Delia and me. 'I thought you meant the house in the city.' She shook her head and rubbed at the red line of dried blood on her neck.

'We could have tried to get to it before now if you'd told us he lived here,' Delia said. She was clearly furious with Oliver.

'Why?' Oliver said. 'So this bastard could kill Michael as well?'

'Was Michael on the Antarctic expedition, Mr Oliver?' I asked. 'Did Michael kill Jacinta and her baby, too?' It was a low blow but I couldn't help it. I was sick to death of Oliver and his demands and whimpering.

'You're going for assault,' he said, jabbing his finger at me. 'Don't forget that.'

I grabbed his wrist and twisted it as hard as I could, until he cried out in pain and sank to his knees. It was a brain explosion, I admit it, but it felt so good.

'Might as well make it worthwhile then, don't you think?' I said. 'Let's go and make your brother a target, shall we?'

Delia and Sarah Harding stared at me and at Oliver on the ground rubbing his wrist, and then the three of us walked on towards the light.

CHAPTER 53

Michael Oliver was a sad-eyed, balding man in his late sixties whose neck was slowly sinking into his shoulders. He had the look of a dog whose treats were long overdue, and who suspected that maybe no more treats were coming his way, ever. It didn't help that he wore a crumpled, oversized beige tracksuit. He'd either lost a lot of weight recently, or he'd borrowed it from his obese brother.

I didn't know what to make of Michael's reaction when he answered the door to our quartet of wet, dirty, frightened people, one of whom just happened to be his own youngest brother. He ushered us in without a word, eyebrows raised, and I couldn't tell if he was mute with shock, or surprised, or bemused that it had taken this long for his brother to end up in such an obviously nasty predicament.

'Mick,' Dave Oliver said, 'these are - they're with me.' He waved a hand in our direction. 'We've been at the Eyrie the last day or so.' He hobbled over to the kitchen table and sat down heavily as though the effort of even uttering a few words was too much for him.

Since Dave wasn't interested, I introduced Delia, Sarah and myself to Michael and he replied with, 'Mick Oliver, writer and bankrupt.'

The writer and bankrupt's house was more of a cabin, most of it taken up with one medium-sized room incorporating the kitchen with its table and four chairs, a lounge section with a two-seater sofa and two mismatched single lounge chairs, and a study area where there were some cluttered bookshelves, a four-drawer cabinet, and a small pine table and chair. On the table were a laptop, a printer and a correspondence tray half-filled with white paper. There were three closed doors running down the right-hand side of the room, which I assumed opened to the bathroom, toilet and bedroom. The floors were polished boxwood, now dull, and there was a large, frayed, oval-shaped brownish rug on the floor in front of the grey sofa. It was a pretty spartan set-up.

'Strike some trouble?' Mick asked me, ignoring his brother.

'Yes, a lot,' I said. 'Do you have a phone?'

'Only a landline,' he replied. 'Over there.'

'Mind if I make a call?'

He gestured for me to go ahead, and then looked at Delia and Sarah Harding.

'A cuppa?' he offered, and they nodded, silently making their way to the kitchen table.

I dialled Henry's number. He answered on the third ring.

'Henry, it's Gar.'

'Where are you? The police are on their way to the Eyrie. I gave them what I could about the Auroras. What's been going on there? Are you all right? This isn't some kind of hoax, is it, Gar, because if it is, our business is down the toilet.'

'We're at a house along the creek from the Eyrie. We escaped from the killer.'

'Who is this bastard?'

'How should I know, a bloke on a mission,' I said. Henry would have had an apoplexy on the spot if he knew it was Gianni. 'He's killed four of them, at least two here, and there are body parts from another one, but I don't know if everyone's here, their bodies.' Philip Downer's head and detached ear swam into view in my mind's eye, and Melanie Rogers-Hilton's diamond stud rolled out of Downer's cooked mouth, again. My stomach began a slow churn. I looked over at the kitchen table, and could see that the others were as white-faced as I felt.

'Jesus. Look, the police'll be there soon, so don't worry.'

'No, we won't worry, Henry,' I said, frustration creeping in at the end of a very long couple of days. 'He could be outside the fucking door as I speak, ready to gun us all down, or chop us up.' I'd bet Belle's house that he wouldn't be, but Henry should share some of our distress.

Did I really think Gianni would do that, now, when he and I had - what had we done? - had a conversation whose tacit content was a request to me to protect his identity, right before he blinded me with capsicum spray and left me to the elements.

'Calm down, sport, if he'd wanted to do that, you wouldn't have had the chance to call me or anyone else, would you? Think about it.'

I could hear Henry breathing into the phone. Neither of us knew what Guy Friendly might do, but at least Henry had the glass half-full attitude.

'Sorry, we're a bit twitchy at the moment.' Then I remembered. 'You'll have to tell the cops the bridge to the Eyrie is gone. They'll have to go further down if there's another bridge or crossing, or get a boat. We're along the creek at Mick Oliver's house. Hang on.'

I looked over to the kitchen where Mick was pouring boiling water into a large teapot.

'Mick, what's the address here?' I asked.

'Mail Service 43, Six Mile Creek, take the Avalon Bridge off Lamington Rocks Road. I'm four kilometres from the bridge. Dirt track.'

I relayed the information to Henry.

'I'll call the police now. Do you have any weapons, Gar?'

'I'm not sure, I'll check with our host.' I gave Mick's phone number to Henry, and went to join the others at the kitchen table.

'Thank you for your hospitality,' I said to Mick Oliver. He handed me a cup of tea. I didn't know how much Mick had overheard of my conversation with Henry, and although he deserved better, I didn't have the stomach for a full explanation. 'The police are on their way.'

Mick nodded and then turned to his brother.

'I suppose you've made me a target again, Dave. Would that be right?' Mick stared at Dave until Dave raised his head and stared back at Mick.

They sat like that for at least a minute, in some kind of hostile sibling standoff during which Delia, Sarah and I stared at our tea cups. It was quiet in the cabin, which was just as well; I could listen for unusual noises coming from outside. I don't know what I expected to hear: Guy Friendly in a tank, ready to bulldoze the cabin? Guy Friendly kicking the door in and machine-gunning us? How did I know what Gianni had become in the years since we'd been close, and since he'd turned into Guy? He'd fallen in love with a woman, Jacinta, they were going to have a baby, and then the worst possible thing happened. But the Gianni I had known was a gentle, quiet person, relatively speaking. Sure, he'd joined the army, sure he was a bomb expert, and yes, he'd had to kill or be killed. He'd been a man in uniform, and that was his job, it was nothing special, and there were thousands like him out there, trained killers, within very specific boundaries and regulations, most of the time. But Guy Friendly, murderer, determined on revenge? Would he see himself that way, as a serial murderer, or did he simply see all this as another operation to be completed? Completed.

'Garfield?'

Delia touched my shoulder. 'Garfield?'

'Yes, Delia, sorry.' I hoped Delia hadn't tuned into my thoughts at this moment.

'What now?'

'Now, we wait,' I said. 'I'll go outside, you won't see me, but I'll be there, looking out for our stalker, just in case.' Henry's line was as good as any. 'Don't worry. The police will be here soon. Maybe you could keep an eye on those two.' I nodded at the two remaining Auroras in the kitchen. Delia agreed, reluctantly.

I thanked Mick Oliver again for his help before I left the cabin.

181

'You looked like you could use a hand.' He glanced over at Sarah and Dave, sitting silently at his kitchen table. Delia had only made it as far as the sofa where she sat with her eyes closed. She may have been meditating.

'Aren't you curious about what's been going on?' We looked like a bunch of refugees from a psychopath, or at the very least a tsunami, an earthquake, a wildfire.

'I figure Dave and his gang of greedy brokers have finally been brought to account by an unhappy investor. You're not a stockbroker, are you?'

'I'm the security. We were outgunned.' But with no guns in evidence.

Mick gestured towards his laptop. 'I'm writing my own version of Dave's coterie - it's therapy. He helped turn me into - this.' He glanced down at his tracksuit. 'I know what I look like. I used to be somebody, not a big somebody. All I wanted to do was give people some fun, a bit of entertainment for a week or two for their holidays. Walk in the rainforest, pat the snakes, feed the leeches, eat slap-up meals from the Eyrie's kitchen. And then, Dave's bunch lost everything. He encouraged me to overcapitalise, and I was stupid enough to do it.' Mick shook his head and walked me out to the narrow veranda that ran along the front of the cabin.

'Sure you don't want to stay here?' He pointed to the rocking chair near the door.

'I think I'll be more use somewhere over there.' We both looked out at the dark forest. It was as black as things could get.

'Take this with you.' Mick handed me a roll-on mosquito repellent from the little table next to the rocking chair.

'Thanks.' It was a weapon, of sorts. Dave Oliver's brother had shown more consideration in one simple gesture than all of the Auroras put together had managed in probably a very long time.

'Would you mind telling the cops I'm out here, and that I'm not the killer.'

Mick Oliver smiled. 'It's the least I can do.' He put out his hand and we shook. Then I disappeared into the night and hoped Gianni was on his way back to his grave.

CHAPTER 54

What was Guy Friendly thinking when he lurked in the rainforest waiting for an Aurora, or, as he must have thought of them, a Polaris, to happen by? How did he maintain the rage for such a sustained period of time in such trying circumstances? He'd planned everything carefully, from finding out, somehow, what had really happened to Jacinta, to faking his death, and then organising a comprehensive plan to corral the Polaris/Aurora crowd at a place like this in order to pick them off. But he'd jumped the gun with a couple of them, it seemed, and taken them out beforehand. He'd set up the roasted head and frozen ear, blown up the bridge, created the DVD, turned Graham Butler into pink mist, and ended Peter Leason's life like a rabbit's. I guessed he'd see Dean Porter as collateral damage. He loved Jacinta, loved her deeply, but his hatred for these finance people demonstrated a depth I couldn't fathom.

Could Gianni really have become a psychopath, the little boy who'd been my best friend, the adolescent who'd been my good-time-bad-time mate? He hadn't been a fire lighter or a bed-wetter, and no one had dropped him on his head, as far as I knew. Had he taken any trophies from his victims? I couldn't be sure, but the most obvious totems - the diamond studs - he'd left behind for us to discover, or else he'd simply discarded them.

What did I know for sure, then? Only that he'd killed four people, and that when he'd had the chance to kill me, he didn't, and when he'd had the chance to finish us all off, he hadn't, for surely he had a gun, somewhere. But his inaction may have been because of injury, so he decided to beat a strategic retreat. That didn't sound psychopathic, did it? That sounded reasoned and logical, militarily sensible, the actions of a well-trained soldier. What would I prefer, then: psychopathic Guy Friendly, nutcase abroad, hellbent on gory revenge, or Gianni Magiolo, the almost-white knight, dispenser of justice, and champion of his slain lover?

It seemed to take all night for the police to arrive, but in reality, it was only a couple of hours. It was my circular thoughts, and my inability to decide what to do, my paralysis, that made it seem like forever in a rainy, dark purgatory. Eventually, I heard them move in and scuttle about. There were at least half a dozen, probably more, judging by the separate movements I could detect. They took up positions around Mick's cabin and I wasn't far away from them in my spot within a nest of large boulders. A light mist had begun to fall, and I was glad they were here at last. I could move, take some action, but carefully. If they had their fingers on their triggers - and there was a middling to high probability that they did, given the circumstances - then it was shoot to kill rather than capture and contain.

'Hello,' I yelled, 'I'm Garfield Fletcher. I'm Garfield Fletcher, from Pinkert Security. I'm unarmed. I'm unarmed.' I tossed the mosquito repellent to the ground, in case they thought it could be some kind of incendiary device, a grenade, or even a remote detonator. Some of these guys were steroidal and seriously trigger happy, or so my paranoia told me at three in the morning. 'I'm coming out into the open.'

'Arms up, over your head,' screamed a voice. 'Arms up.' Spotlights from the police vehicle parked back along the track lit up the area in front of the cabin.

I did as I was told, and as I walked out very slowlly to the clearing in front of the cabin, Mick Oliver stepped out onto the verandah.

'He's with us,' he called. 'He's one of us.' Mick put his hands up, too, and stood there framed in the doorway. I could see movement behind him as the others in the cabin came forward to stand with Mick.

A voice right behind me said, 'Don't move,' and proceeded to pat me down. 'Turn around.' I turned to face two emergency response officers in blackout camouflage gear, helmets, and bullet-proof vests. One of them held his automatic rifle on me.

'Is the safety on?' I asked him. He didn't answer, but he flinched slightly, not a great sign, and then his mate, the one who'd patted me down, turned and flicked him an eye code of some kind, and he raised the rifle so the business end pointed at the sky.

'Thanks,' I said, my legs rubbery, my heart racing at three times its usual leisurely pace. If anyone was going to kill me, I'd rather it was Guy Friendly.

'Into the house, Mr Fletcher,' the first man said. The second man drifted back into the darkness.

Inside, I gave the officer, Becker, a summary of what had happened to us over the last two days. I mentioned Guy Friendly's DVD revealing what had happened to Jacinta Hurley on and off the cruise ship Magellan, and Friendly's determination to avenge her death. It was a very powerful motivating force, responsible for everything we'd experienced. I offered the opinion that Guy Friendly wasn't interested in harming anyone else, and Dean Porter had been a wrong place, wrong time disaster.

Becker maintained a professional exterior of calm neutrality, but I sensed a level of excitement lurking beneath, a desire to get moving and hunt the bastard down, regardless of his specific motives and related targets. It was a police safari. He explained that his tactical response group would comb the rainforest up to, and around the Apostles' Eyrie and secure the place before the forensics team arrived in the morning to begin their investigation. We would be evacuated immediately and we'd have police protection, more of it for Dave Oliver and Sarah Harding, and Delia, and drive-by patrol cars for me, the non-Aurora. Delia was only technically a member of the Auroras, but it was better to be safe than sorry. They'd worry about the specifics of Guy Friendly's targeting strategy later.

'Did any of you recognise the assailant?' Becker asked.

'Only from his visits to the office,' Sarah Harding said. 'He was a delivery man, but I'm sure that isn't his real name.' Delia and Dave nodded in agreement, although I doubted that Dave had ever done reception duty in his life.

'Homicide will interview you about everything,' Becker said. 'Tomorrow.' He turned to me. 'How about you, Mr Fletcher. Any idea who this bloke Guy Friendly is? Did he look familiar?'

The moment had come. Opportunity knocks only once in these circumstances. I couldn't afford to blow it, and blow the rest of my life, one way or another. Becker wasn't asking because he thought I knew Guy, he was asking because it was procedure, so I responded in kind, as expected.

'No idea,' I said. 'Never seen him before in my life.' And really, that was true, I told myself. I'd never seen this man, Guy Friendly, before yesterday. Gianni, on the other hand, was an entirely different prospect, and I had to find him, whatever the cost.

Becker nodded and we all got up to leave. He offered Mick the opportunity to evacuate with us, but Mick declined, so he told him to stay vigilant and keep his cabin locked. Mick smiled and shook Becker's hand, and I thought he'd be just as likely to offer Guy the same hospitality he'd extended to us, should he happen by. Not so, his brother.

'If you see this prick,' Dave Oliver said, as we all trooped out of the cabin behind Becker, 'shoot first, and often. Don't bother with questions. The bastard killed my friends.'

Becker didn't break his stride or reply to Dave, but I suspected that if Guy Friendly was still somewhere nearby, Becker would love to fill him full of lead and fit him for a wooden overcoat long before any pertinent questions even occurred to him. I, on the other hand, had nothing but questions for a man I'd never known, and who no longer existed.

CHAPTER 55

It was almost dawn by the time the police dropped me off at Belle's house. Henry was sitting on the verandah, waiting by the elephant's foot umbrella stand, twirling Belle's old black brolly.

'All right?' he asked, as I walked up the steps.

For a moment, I couldn't remember if I had keys, and then I realised that the one thing I'd managed to hang on to was my key-ring with its menacing apple-peeling pocket knife.

'Garfield? Are you okay?' Henry was genuinely concerned.

'Sure, Henry, I'm alive, so I'm okay.' I opened the door and went in. Henry trailed behind me. I flicked the switch in the lounge-room. Nothing. I continued on to the kitchen. The double fluoros still worked. Good on you, Belle. There was a momentary flash as the starters kicked in, more gloom, and then they lit up. I went to the French doors Edie had installed so Belle could easily wheel herself out to the big deck Edie had built and get some sun-bathing in on mild days.

'Cuppa? Scotch? Xanax?' Henry asked, watching me take the key from the hook near the door.

We stepped out and stood side by side on the deck and watched the sky lightening. There was still a lot of cloud cover, but every so often there was a break, and the tease of a patch of blue. Would the sun ever shine again?

'Cuppa, that'd be good,' I said.

Henry shot off to the kitchen and I sat in one of the outdoor recliner chairs Edie had bought for Belle in case she ever felt the urge to really and truly relax. I leaned back on the padded headrest and closed my eyes. Somewhere nearby someone was already burning toast. Maybe it was Henry. The local magpies were singing in the day, along with an assortment of other chirpy birds and screeching, zooming parrots. The crows had the loudest word with their long, atonal caws and clicks, but the magpies, they were something else. They sing for no other reason than that they're born to do it every day, every day without fail. I hadn't heard a single magpie in the rainforest.

'Here you go, pal.'

Henry was standing over me with a tray.

'I must have dozed off,' I said, pushing myself up to a straighter angle.

Henry had made tea and toast, half a dozen slices smothered in a variety of substances from Belle's fridge. Marmalade, rosella jam, lemon curd, peanut paste. I wolfed them down and poured cup after cup of tea.

'Slim pickings down at the Eyrie?' Henry said, sipping away at his coffee as I worked my way through the toast.

'Not much time for eating,' I said.

After a while, I slowed down and leaned back. I hadn't realised how hungry, or how fatigued I was until I'd come to a standstill.

'I'm sorry, Gar,' Henry said. He was perched on the edge of his matching recliner chair, teetering on overbalancing.

'You didn't know.'

'I should have done more checking, made them wait. They paid up front; the cheque cleared, I didn't give a shit about the rest. Some detective.'

'Don't worry,' I said. 'I think they're going out of business.'

'This bloke, the killer. What's that all about?'

Henry had only the bones of the story. All he knew was that we'd found a roasted head and a frozen ear, and that someone was trying to kill us.

'It's to do with his partner, his lover,' I said, and I proceeded to give Henry the Reader's Digest version of our weekend in hell with Guy Friendly. I tried to feel detached, but the only thing giving me any distance from it all was sheer exhaustion.

'Jacinta Hurley. Why does that name sound familiar?' Henry stood up and wandered across the deck.

'Maybe you read about the inquest at the time. I thought a couple of the Auroras looked familiar when I met them on Friday. It was their photos in the paper after Jacinta died, when they claimed she'd managed it all by herself.'

'No way he could be the husband?'

'I doubt it,' I said. 'Anyway, the police will take care of it.'

Henry looked at me for a moment and then kept walking back and forth across the deck. 'If he's as smart as he seems, and this determined, they'll have trouble. Unless he decides to come to them.'

'Does that even happen?' I couldn't imagine Gianni, or Guy, turning himself in to the system he'd rejected to champion Jacinta's cause.

'Sometimes, with the suicide jockeys - death by cop, you know, but it's more likely he'll try and finish the job, with the other two. There's Sarah Harding, the one who hired us. Who's the other survivor?'

'David Oliver,' I said, 'the CEO.'

'And who died?'

'Philip Downer, the Chairman of the Board, the biggest honcho. He's the roasted head. Melanie Rogers-Hilton, Chief Investment Advisor - it's her ear ring we found in Downer's mouth. The bodies are missing and I reckon they were already dead when we got to the Eyrie. Then Graham Butler, the Chief Finance Officer, was blown to smithereens out the front of the main Eyrie building, and Peter Leason, the Chief Operating Officer - Giann - Guy Friendly slit his throat just before he capsicum sprayed me and left the scene.'

Had Henry noticed my near slip with Gianni's name? I had to be extra vigilant around an ex-Homicide detective. I was too tired to be having this conversation, even with temporarily kindly Henry.

'If I was Dave Oliver, I'd be checking my Will, and going on a long vacation, maybe permanently. One with constant movement and no fixed address.'

'What are you saying? That he'll strike again?'

'He's on a mission. He'll probably go for both of them, definitely Oliver. There doesn't appear to be a sexual element to any of it, so he's not into raping the women, or torturing. But that's to be confirmed. They haven't found the other bodies yet.'

'He'd never do that. No way.' The words were out and they weren't coming back.

'What? You sound like you know the man.'

Now Henry watched me like a former homicide detective. My only consolation was that this was good practice for when the real homicide team interviewed me later and took my statement.

'If he was into torture, Henry, would he have put me on that ledge so carefully and left a rope for me to save myself?' Good save, Garfield the dopey.

'Why do that at all?' Henry asked. 'That's one peculiar perp.' He shook his head. 'Maybe you reminded him of someone he knew, and liked, instead of hated. Consider yourself lucky.'

I forced my lucky self to get up. It was time to go to bed, go to sleep and get some sharpness back. Lying is always such a challenge.

'Did he say anything to you, Gar? Did he seem rational?'

'He's - he seemed very focussed, very specific. Operational.' That was the truth. I turned from Henry and took the breakfast tray into the kitchen.

'In that case,' he said, following me in, 'Sarah Harding should take the farewell tour as well.'

CHAPTER 56

My interview on Monday with a detective from the taskforce investigating the multiple murders went as well as I could have expected. After I'd had an afternoon's and an entire night's sleep on Sunday - no nightmares due to exhaustion - I didn't make the same mistakes I'd made with Henry. I managed to explain the entirety of my participation satisfactorily, judging by the detective's responses. He didn't even try to denigrate my position as a private security officer, but that could simply have been due to Henry's history as one of them - once a copper, always a copper - even though it had been in another state. I think they were all so awestruck by what had landed in their laps - an actual serial killer, a career maker or breaker - they'd be processing their own reactions for some time to come. Taking the piss out of a lowly private investigator like me was the least of their interests.

The detective put me on notice to expect the possibility of further questions as the team sorted through the crime scene and searched for everything linked to Jacinta Hurley. In the meantime, I should contact them immediately if anything occurred to me that I hadn't already mentioned. Yes, officer.

Through his police connections, Henry learned later in the week that Philip Downer had been reported missing by his daughter, but, as was usual with adult missing persons where there was no obvious evidence of foul play, no immediate action had been taken. Then, the events at the Eyrie came to light. The police quickly traced Downer's movements to the university and a knees-up at the staff club with some of his business faculty soulmates; but it seemed that he hadn't made it home.

Coincidentally, a cleaner doing the once a week vacation period dust over of lecture rooms and so on, happened upon a dismembered body all over one of the music department's recording studios. The head was nowhere to be found, and while the body was naked and had no identification, the police were fairly certain it would prove to be Downer. The cleaner had reported that a CD of his favourite jazz player, Dave Brubeck, was playing on a continuous loop in the studio. Gianni had loved jazz, and Brubeck; he'd seen himself as a musician, but his father had other plans, business plans, and Gianni had taken Gianni Senior's road because he was a dutiful son. No music, not professionally, anyway, just the piano for fun. Then, Gianni Senior died in the kitchen explosion, and Gianni joined the army.

'You should take some time out, Gar,' Henry said. We were sitting at the meeting table in his premises. 'In fact, I insist.' He fumbled his wallet from his trouser pocket and removed a wad of fifties. 'Here.' He held the money out to me.

'Aren't you going to count it, get a receipt?' I asked, which was a bit churlish of me, really. 'Sorry.' On the other hand, Henry would know exactly how much was there.

'It's okay, I know I'm a tight-arse,' Henry said, smiling. 'Take it.'

'Thanks.' I took it, folded it and pushed it into the top pocket of my shirt. 'Don't worry, it'll be safe.' I patted the pocket, buttoned it up, and made a mental note to get to the bank and check my balance.

'Things are quiet at the moment, anyway. You need to settle in, next door.' Henry's mobile rang and he glanced at the number calling before he answered it. 'Why don't we meet up for lunch later? Fancy a curry at the Taj?'

'Sure,' I said. I may have been a fake P.I. and security expert, but I knew when I was getting the bum's rush. Henry was through the door to the kitchen and muttering into his phone before I stood up.

I was at Belle's front door when her landline rang. It reminded me my mobile was gone, thanks to Gianni.

'Hello,' I said, wondering if it was one of Belle's old friends, still not caught up with her demise.

'Garfield?'

'Delia?'

'Yes, it's me.'

'Why are you whispering?'

'I - I don't know,' she said, returning to a normal volume.

'How did you get this number? I don't even know what it is.' I looked down at the phone, but the number was long gone into a smudge of HB pencil.

'I rang Pinkert's. Henry gave it to me. Gar, I need - I'd like to talk to you.'

'No time like the present,' I said. 'Delia, how are you? Are you okay?' I hadn't seen or spoken with Delia since we'd been dropped off at our respective homes by the police. We were all so exhausted, we'd been like a bunch of zombies, eager only for our own familiar surroundings and loved ones, if there were any left to us.

'Not on the phone, Gar. I'd like to catch up, in person.'

Why did Delia's tone sound so false to me? She could have been an airline steward describing the in-flight movie and available snacks.

'That's fine,' I said. 'I've missed you, too.' It would be a treat to see her, even after all that had happened.

'Where can we meet?' she asked.

'I don't have transport,' I said. 'Would you be able to come to my place?'

'No,' she said, emphatically. 'I mean, um, coffee, how about coffee, somewhere near you?' The in-flight movie tone again.

'Do you know Boundary Street?'

'Yes.'

'Café Babylon, upstairs. Okay?'

'I'll be there in half an hour.'

'Sure,' I said, but she'd already hung up.

CHAPTER 57

I decided to postpone worrying about Delia's strangeness on the phone and just go. I checked myself out in the long, narrow mirror handily fixed to the back of the front door. That was one way to ensure you didn't forget your hat, or coat, or miss a run in your stockings. Good on you, Belle.

As I neared the Magiolo house at the top of the hill, I couldn't help but wonder whether or not Nonna Lucia knew about Gianni's fake death. I hadn't mentioned him when I saw her previously because I didn't want to upset her, or me. She'd loved Gianni, adored him like a son and grandson rolled together, a powerful combination. If she didn't know, his death must have almost killed her. No wonder she'd developed diabetes.

I stopped in front of her house; the ginger cat whose name I still couldn't recall was sitting on the fence grooming himself. I went over to him and said hello, reaching down to see if I could give him a chin rub, or if he'd slash me. It was as though we'd been a couple forever; he pushed against my hand and made sure he got in a good rubbing.

'It must be the complexion,' I told him, wiggling my fingers against the side of his face. 'We're made for each other.'

I sat on the fence beside him for a minute or so, and I thought if Gianni was in there, he'd see me and know I was back. Somehow, he'd intuit that I needed to see him, and somehow he'd get a message to me, maybe through the cat, a note attached to his yellow collar with its fish shaped silver studs. But cats were unreliable messengers; it would have to be the Nonna, and if she knew about Gianni, did she know what he'd been up to as well? Had she known Jacinta Hurley, and loved her like a daughter and granddaughter? Could she possibly endorse Gianni's actions? The police might regard Lucia as an accessory if they discovered Guy Friendly's identity.

I needed to know more, but I couldn't bring myself to knock on the

Nonna's door. I leaned down and gave the cat a kiss on the top of his head. As I stood up to go, he jumped off the fence and disappeared under the house. Safe from me, and everyone.

Did I see the curtain in the window move, or did I wish that it had? No, I wished for the Nonna to know nothing, to endure her grief and say goodbye to Gianni, once and for all, and I wished I could do the same. I waved at the house and continued on to Café Babylon.

Delia was sitting upstairs in one of the small rooms when I arrived. She was wearing black jeans and a white T-shirt and she had her hair pulled back in a ponytail. She looked as though she still hadn't managed to catch up on much sleep. There were dark rings under her eyes and she was paler than usual. When she saw me, she picked up the two drinks on the table and walked towards the verandah that overlooked Boundary Street. I followed her out. She was even paler in the brighter light.

'I ordered you a Coke,' she said. 'I hope you don't mind.'

'Not at all. Have you been here long?' The Coke was sweating, but it was a hot day, and Babylon wasn't known for its air-conditioned comfort.

'Not long,' she said.

We sat opposite each other and sipped our drinks while we watched the street below. People were walking, running, strolling, driving, drinking, eating, calmly or rabidly getting on with life as they knew it. The tropical low hadn't quite left the area yet; there were gusty winds still, and the sky turned grey every so often and splashed down some more rain. As a result, the humidity was up and sweating had become a second occupation for everyone but the coolest of us.

'See that car down there?' Delia nodded her head at something behind me, but when I turned to look she said, 'No, don't look.'

'I can't see the car if I don't look,' I said, and turned to where she'd indicated.

'The red one, the sedan there near the kebab shop.'

'Nice colour,' I said. As we watched, a man in blue jeans and a black polo shirt emerged from the kebab shop with two long white packets in one hand and a couple of juice bottles in the other. He opened the passenger side door of the red sedan and got in. The car remained stationary, but the windows were too dark and the car too far away to see what was going on in there, presumably eating.

'Does it look like an unmarked police car to you?' Delia asked.

'What does an unmarked police car look like?' I asked back. I had no idea. Or I might have known had I actually completed my security and investigation course. 'Henry might know.'

'No, don't say anything to Henry.'

'Delia, you're really anxious – what's going on?'

'Nothing, nothing. Look, I had to talk to someone, and I thought you might - I don't know.' She looked away from the red car and sipped more Coke.

'Just relax,' I said. 'It'll take a while for things to get back to normal.' They never would, but why rub it in, and Delia was no fool; she knew the drill.

She sat back with her Coke and twirled the straw around the ice in the bottom of the glass.

'Would you like another?' I asked. She shook her head.

'The police seem to think Dad is connected with Guy Friendly, and therefore I'm connected with Guy Friendly.' She took a deep breath and let it out slowly.

'That's ridiculous,' I said. 'They're trying to make the pieces fit together - they're forcing it because they've got nothing on Guy. Did they say if they knew anything about him yet?' They wouldn't tell a witness and potential accessory anything, but I had to ask and besides, Delia would have her own take on our man; she held him responsible for her father's death.

'Well, they've got our descriptions of him, and they've got his DVD - they know he can sing and play musical instruments. They know he's smart, and efficient, and determined. They know he can blow things up with precision, he can travel around in the scrub undetected and literally scare the life out of old men.' She stopped twirling the straw, put her glass on the table and rummaged in her bag, pulling out her sunglasses. I saw the redness in her eyes before she managed to get the glasses on.

'Delia,' I said, but I didn't know what to say. I watched a tear sliding down her face, and another, and more. She didn't bother wiping them away.

We sat there silently for some time, long enough for the red car people to finish their lunch and drive off. I'd turned my chair around so I could keep an eye on them for Delia. Who knew what the police might do with such an outrageous case? They'd put every resource they could on it, and do everything that would make it obvious they were seriously investigating, including tailing Delia, I suppose. Maybe they were tailing me, too, regardless of Henry's connections. And it wouldn't matter that Guy Friendly was no real threat to the public - the public would see Guy not as a man on a specific mission, but a Frankenstein monster about to descend on their suburb and kill at random.

Delia wiped her tears and blew her nose and we sat on. The café was beginning to fill up with hungry, thirsty people. I didn't expect to hear from Henry; he knew I didn't have a mobile yet, so if I was out, lunch was out, too.

'Lunch?' I asked.

'I have to go,' Delia said. 'But Gar, just to be sure, can I ask you a personal question?'

Here it was. Somehow, Delia had sensed a connection between Guy Friendly and me during that last confrontation at the Eyrie, something in our body language, our eye contact. It had taken this entire time for her to work herself up to asking.

'Anything,' I replied.

'Did you phone me yesterday?' She gazed at me from behind her sunglasses.

The unexpected. 'Phone you?'

She nodded.

'No,' I said. 'Why did you think it was me?'

'I'm not sure,' she said. 'You - sorry, the voice, it sounded - I thought it sounded like you, but now - '

'Delia, what did he say?' It had to be him.

'He said, 'You're safe, Delia,' and when I didn't say anything, because I was confused and shocked, he said, 'Did you hear me?' And I said, 'Yes.' He said, 'You're safe. Don't worry."

'You know who it is,' I said.

'And he said something else. Maybe that's why I thought, for a minute, that it might have been you, because how could someone so callous - ' She stopped and I thought she might break down again.

'It's all right, Delia,' I said, 'he's right, you're safe. He only wants the Auroras - he knows you've got nothing to do with it.'

'He said, 'I'm sorry about your father, Delia - if I could bring him back, I would.' And then he was gone. He really sounded choked up. But he's a killer, a psychopath, Garfield. I don't get it.'

'Come on,' I said, 'let's get out of here.'

We went back down to the street and I walked Delia to her car in the lane off Vulture Street. I could have tried to explain, in generic terms, that even psychopaths - which Gianni wasn't - have regrets, even killers have hearts. Especially this killer. But I didn't dare draw any attention to myself where Guy Friendly was concerned, even with Delia.

'What are you going to do now?' I asked her as she put on her seatbelt.

'Organise Dad's funeral. They've released his body. There's some other tests, but the post-mortem said it was a heart attack.'

'Will you let me know when? I'd like to come, if that's okay with you.'

'Of course, what's your mobile number?' She reached for her bag and took out her mobile, ready to input my number. I didn't have one, and I didn't know Belle's, either.

'Um, can you call Henry's business phone? It'll be under Pinkert. I'm getting a new mobile today. Now. I'll give Henry the details.' I leaned down and kissed Delia's cheek. She gave me a strange smile, wrote her number on a page of her notebook, ripped it out and handed it to me.

'Thanks,' I said. 'Don't worry, you're safe. Don't even think about Guy

Friendly, he's gone. He's got more important things to do, like leave the country.'

I waved Delia off and walked back to Boundary Street. If Gianni wanted to contact me, he'd use Henry's number. I had to get back in the game. If he was calling Delia with apologies, did that mean he still had plans for the other two? I found the nearest phone shop and spent some of Henry's guilt money.

CHAPTER 58

Henry came good with dinner at the Taj, one of their famous curry banquets. His guilt trip's half-life was lasting longer than I'd imagined it would, but I found it hard to settle down and enjoy the ride. Instead, I quizzed him about the investigation and sipped my ginger beer. I was the designated driver.

'So what's the taskforce up to now?' I asked.

Henry shifted in his seat and scooped another few tablespoons of mango chutney onto his plate, followed by another helping of steamed rice.

'The Madras, Gar,' he said, indicating the smallest casserole dish on the table.

It was a thick, grey, round container with a heavy lid and was only about six inches in diameter. That, of course, was part of the appeal, presenting the restaurant's, and probably the country's hottest curry in a compact, menacing looking dish. Open at your peril, Superman, there could be kryptonite inside.

'Some more?' he offered, removing the lid and glancing inside and then up at me.

'Go for it,' I said. I'd already had to ask for another carafe of water as we made our way through the various curries on the table. There seemed to be a shortage of the mild varieties, and a few teaspoons of the Madras extra special that Henry was now spooning onto his rice had satisfied me for life. No wonder Indian desserts were so luscious and sweet; the curries necessitated a strong counterpoint.

'The investigation?' I said, as the waiter whizzed by. Henry caught his eye and ordered more pappadums and beer. I asked to see the dessert menu.

'Dessert?' Henry said. 'The night is but a pup, Gar.' He laughed and forked down a mess of curry, chutney and rice. 'Mmmm, it's been too long.'

'We were here last week,' I said.

'Like I said, too long.' He forked in another couple of mouthfuls, his beer arrived, and he sat back with a glass and gazed down at his plate, smiling with undisguised satisfaction.

The waiter gave me the dessert menu, and I waited. That was my job, to wait for the master to speak.

'The investigation. You know they found Philip Downer's body, the rest of it.'

I nodded. What appeared to be the torture of Philip Downer didn't seem like Gianni's style, but then, how could I claim superior knowledge of what Gianni may be like after what he'd been through with Jacinta? Now, was he both Gianni and Guy?

'No sign of the Rogers-Hilton girl. The tests on the bodies at the Eyrie and the content of the DVD confirm what you already know - they're murder victims from an apparent hit list of people who went on an Antarctic cruise and did some very naughty things to a girl named Jacinta Hurley.'

'Guy Friendly's girlfriend.'

'Bit more than a girlfriend, wouldn't you say?' Henry raised an eyebrow. 'More like a bloody obsession. Anyway, the husband's out of the picture, so no joy there.'

'Husband?'

'Jacinta was married, to a Mark Barrett, mild-mannered suburban solicitor, conveyancing specialist. Not a mean bone in him, according to Cooper, but he bores for his country.'

Cooper was Brad Cooper, the senior detective in charge of the Eyrie taskforce. Henry's connections went higher than I'd imagined.

'Totally torn up about Jacinta, even though they'd been separated for a while.'

'Separated?'

'Not for long enough though. Things were happening long before the separation. Barrett had no idea about the baby, or the affair, obviously. He even thought they might get back together. Coop's speculating that she could have met this bloke on one of her photographic expeditions. If he was on the cruise, unlikely, but if he was, he could have kept his head down until after the inquest, then decided to deliver his own brand of justice. They're looking at the passenger lists.'

I had my doubts about Gianni being on the cruise. He wouldn't have let Jacinta out of his sight, and he especially wouldn't have left her in the hands of a bunch of yahoos.

'So they don't have a clue who Guy Friendly is?' The Gianni I knew was methodical, careful, and left no trace of himself if that was his choice of behaviour.

'Things are just beginning, Gar, we'll get him, don't worry.'

Henry started eating again. I ordered a creamy, fluffy, sugary dessert and coffee and wondered how they'd find a man already dead and buried. What kind of forensics would a deceased killer produce, if they ever could identify him?

'Oh,' Henry said, crunching a pappadum into submission, 'by the way, they're reopening the inquest into Jacinta Hurley's death, in light of what's come to light, so to speak. Even if it's just cosmetic, it'll be better than nothing. Make the husband a bit happier now he knows what really happened with those stockbroker pricks.'

'What do you mean, cosmetic?'

'Proof, sunshine, proof. All they need is a 'he said, she said' scenario and they're buggered.'

'You've lost me,' I said as the dessert and coffee arrived in double quick time.

I wasn't sure I could even begin to eat it, let alone finish. My appetite had slowly evaporated after talking about Jacinta, but it didn't faze Henry. If anything, he seemed energised. Did the police force invite the return of old homicide dicks to active service in the same way the air force welcomed back pilots? Henry would surely accept in a second, based on his current level of interest. I couldn't imagine what he'd be like if he knew about Gianni.

'It looks as though the Harding woman is willing to tell the truth about what happened down in the icy blue. Coop thinks finding out about Jacinta's pregnancy was the last straw. But it sounds to me like our Mr Friendly scared her straight, only Oliver insists the inquest got it right. We all know the DVD is probably 99% accurate, but proof, Gar, proof's the thing. We'd need corroborating evidence, something indisputable.'

He sat back and eyed off my dessert. I pushed it towards him and watched as he hoovered it up. If Gianni knew that proof would bring the surviving Auroras unstuck and into a courtroom to be tried, would he cancel the rest of his project and reveal how he knew what had happened? Would that excuse me from going to the police and dobbing him in? Why was there no one I could turn to for wise advice and guidance? When we were kids, it was Gianni, but now?

Henry finished my dessert and licked his spoon clean. There was a moustache of cream on his top lip. I couldn't bring myself to tell him about that, either.

CHAPTER 59

For the next several days, I attempted to establish a comforting, home-style routine at my new house. Belle's house. It would always be Belle's house, Edie told me in a phone call from her retirement home on the north coast. Always. She was happy for me to stay in perpetuity, but it was Belle's house. Check. And she was happy I'd survived my first assignment for Pinkert Protection and Investigation Systems and Services. 'You might tell Henry he could reorganise the business name, Garfie love.' I told her I would.

I omitted the goriest details from the Eyrie weekend and gave Edie the MA15+ rather than the R-rated version. There wasn't a big difference and she'd already seen the news and knew about the manhunt for Guy Friendly, suspected psychopath. My story didn't fool her and we both knew it; it simply served a purpose and got us through the worst of it. 'Well, love,' she said at the end of our call, 'it isn't like they were family or friends, those dreadful Auroras. I don't know any stockbroker types, but I imagine they find their own level, somewhere.' She said she'd call me every Sunday night, 'for updates' and street gossip. 'You know, Gar,' she said, 'if I was Guy Friendly, I'd probably do something similar to my soulmate's killers.' I forgot to ask her the cat's name.

I bought light bulbs and replaced every one in the house, including the few that were still working. I installed new starters for the fluoros in the kitchen. I turned on every light in the place and stood across the road after dark just to see how brightly it could shine. It shone like a modest little cottage with all the lights extravagantly on.

In the afternoons as the sun set, and on into twilight, I sat out on the front verandah with my new citronella bucket burning away, and watched the world go by. Henry joined me once for a beer and to let me know there was nothing new to know on the Guy Friendly hunt and the surviving

Auroras were still under protection, but otherwise he left me in peace to make my own way for a while. If I chanced to gaze up the hill towards the Nonna's house, I was likely to see the ginger cat preening himself on the fence, or darting across the street in advance of a car or motorbike. Daredevil.

Each morning, I relaxed in the recliner chair on the rear deck with my oats and coffee and watched the birds waking up before dawn and deciding what to have for breakfast with me. Invariably, they chose seeds, insects and worms, or swooped around the next door neighbour's vegie patch. I made a mental note to buy a combination bird feeder and bath next time I was at the hardware shop.

During the day, I did a lot of walking around the neighborhood and into the city, wondering what to do next, or distracting myself from wondering what to do next.

I cleaned out the fridge and pantry, and bought another order of groceries, staples, things that meant I was here to stay: sauces, spices, herbs, marinades, curry pastes; pastas, noodles, jams, salad dressings, vinegar, mayonnaise; coffee beans, tea, sugar, vanilla essence; yeast, flours: self-raising and plain; lentils, chick peas, rice. I loaded the freezer with puff and shortcrust pastry, white and wholegrain bread loaves, burger rolls and croissants; snap-frozen peas, beans, carrots, broccoli, and spinach; a few varieties of colourfully-boxed fish, some lamb and beef mince, and a couple of frozen pizzas, for lazy emergencies.

I was equipped for a siege, and I felt happier, although the stacked pantry and freezer shelves couldn't seem to restore my previously unbroken sleeping habits. Once upon a time, I'd hit the pillow, with or without the calming balm of sex, and wake to sunlight after hours of dreamy, or dreamless rest. Every night since I'd returned from the Eyrie, I woke every hour or two, my heart racing, the darkness pressing, trying to make out what exactly was in the bedroom at that precise moment.

One night, I heard noises in the walls; slowly they moved up to the ceiling. For a very stupid reason - something vague and full of anger, to do with controlling one tiny, pathetic segment of my surroundings - I decided there and then to confront the intruder. I stumbled downstairs and found Belle's ladder, positioned it under the access square into the ceiling, which was located in the kitchen, and climbed up with my new Dolphin torch.

I pushed the cover aside, took another two steps, flashed the torch around, and came face to face with a large, orange possum a metre from my face. She - it was a female, she had a baby on her back - and the baby stared at me from wide, black eyes. Their noses twitched simultaneously, and then the mother took fright, but instead of running away across the dusty insulation batts, she came straight for me. I felt her claws in the top of my head as I ducked and I heard a strange, guttural cry - of triumph over the stupid human? I lost my balance, dropped the Dolphin, and grabbed the side of the access square to save myself, kicking the ladder hard. It tottered and fell over and I hung there for several seconds before dropping the last metre to the floor.

I lay there next to the ladder, cursing, panting and shaking, dusty and clawed. When I felt my head where the possum had used it for a launch pad, it was wet: blood. In the bathroom mirror, I could just see enough to know that they were superficial lacerations. I treated them with methylated spirits and forced down the gasps of pain as it hit the broken skin. Then, very gently, I rubbed some petroleum jelly into the wounds and left a healthy dollop along the top of each scratch to protect the skin from drying out too much. It was an old sailors' trick - in salty air with sea water everywhere, Vaseline provides a means of protection not offered by other creams and salves. In a couple of days, I'd be able to change to Vitamin E cream for speedier healing.

My carefully planned routines were interrupted by a call from Delia about Dean's funeral the next day. It had been a week and a half since his death, but at different moments during those days, it could have been five minutes or five years since the Eyrie.

The next morning, I put Belle's landline on call forward to my new mobile, borrowed Henry's car, and set off for the monumental and lawn cemetery where my parents, and Belle, were buried.

CHAPTER 60

The cemetery was located in what used to be an outer northern suburb. Used to be, at the time my parents were buried there. In the years since, the city had continued to sprawl through every compass point, and outer northern had grown closer to simply suburban. Among the residential developments in the area, there were still pockets of acreage and low-lying land, the latter unusable for housing, or commercial and industrial precincts due to flooding potential and underground streams.

The acreage owners were holdouts, reluctant to sell to a sub-dividing builder for as long as they could afford the property rates, so there were some beautiful fairway expanses of tractor-mown green lawn surrounding ranch or hacienda style homes. Some of them had horses in the back yards and an occasional goat strolling around. The cemetery, St Bart's, or more formally, St Bartholomew's Monumental and Lawn Cemetery, was in the middle of it all, and it had room for expansion into some uncleared hectares the owners had bought for a song a few decades previously. There's always money to be made from the inevitable growth of the death industry.

I arrived late and had to park at the far end of the packed car park. The chapel was a two-minute walk away through a carefully manicured garden of native shrubs, bushes, and flowers. I could hear the pastor speaking as I approached the entry, but there was no hope of getting a seat or even getting inside. The place was overflowing with mourners. About 30 of them stood outside the main doors and others lined up down either side of the seating and spilled out the side doors and into the garden. I had no idea who Dean's friends were, but he had plenty of them, it seemed.

I tried to locate Delia in the crowd, but realised she would have been down the front, close to the action for Dean. The place had been repainted and there were cheerful bunches of flowers and white gauze curtains billowing in the breeze, but you couldn't get away from the reason why people gathered here. The atmosphere hadn't really changed at all since my last visit, for Mum and Dad's funeral after the car accident. I was at sea for Belle's farewell.

A couple of hard case smokers had removed themselves from the body of people at the main door, and were dragging on their gaspers as though they were next to be fitted for their wooden overcoats. It wouldn't be too long. I went over to stand near them, feeling out of place and out of sorts. Delia had blamed Guy Friendly for Dean's death, and in a way, she was right. But Dean had chosen to be there to scare the daylights out of the Auroras, and I think he would have taken all of this in his stride. What did his friends think?

'Known Dean long?' I ventured, standing between the smokers and a stand of coral ardisias.

One of them, a man in his sixties, with steel wool hair, faded green eyes, and dark brown nicotine stains on his smoking fingers, raised his eyes from his fascinating black loafers and squinted at me through his latest exhalation. He glanced at his watch.

'About the last 25 minutes,' he said. 'You?'

'Not long,' I said. 'Are you with the funeral home?'

'Nuh,' he said, and flicked his spent cigarette to the ground in front of him. He pressed it into the grass with the ball of his right shoe, and then strolled off to stand at the main door with the big group.

The other smoker was perhaps a little younger, with obviously dyed brown hair, mutton chop sideburns and an ill-fitting grey suit that made him look like an elderly schoolboy. He'd begun to nod when the first man told me he'd known Dean for less than half an hour, and he kept nodding, intent on his drawback and the effort required to produce smoke rings.

'Did you know Dean Porter, sir?' I asked him.

'Only by our dividends,' he said, and laughed a bitter-sounding laugh before he began to cough and went very red in the face.

I thought he might be ready to check out, since he was already here, but he recovered and moved off toward the bubbler beyond the ardisias. I could have followed him and asked him what he meant, but there was a sudden energy in the air around him that cut through the cigarette smoke and made him seem unapproachable. Or else I was suffering too much from the effects of either being at my least favourite place in the world, after the Apostles' Eyrie, or inhaling too many chemicals from his smokes.

Back at the main entry there was movement. The spillover people were turning to head out and clear a path for Dean in his coffin and the rest of the congregation to exit. Funeral home pallbearers dressed in cobalt blue suits, pale blue shirts, black ties, black shoes, and black Akubra hats wheeled out the coffin.

Delia followed them out. She wore a plain black dress and her hair was tied back with a narrow gold clip in a loose ponytail. She was pale and severe and dry-eyed, and she supported two elderly women, one on each side clinging to her arms. They were pale and wrinkled and crying, and it appeared that the three of them were the official mourning party. Everyone else exited like a crowd at a concert or a football match, each individual or group intent on their own thoughts or sharing an observation or two with each other. Most of them headed for the car park; some approached Delia and the old ladies with a quick word of sympathy before they left.

The rest of us saw the coffin into the hearse and one of the Akubra men announced that we could all follow Dean to his final resting place about 800 metres from the chapel where there would be a brief interment ceremony. I caught Delia's eye and she motioned me over.

'Garfield, thanks for coming,' she said, stepping towards me and out of the clutches of her two friends. I pulled her close, hugged her tightly, and kissed her cheek as we separated. She smelled of lavender and jasmine. 'These are Dad's cousins, Gemma and Gloria.' She turned to each one. 'This is my friend, Garfield Fletcher.'

Gemma and Gloria nodded hello and continued their quiet crying. Delia handed them over to a hovering Akubra man who proceeded to position himself with them behind the hearse in readiness for the walk.

'How are you?' I asked.

'Oh, you know, okay, tired, had enough.' She looked around at the departing congregation. 'I have no idea who most of these people are. News travels fast in the financial world.'

'They're from the stock market?'

'Not stockbrokers. Investors, like Dad and Max. These are Aurora victims from what I can gather. The shareholders protest group.'

'Ah,' I said. The dividends remark made sense now. 'Why did they come?'

'I'm not sure, probably some of them out of respect for a fallen fellow investor. They would have seen Dad's name in the paper and made the connection with the company and all the stuff about the murders. Maybe they think he topped himself, too, like Max. Or that he's a hero.'

'Well, he is, kind of,' I said. 'Don't you think?' Everyone was a hero these days, so why not Dean, who turned his anger and outrage into a practical project. Just like Guy Friendly, only ineffectual in the end.

'No, I don't. I think we were foolish and I should have stopped him before he could even have started his vendetta, or whatever it was supposed to be. At least Guy Friendly got results, the bastard.'

The hearse began its slow roll away from the chapel and we followed. From somewhere - the hearse? - came the sound of bagpipes.

'Dad loved the bagpipes, Irish pipes. Sorry about the noise.'

'I love bagpipes, too.' I took Delia's arm and linked it with mine and we followed the piping hearse in silence along the main cemetery avenue, and then off to the right and down to an older section where Dean's wife and Max were buried.

We could see the grave about halfway along our walk, just after we turned right before the downhill run. The mound of dirt was large and stood out clearly in the midst of the headstones. When I looked behind us, no one else was following. Several people had peeled off halfway along, visiting their own relatives I assumed.

When we arrived, things progressed quickly at first. The funeral people placed the coffin on the fake grass next to the grave and the pastor called all four of us to order with the sign of the cross. Gemma and Gloria sat on the chairs provided beneath the small marquee; it was a hot, humid day, and already clouds were gathering for an afternoon storm. I stood with Delia next to the women and we listened respectfully as prayers and blessings were offered for Dean.

After he was exhorted to rest in eternal peace with perpetual light shining upon him, the coffin was supposed to be lowered. Delia let some tears out then, and I remembered Mum and Dad at the joint ceremony we had for them. Each coffin lowered, one by one, into the dark, deep hole. It was horrible. But Dean's coffin stayed where it was beside the grave with the lowering frame poised above. I saw two of the Akubra men whispering with a man in khaki work clothes. He was shaking his head. The pastor looked impatient.

Eventually, the whispering ceased, the man in khaki walked off, and the head Akubra man came over to me.

'I'm very sorry, sir,' he said, ignoring Delia, 'but we can't inter your loved one at the moment.'

'You should speak with Delia Porter, Mr Porter's daughter,' I said, gesturing at Delia. I took a step back as she stared at the man. His embarrassment was clear in the colour that suffused his face all of a sudden.

'I'm terribly sorry about this, Miss Porter,' he said. 'I didn't - um - the groundsman informs me that the sides of the grave are too unstable for us to continue with the interment. There's a risk of collapse.'

'So what's going to happen?' Delia asked, wiping tears from her cheeks.

'He'll have to bring in his tractor and shore up the sides, then we'll be able to proceed.'

'How long?'

'It could be a while, he doesn't want to collapse the whole thing, so he'll take every care.'

Delia said nothing. She walked away from us and stood gazing up the hill. Then she went over to the pastor and spoke with him. I saw him shaking his head. She took his hand and shook it briefly, and then went to Gemma and Gloria and spoke to them. They murmured and pulled tissues out of their bags and wiped their eyes. Delia walked over to the coffin, placed her hand on it and whispered something to her father.

'There's no problem about the interment, it will happen,' the Akubra man said to me. 'I can reassure you of that, sir.'

Delia returned to my side. 'I can't risk the old girls getting sunstroke or dehydrated, Gar. I have to take them home. Dad would be livid if he thought they were waiting around for him.' A little smile crept out to the edges of her mouth and was gone just as quickly. 'The pastor has another service shortly, so he can't stay.'

'I can assure you, madam, you have nothing to worry about. We'll take care of your father.' The Akubra man stood tall. 'We'll post a sentry.'

'For as long as it takes?' Delia asked.

But the Akubra man hesitated a moment too long.

'For a maximum of one hour,' he said, finally, shifting his feet around on the damp ground and breaking eye contact with Delia. 'But the groundsmen are here, this is a controlled environment, and nothing bad can happen.'

After our weekend at the Eyrie, that was exactly the wrong thing to say.

'I'd be happy to stay with Dean,' I said, turning to Delia. 'I have plenty of time, Delia. I'll stay, and I'll give you a call when it's done.' Since I'd missed most of his service, I could try to make up for it by sitting with him and waiting.

'Gar, are you sure?' Delia asked.

'Of course. You take care of Gemma and Gloria, I'll take care of Dean.' I took her hand and held it in both of mine. 'What do you say? Fair enough?'

CHAPTER 61

At the 35-minute mark of the sentry's hour of vigilance, he removed his coat and tie, placing them on the passenger seat of the hearse, rolled up his sleeves and began dismantling the small marquee, which meant I lost the only shade in the immediate vicinity. He declined my offer of help, so I sat on the concrete border of the nearest grave and watched. As he was working, a groundsman drove up in a utility, jumped out and helped him fold the half dozen plastic chairs. They put everything in the back of the ute, the two of them picked up the lowering frame and moved it away from Dean's grave, and then the groundsman took off. The Akubra man rolled down his sleeves and rebuttoned the cuffs, then walked towards the hearse.

'Hang on,' I said, 'are you leaving?'

The man stopped and turned back to me. 'Got another funeral in 20 minutes,' he said. He reached in through the hearse's passenger window and pulled out his black tie, which he'd merely loosened when he took it off, so it was a simple matter of looping it around his neck and tightening rather than re-tying.

'It isn't an hour yet,' I said, standing on the technicality. They'd already buggered around enough and upset Delia, and I was getting hotter by the minute.

'But you're here,' he said, smiling at me. 'You'll do. I have to get over to the lawn and set up.' He walked around to the driver's side and opened the door.

According to the map I'd consulted on my way in to the complex, the lawn cemetery was up and over the hill we'd walked down on our way to Dean's grave.

'When's the tractor guy coming back?'

He checked his watch. 'Half an hour or so, most likely. He'll be on lunch now.' He adjusted his tie once more, tipped his Akubra at me, got in and drove off. Once the engine noise abated, Dean and I were left in peace.

'Things move slowly in the land of the dead, Dean,' I said to Dean's coffin, 'and the barely alive here at St. Bart's.'

I hadn't planned on any of this, and had no water or food with me. I'd noticed a bottle of water in Henry's car up in the car park, but I couldn't leave Dean and claim to Delia that he hadn't been abandoned again while he was still above ground. She'd been distressed enough when she had to leave him at the Eyrie for the police to discover, check and remove to a post-mortem. It was the principle that was at stake, not the benign reality of a quiet cemetery and a well-secured coffin. Then I remembered passing a tap on our walk here and it was close enough so that I could continue to keep an eye on Dean resting on his bright green grass carpet.

The tap was at the top of the hill, beneath a group of poinciana trees. Once I reached their shade, had a drink and splashed water over my head and face, I decided to stay and watch over Dean from a cooler distance. I knew he wouldn't mind.

It took me a few minutes to realise I was sitting only a couple of rows away from Mum and Dad. My hand went up automatically to the scar on my forehead. I didn't need to visit them in these acres of buried misery; I carried the reminder with me on, and in my skin, of what had happened to us. I rubbed at it, and knew that it was fading, felt it getting shallower with the years of wear and tear and simply living. Oceans of sea salt and swells had helped.

The last time I was here, the poincianas had been far less impressive, and the cemetery had been smaller; its growth in all directions since was disorienting. I remembered the tap, too, now; it was where I'd sought relief after I'd thrown up at the gravesite. Instead of a scoop of sand, Mum and Dad had copped a layer of vomit. I'd been mortified, appropriately enough, but Henry and Gianni had simply helped me up and taken me over to the tap for a mouthwash. Gianni told me they'd be laughing their heads off in heaven.

They were still where I'd left them, but the grave had subsided and the thin sheet of charcoal granite on top had cracked in several places. I couldn't even remember who'd decided that granite was a good idea, or that a monument rather than a lawn burial was in order, or even who'd authorised the wording on the headstone: 'In loving memory of Martin Paul and Victoria Helene Fletcher. R.I.P. Always Remembered by their Devoted Son and Family. Died Tragically 1987.'

'Every death's a tragedy, when you think about it,' said a voice behind me. The tractor man at last, and earlier than I'd expected.

'I guess so,' I replied, reaching over to pull some weeds, 'how long do you think you'll be?' I turned around to face him and looked up. He had a moustache now and he was wearing the groundsmen's khaki work shirt and shorts ensemble with a broad-brimmed hat.

'As long as it takes,' he said. 'How about some shade?'

CHAPTER 62

We walked back to the poincianas and made ourselves comfortable perched on the edge of Judith Rixon's slab.

'How's the pneumothorax?' I asked, trying for calmness. 'And the arm, healed up yet?'

'Getting there,' Gianni replied. 'Breathing easier.' He waggled his arm, pushed up the sleeve and revealed a red scar about 12 centimetres long.

'Where've you been?'

'Lying low, recuperating. It was a pretty intense couple of days, Gar. I hope you're taking care of yourself. You've probably got PTSD by now. And poor Delia, she can't be travelling too well.'

'If you go near Delia, Gianni, I'll find you, and I'll get you.'

'Gar, Garfie, I wouldn't hurt Delia, not a hair on her head. I've already told her that.' He leaned over and patted my arm. 'Who do you think I am?'

'What are you doing here?' I felt more anger than shock at seeing him. If anyone twigged that it was him, and that I was talking to him like some long lost pal - which was exactly what he was, long lost - that would truly be it. I'd spend the rest of my life in jail, convicted as an accessory to four murders. Who would believe otherwise?

'Checking in, Gar. Wondering what you've decided to do.' He pushed his hat back and wiped his hand across his forehead.

'Do you know how monumentally unprepared I was for the Eyrie? You turn out to be Hannibal Lecter in the fucking rainforest. My oldest friend. Jesus, Gianni, what happened to you?'

'Hannibal Lecter?' Gianni raised his eyebrows. 'Oh, I get it. Downer.'

'Henry said Downer was tortured, apart from having his head roasted.' The memory of Philip Downer's head in the roasting dish at the Eyrie floated back to me and gave me the beginnings of queasiness.

'Listen. I didn't even nibble, no interest in cannibalism. I've seen it too often in darker places than sunny old here.'

'But the torture, Gianni.' I couldn't get my head around Gianni as a torturer. It was unthinkable but he did it, didn't he?

'Opening night nerves, Gar,' Gianni said. 'He was the man, the one who made the final decision about Jacinta, and the sheep all followed. I wanted him to be an example. I stabbed him in the knees, and you know what, it felt good. It felt bloody great.'

'And that's it? Stabbed knees?' Could I live with that? Knees only, then death, decapitation, ear removal, roasting. Post-mortem abuse was disrespectful and creepy, and just plain outrageous, but it wasn't painful, not to the victim anyway. They weren't at the top of the psychopathic hierarchy of needs, were they, these après death hi-jinks?

'He was dead before most of the rest happened.'

I stayed very still. Most? 'Most?'

'Exsanguination, Gar. Excessive and speedy blood loss. People are unconscious so quickly, they don't feel anything.'

'How would you know? Had a lot of practice lately?' It couldn't be true. I almost prayed to the cross on the headstone in front of me I was so desperate for it not to be true. If it was true, then what did that make me? Did it make me a different person from the one I thought I was when Gianni was Mr Straight and Narrow, before Jacinta?

'You have to know where to place the blade.' He pointed at my chest. 'You don't want a cardiac tamponade, for instance, do you?'

I looked at him; he was smiling at me. 'What?'

'What you want - what I'm trying to explain to you - lest you think I'm the beast from Nietzsche's abyss - is a more or less instantaneous unconscious state.'

'More or less?'

'Within seconds, half a minute.' He reached towards my throat and I flinched back and away. I couldn't help it.

'You aren't frightened of me are you, Gar?' Gianni dropped his hand.

'What happened to Melanie Rogers-Hilton?' I had to think about his question.

'I was going to show you how to depress the carotid arteries to effect unconsciousness, then it's a simple matter of - '

'Melanie.'

'She's cool. Don't worry, she's in a better place. Knees intact. Everything intact. Except for the ear-ring, removed humanely.'

'The one you stuffed in Philip Downer's mouth?'

'It had to go somewhere.'

'There's too much unexplained. If you went to the police - you must have hard evidence proving how Jacinta died. You wouldn't have done all

213

this otherwise.' Let him prove himself to me. Let him justify the unjustifiable. 'That wasn't on the DVD.'

'Isn't it enough that you can trust me, Gar?'

'Don't play silly buggers, just bloody tell me.' I wasn't frightened, if I had been before. Now I was curious, and still angry. If I'd had a plan for my future, which I didn't, prison wouldn't figure in it.

'Fair enough. When they brought Jacinta back to the main vessel, they had her backpack as well. But instead of putting it in her cabin, one of the gang, I don't know who, an idiot, thankfully, got rid of it on the ship, pretty much threw it away and forgot about it.' He stopped talking and looked out over the headstones.

'Gianni?' I turned to see why he'd stopped.

'They threw her away, Gar, Jacinta,' he said, and there were tears in his eyes. 'My girl. And her baby. Our baby.'

Somewhere, a mower started up.

'I'm sorry,' I said, and I was. Gianni had always had plenty of love ready to go.

It took him a while to continue, and the mower kept buzzing in the distance to keep us company, so I focussed on that and tried to stay objective.

'One of Jacinta's cameras was around her neck when they found her, but the other one, and her mobile phone were in her backpack. Those fools that killed her didn't think anything of it, but eventually, someone on the Magellan found it, identified it, and sent it to her husband. By then, the inquest had come and gone - they did it fast because Downer had connections and he didn't want the whole sorry scandal to linger. Did you know that? Can you believe it?'

'I didn't know, but I believe it,' I said. The entire world seemed to run on a who you knew basis. I wouldn't have the job with Henry if it hadn't been for Edie's insistence. Henry's firm wouldn't have gotten the job with the Auroras had Gianni not recommended him as part of his operation. We were very small beer.

'When I decided it looked like a dodgy deal, I broke into Jacinta's house and found her stuff from the cruise. I didn't know where else to start, and I wanted something to remember her by. No one else knew about us, Gar. Not a soul anywhere. Jacinta was going to divorce him.'

'So, where was the evidence, and why did you think it was dodgy?'

'Gar, Jacinta was a smart woman, seriously smart - there's no way she would have gotten herself into that kind of position without something going very wrong. The inquest just - it didn't sound right - I know Jacinta, she would never have ended up pissed in a dinghy. Somehow, at some point, she trusted those pricks. Of all the people to trust with your life.'

'So were there photos or something?'

'There were some photos of the Polaris Aurora bozos, and a few landscapes and so on. They helped me to verify their identities. But she sent me text messages from her mobile when she realised they'd forgotten her. She told me where she was and that she'd been left there. She was desperate - and somehow, poor little thing, she thought I could help her. I was thousands of kilometres away in the desert, Gar. The messages failed to send anyway, I never got them, then the battery died. And then Jacinta died.'

'But you found the messages.'

'When I juiced up the phone and checked it out, there they were, ready to go. She named them all. She was a very thorough person - she reminded me of me.'

'And then you could be certain they'd lied and covered it up. Why didn't you go to the police?' I had to ask.

'For a death by misadventure verdict, a slap over the wrist? You must be kidding. You're kidding, right? They would have lied through their teeth.' He stood up and walked a few paces along the path between two rows of graves. He was angry. 'What would you have done, Gar? Let it go? Tell the cops and hope for the best? Or do it yourself?' He came back to me and stood above me. He wanted me to lay my cards on the table. I stood up and faced him.

'I don't know.'

It was the wrong answer.

'Come on,' he said, and gave me a little shove. I staggered back a step. He'd taken out his rage on the Auroras; he'd tortured, however briefly, decapitated, blown up, sliced, and he'd done God knew what to Melanie Rogers-Hilton. But no one knew how much he must be hurting. I was the only one in the world. Unless.

'How does the Nonna fit in here? Does she know about of any of this? That you're even alive?'

'Of course she knows, she's the one who's saved my bacon since the Eyrie.'

'You've been hiding there, at her place?'

'Family, Gar. You and I don't have many of them left. We have to cherish what we have so they'll cherish us.'

'She knew you didn't die in Iraq.' She would never tell a soul. She'd die before she'd betray family, especially Gianni, her one and only prince.

'I had to go back there and check myself out of the game. It took some organising, but if you have the money and the connections, you can do anything, particularly in a war zone. You know that.'

And if Gianni went down, so did Nonna Lucia. It was a neat package. I could almost imagine he'd planned it that way in case something like this happened and he was found out by someone like me. Or Henry. He probably could bring himself to kill Henry, if he had to. I was 98% certain that Gianni wouldn't decapitate, explode or exsanguinate me. But what could I, the so-called law-abiding citizen, do to him?

CHAPTER 63

'So Gar, what's the plan?' Gianni stood up and began to stroll down the hill to Dean's grave. I followed him.

'I don't like to make plans,' I said feebly.

'Which is why you're where you are,' he said, turning to smile at me.

'And your plan worked out so much better,' I said.

He feinted a jab at me and I dodged sideways, almost falling on top of a grave.

'Come on, give it up.'

We reached Dean's plot and Gianni walked over to the open grave and stood on the edge. Graves are surprisingly narrow structures, and dark, very dark, after the first metre or so. They seem to disappear into a black nothingness rather than more dirt. Dean's already contained Max, and Dean's wife. Did Delia think she'd end up here, too?

'Stay dead,' I said. 'Get out of the country, and don't ever contact me again.' I paused and waited, but Gianni said nothing. 'That's the plan.'

When he turned to me, I could tell he was choked up.

'Good plan, Garfie.' His voice was hoarse. 'I couldn't have put it better myself. Will you look after the Nonna for me?'

'Like she was my Nonna,' I said.

He held out his hand and I took it. We shook, but it wasn't enough. I pulled him to me and we hugged for a while. Then I heard a shout and machinery noise from across the lower intersection 20 yards or so from Dean's grave. The tractor man, the real one this time.

'Time to go,' Gianni said, disengaging himself. He leaned in to me and kissed me on both cheeks. 'Stay alive, Gar.'

He trudged off up the hill towards the poincianas and I lost sight of him as he turned off down a path that I thought would take him to the vacant land at the rear of the cemetery. When the tractor guy arrived, he offered me condolences on my loss. He could see that I was crying, but he didn't need to know who the tears were for.

I watched him shore up the sides of the grave, delicately placing the tractor's shovel here and there, tamping the soil carefully but firmly into place. Another groundsman arrived in due course, and between the three of us, we returned the lowering frame to its position, mounted Dean's coffin on the straps, and they gave me the privilege, so they thought, of pressing the button to send him off to oblivion and the worms. The coffin creaked down and down, the rollers squeaking and groaning like some old, old wagon wheels.

When it was all done, they quickly packed the lowering frame and the fake grass carpet into the back of the second man's ute. He offered me a lift to the car park. I didn't see any sign of a moustachioed groundsman wearing a broad-brimmed hat on the trip back.

In Henry's car I wound down all the windows, backed out and drove a short distance to the nearest shade next to the gazebo at the entrance. The bottle of water rolling around on the passenger side floor was hot and tasted horrible but I took a few sips anyway.

I waited for a while, until I felt relatively calm, then flipped open my new mobile and called.

'Dean's okay,' I said when Delia answered.

'Thanks, Gar. I really appreciate it.'

Then we waited. For each other? A plan. Gianni was right.

'How are you?' I asked.

'Okay, you know. I took the cousins to lunch. They thought the rollup for Dad was wonderful - they go by numbers. Dad never had that many friends in his entire life. Some of them said I should be proud of him because of what happened to the Auroras. They seem to think he had something to do with their murders, and they're happy about it. What am I supposed to do with that, Garfield?'

'Um - I don't think they know what they're saying. They're angry, and bitter. They feel like Dean got their revenge for them.'

'I know, but it's wrong, Garfield. I don't want people to remember Dad like that; he wasn't a criminal, for God's sake. And I'm still working for them.'

'The Auroras?'

'What's left of them.'

'Why?' How could Delia stand to be near them? If it wasn't for them, Dean would still be alive. Max would be alive. Jacinta would be in Gianni's arms and they'd be watching their baby grow up. They might have invited me to be a godparent.

'I feel sorry for Sarah Harding. I don't give a shit about Dave Oliver, don't get me wrong. But she's - she seems genuinely sad about everything.

She's a wreck. She's been going to the funerals for the others.'

I'd forgotten that Downer, Butler and Leason would have to be buried, although Butler's coffin would surely be symbolic, given the circumstances of his death. How would his family feel, staring at an empty box, knowing most of his remains were still at the Eyrie, and always would be?

'I'm helping her wind things up,' Delia said, interrupting my unpleasant thoughts. 'Don't worry, they're paying well - a thousand a day from Downer's so-called petty cash stash.'

'They're going out of business?' I was surprised. Somehow, I thought Harding and Oliver would rise from the ashes of their financial and homicidal ruin, and start running again faster than ever. Wasn't that what stockbrokers did? Wasn't their mantra 'So what?'

'In a manner of speaking,' Delia said.

'What do you mean?' Dean would have been pleased they were finished, but I knew Gianni wouldn't care either way. He's always known what he wants, and it's never been about money.

'Sarah's leaving the business completely. Her brother's set her up with a job in London working for a refugee organization. She's off with her son as soon as she dots the last 'i'.'

'And Oliver?' I was betting that he was a creature of habit, despite the fact that Guy Friendly was still at large.

'A new start-up company, so he says. I don't know where he'll get backing after all this. But these people bob up all over the place just when you think they're completely and utterly screwed. They have networks everywhere.'

'Perhaps he needs a laxative muffin, and a fish poo latte.'

'Perhaps. Maybe I'm keeping my powder dry, until the big send-off. And the police are still watching out for him and Sarah, you know.'

I could hear a little of the old Delia in her tone, although it hadn't lightened much.

'Maybe we could get together for coffee sometime. When you've put the Auroras behind you.'

'You've got my number, Gar.' Then she was gone.

Since I was on a roll, I checked through my contacts list and picked another number. It took a while to get through, and then to find someone who understood enough English to help me with my enquiry. They went away for a while, and I wondered if I'd have to declare bankruptcy over my next phone bill.

'Hello,' said the familiar voice.

'Rita. How are you?'

'Gar. What's up?'

Her voice sounded different. It was soft and calm, nothing like the Rita I'd known on the high seas.

219

'I was just - thinking about you. I wondered how you're going?'

'Great,' she said. 'This is the best thing I've ever done. At first, I wasn't sure, you know, after what happened, I thought maybe I was just reacting to the whole near death experience syndrome.'

'But you weren't.'

'No, no, I wasn't. This is home, Gar. You should try it.' She laughed a cool, sweet laugh that made me want to floor the accelerator and escape from the clutches of all the dead people around me. Life was what I needed.

'Are you a guru yet?'

'Maybe in another hundred or so lifetimes. A thousand. I'm just an apprentice.'

'So you can't give me any sage advice?' Someone, anyone, give me advice.

'Are you in trouble? Could Garfield the Laidback Wonder of the World be in trouble?' She laughed again.

'No, I don't think so. Not any more.' Indira Rahnee Devi wasn't about to give her apprentice's advice to another apprentice.

'I don't know anything, really, but you can only do your best, Garfie,' she said. 'With what you know at the time. Try to be kind - I know you are, so you shouldn't have any trouble at all with that.'

'Rita - do you think they'd let me in - where you are?' What was I saying? Clutching at straws of comfort from someone else's perfect life. Idiot.

'Come for a holiday, and see how you feel.'

I heard bells ringing in the background.

'I have to go now. Meditation session. I love you, Garfie. Always remember there's someone who loves you, no matter what.'

'I love you, too, Rita.' The bells got louder, and I couldn't hear her anymore, and then the connection was cut. I sat in the car near the gazebo for a long time, planning my future.

TWO MONTHS LATER

CHAPTER 64

Nonna Lucia's wide back verandah had a million-dollar view of the city in the near distance across the river, but the Nonna couldn't have cared less. As far as she was concerned, those that wanted the city could have it, she was interested in her vegetable garden and her avocado trees. Enough said. No property developer would buy her out, and she'd be there for as long as she breathed. I suspected she didn't want to move in case Gianni came back looking for her, but I'd never know for certain because I'd decided never to ask her about Guy Friendly.

'Garfie, darling, can you turn the telly around, please?'

'Sure Edie, just a sec.' I put the tongs down and left Henry at the barbecue to splash more beer onto the steaks, sausages, and fried onions. Our fortnightly Friday night cookout. Tonight we were at the Nonna's, and we maintained a roster that took us in a tight triangle from here to Henry's, to Belle's. The menu changed according to whim, but the guest list was exclusive.

'News in a minute,' the Nonna said, smiling up at me as I walked past.

The two of them, Aunt Edie and Nonna Lucia, sat in their recliner chairs like a pair of dowager princesses, waited on by their faithful manservants. And one cat.

'Caitus, get down from there,' Edie yelled, but her heart wasn't in it. The yell sounded more like a loving caress than a warning.

The orange and white striped cat, Caitus, had jumped onto the table where our salads were waiting and proceeded to inspect each bowl for feline friendly edibles. He preferred fresh, boneless cod, and most days that was what he got, especially since reappearing after an absence of three weeks. We thought he'd gone to the cattery in the sky, but when I found him sitting on the fence outside the Nonna's, looking sleek and well fed, if a little flea-ridden, I concluded he'd just been on a holiday, probably a few streets over where a new fish shop and sushi bar had recently opened. Maybe 'Caitus' meant wily.

On my way back from turning the television around for the ladies, I veered past the salad table and slotted Caitus onto my forearm with his paws dangling on either side and pressed him gently against my hip. It was a position we'd arrived at by trial and error. I took him into the kitchen and found some cod waiting for him in the fridge.

'There you are my good fellow,' I said, placing the bowl in front of him and giving him a pat. 'The ocean's best.' Belle had always named Edie's cats Caitus, every one of them, and no one, including Edie, had ever bothered to ask Belle about the name. Another reason for a séance, apart from asking Belle to stop turning the lights at 58 on and off whenever she felt like it. It was either Belle, or the possum chewing through the electrical wiring.

When I returned to the verandah and my post at the barbecue, the news had started.

'There was a grisly find today at a vacant ice factory east of the city near the river mouth,' said the anchorwoman.

Nonna Lucia grabbed the remote and turned up the volume.

'A routine safety check prior to the iceworks re-opening next month revealed a body in one of the freezers.'

The scene showed a helicopter shot of a large non-descript building on an industrial estate. Police cars were everywhere, lights flashing. I glanced at Henry, but he was busy pushing the onions around and didn't seem very interested. The dowager princesses were rivetted.

'The body is believed to be that of a woman in her thirties reported missing over two months ago. Police will not confirm her identity, but a source close to the investigation said she was found lying on a mattress fully clothed and there were no obvious signs of physical trauma. Beside the mattress, she had apparently written the word 'Sorry' in the dust on the floor. A post-mortem will be carried out to determine the cause of death.'

'Henry?' I watched him turning the sausages carefully, one by one.

'Melanie Rogers-Hilton,' he said quietly so the ladies wouldn't hear.

'Are they sure?'

'As sure as photographic comparison can be. They'll do DNA and other stuff, but it's her. She's well preserved.'

'Fingerprints? Any idea who did it?'

'Gar, we know who did it - the incredible vanishing man, Guy Friendly. The only trouble is, who's Guy Friendly?'

Henry raised his voice at the second mention of Guy Friendly, and I saw the Nonna flinch and then relax. She changed the channel to a lifestyle show about vineyards, which prompted us to toast her great blood sugar reading five days in a row, Edie's liberation from the retirement village, and

Caitus's triumphant return.

There was only one other part of my plan still awaiting finalisation, but I couldn't do anything about that until the next day.

CHAPTER 65

OPERATION BLUEWATER POLARIS MOP UP #001

It appeared to be a very jolly Saturday night dinner party, although his vantage point meant he could only observe but not hear the conversation. The group was aggressively boisterous, all male, all suits, and there was little variation in age. He was grateful he couldn't hear them.

They were all in their fifties, and mostly overweight with one or two exceptions. As they left the restaurant in ones, twos, and threes, calling their farewells to each other along the street, he noted that they all wore the same old school tie: the red, blue and yellow stripes of a private school whose alumni were proud to call their own.

'Next time, Oliver Bolivar,' one drunk diner called down the street.

'Your shout, monkey man,' Dave Oliver yelled back. He staggered across the road to the waiting cab and pulled open the passenger door. 'You right?' he asked, falling heavily into the seat. 'North. Ascot.'

'No worries,' said Guy Friendly, starting the meter. The cab glided away from the curb at a leisurely pace.

'I'm a free man at last. A week ago tonight.' Dave Oliver relaxed into his seat and idly gazed out at the streets passing by.

'That's great.' And a lucky night when Oliver chose to travel alone and to hail a cab home. Friendly had been watching him since he'd gained his 'freedom.'

'No more bloody bodyguards for this boy,' he said. 'From now on, I'm flying solo.'

'Bodyguards?'

'It's a long story, pal, long, bloody, messy story. Murder. Police. Private security. But in the end, the others are dead or gone, and I won. Me. I won and the other bastard lost. Coward.'

'Fantastic,' said Guy Friendly. He leaned towards the console and pushed a button. The cab continued on its northern route and he watched Dave Oliver close his eyes as the last two celebratory brandys took effect. The music began to play. It took a couple of minutes and an increase in the volume before it registered.

'Where have I heard that one before?' Oliver slurred his words.

'That's from a movie called Casablanca.'

'One of the greats,' said Oliver, emphasising each word. 'What's that tune called again, do you know, buddy?'

'That one? "You Must Remember This," Mr Oliver,' said Mr Friendly.

Dave Oliver forced himself to wake up and sit up.

'Stop the cab, I'm gunna be sick,' he said.

'No you're not,' said Friendly, accelerating.

'Let me out, you bastard, I feel sick. I'm giddy. Who the fuck do you think you are?'

'Me? I'm the coward.'

Guy Friendly reached out and touched Dave Oliver with the taser he'd bought in Islamabad. Oliver cried in pain and then slumped in his seat, barely conscious and moaning. Should he manage to wake fully before the drive was over, he'd think he'd been hit by sledgehammers and semi-trailers.

Torture. Friendly supposed that would meet the definition. Oliver's terror alone, never mind the pain, would do it, once he realised where he was, and what was going to happen to him. Even in Garfield Fletcher's absence, Gianni Magiolo didn't like the idea of letting his best friend down. He felt for the pistol in his shoulder holster: the better option all round, really. He could have done that from day one, couldn't he, but it seemed important to add degrees of difficulty, for Jacinta. Now, it didn't matter; the operation was almost over; he'd proven his love. It was time to go.

He took a right at the next corner. There was a quiet beach out past the airport where Dave Oliver could spend his last minutes lying on the soft sand, gazing at the night sky. At least he'd be warm and snug in his expensive suit, his special tie firmly tied around his neck.

He might even be able to see some stars that far away from the city lights.

CHAPTER 66

'Cooking two nights in a row, Gar,' Henry said, 'you better watch it, or you'll end up back out at sea chefing up a storm instead of being my ace investigator.' He raised his beer and took a slurp. 'What do you reckon, Delia?'

'I reckon I'm looking forward to dinner,' Delia said, smiling at me.

Henry had a head start on us with his drinking. He'd been celebrating a new contract to provide security services for a large industrial estate in the southern suburbs. Since we were eating at his place, he couldn't see any reason to practice restraint. And now we were celebrating something even better.

'I'd like to propose a toast,' I said. 'Be right back.' I left the deck and went to the kitchen. I grabbed three glasses, the corkscrew, and the bottle of wine I'd chilled. I checked on the goulash and turned the rice cooker on. I'm not a chef, I'm a cook, and I make good, plain food, as my mother would have said. Henry's kitchen felt homey for a change.

Back on the deck, I opened the wine and poured.

'A toast, to Delia joining Pinkert Security and Investigations as our newest researcher and investigator.' There was a freshly minted certificate of accreditation framed on the wall beside mine to prove it. Delia, however, had already indicated her desire to legitimise it with a kosher course, and I planned to join her.

Henry said, 'Hear, hear,' and downed his wine in one gulp. 'I'll just go and get us some more crackers,' he said, and left us on the deck.

'Thanks, Gar,' Delia said.

'For what?'

'For the job. I really appreciate it. I don't think I've had a full-time job in years.'

'It's we who should thank you for even considering us, Delia.'

227

'Mutual admiration society. I like it.' She leaned over and kissed my cheek.

'Why, Delia Porter, you're a flirt,' I said, and kissed her back.

Then my phone rang, and I was tempted to ignore it, but it could have been the Nonna, or Edie. They were tough old birds, but things happen to tough old birds, too.

'Hello,' I said, not bothering to check the number.

'It's over, Garfie.'

'Gianni?'

'Keep taking care of the Nonna, won't you? You're doing a great job so far.'

'Where are you?'

'It's a lovely night, isn't it? I can the stars from here. No city lights to dim them out.'

'Gianni.'

'Your plan has worked to a tee. Or rather, it's about to. I'm still dead, I'm leaving the country, and I'll never contact you again.'

'Wait.' What could I say? What did I want to say? 'I love you.'

'I love you too, buddy. Take care of Delia, Gar. She's a keeper.'

'Gianni.'

But he was gone. I tried the callback, but the number was blocked, of course.

'Gar, are you all right. You're upset.' Delia came over to me and put her hand on my shoulder.

'No, I'm fine.' I sat down and saw that my hands were shaking.

'Bad news?' Delia asked.

'No,' I said. 'Good news, I think.'

Henry returned with more crackers and we waited for the rice cooker's ping.

About the Author

Jay Verney is an Australian author who has published novels, essays, short stories, poetry, memoir, magazine and newspaper columns, book and film reviews, and comics.

Jay's first novel, *A Mortality Tale*, was shortlisted for the Australian/*Vogel* and Miles Franklin Literary Awards (and is available as both a paperback and an ebook). Jay has a PhD (in genre and crime fiction), and a Master's degree (memoir) in Creative Writing from the University of Queensland. In 2009, she received a Dean's Award for Outstanding Research Higher Degree Thesis for her PhD.

Jay's second novel, *Percussion*, is available in both ebook and paperback, as is this, her third novel, *Spawned Secrets*. Her fourth novel, *Summon Up The Blood*, is a result of her PhD and is also a paperback and an ebook, along with the essay that accompanied the novel, *Creating A Custom Fit In An Off-The-Rack Genre World*. Jay's memoir, *The Women Come & Go* includes an essay, *The Women Came & Went*, a reflection on writing the memoir and how writers research and re-imagine history and lives. It's available in, wait for it, paperback and ebook formats, too. Celebrate. Jay has also published poetry. Volumes One and Two of *The Mindful Art of Verandaku*, along with *Zenku 365*, are waiting mindfully for you as ebooks and paperbacks. Very nice.

Jay maintains several blogs: **Transient Total Focus** (www.jayverney.net), the mother ship; poetry blogs **Veranda Life** (www.verandalife.com), and **Zen Kettle**, (www.zenkettle.wordpress.com); and **Last Cat On Mars** (www.lastcatonmars.wordpress.com), a cartoon blog for connoisseurs of Lego and laughs. Enjoy, and thank you for reading.

www.ingramcontent.com/pod-product-compliance
Lightning Source LLC
Chambersburg PA
CBHW060924120626
46557CB00003B/870